# THE HALO EFFECT

# THE HALO EFFECT

The adventures of Harvey Johnson, Book V
Second Edition

## TOM ASHWELL

Copyright 2010, 2015 by Tom Ashwell
Printed by: The Pymander Press LLC.
St. Paul Minnesota USA

Submissions and inquiries: pymander.press@gmail.com

Cover images HST, copyright STScI.
Space Telescope Science Institute.
http://www.stsci.edu/portal/
Used with permission.

For my brother and my father,
two late, great, medical doctors.


Dr. T.R. Ashwell MD

and

Dr. T.O. Ashwell MD

## Acknowledgments:

I can't count how many times I've read in a book that it could not have been done without the help of others. Now I understand that statement more than I ever thought I would. I do believe that I could have finished this work without the contributions of so many others, but it might not have been fit to print if I had. So, I'd like to thank all of those who contributed to this work; by suggesting a change or addition, inspiring a character or even offering moral support. Please forgive me if I forgot to thank someone here, as there have been so many over the years, it was difficult to keep track of them.

In no particular order:

Dayna Thomas, Alan Grosebeck, H. Alan Kantrud, Eric Putkonen, Harvey Johnson, Dennis DeYoung, Joan Richards, Claudia Christian, Linda Bennett, Kim Caruefel, Christine Salokar, Scott Koelbl, Mitch Berg, Patrick Hanson, Debbie Klose, Joan Ruland, Peter Bennett, Julie Canny, Jody Schroeder, Tina Schroeder, Ali Jakubek, Don Preston, Jeffrey Nisen, Mike Busha, Bob Martin, René Holly, Toni Boelke, Lori Schlender, Kim Prescott, Sharon Zepnick, Jack Caudill. last but not least: "M'lady of the summer fields" (She knows who she is.)

# Table of Contents

# A note from the author.

Nobody seems to read to read a 'Forward' anymore so there isn't one this time. Instead, I have been convinced that a few notes from me, that will invariably be read after the book itself, might be in order.

I started on this storyline in 1977 when I heard a particular line from a song on the radio. Being interested in the possibility of extraterrestrial life, speculations about ancient visitors from other worlds starting religions fascinated me. Ancient, antediluvian artifacts hint at the existence of high technology dating back at least 50,000 years made me think. The evidence is worldwide, and convinced me that man probably not only did have high technology in the past but may have had at least one civilization-destroying war to wipe if from all memory. The theory that Atlantis was a hold-out form such a time is not new, and rather than write 'just another story about Atlantis', I looked elsewhere in my research.

I found consistent themes in various theologies that could be interpreted as being about extraterrestrials. Now I am not saying there is not a spiritual component to all of it, but if you created the universe, would you not act within it in accordance to the rules? In other words, why not travel between worlds by space ship? It seems logical to me because many an appearance of angels tells of them flying - rather than teleporting here and there - using wings, like that of a bird to achieve that end. So working within the rules though not being bound by them seemed to be a logical course of action. There are a host of philosophical reasons for this that I will not get into here. In fact, the whole series is, in part, about those very reasons and hopefully they will become clear by the end of the final installment.

Each book is intended to be able to stand on its own as a science fiction story, without the real need to read any of the previous works. In the few events something is mentioned from a previous book, it is noted. Such notation is of course, meant to fill in a blank and possibly to convince you to read that other book as well. (Hint hint )

This is the fifth book in the series and the 'first one published' due to the fact that the book is literally set in stone to start in late 2012. I am told I can be forgiven for prequels that predate the current day more than stories written about the recent past, even if it is all about a parallel universe. So there you have an explanation in a nutshell. There is much more to the 'story behind the story' to be sure, but I won't bore you with it here.

There are many elements to this story you may have seen before. I was noticing a lot of science fiction stories were using similar ideas to my own. However I felt that they were using them incorrectly. For example, 'organic technology' is a logical step beyond what is in use today for a plethora of reasons, and has therefore been used by many an author. However, at least in movies and television, I have been disappointed with its depiction. One does not need to be reminded frame by frame that the ship is organic, by the appearance of dripping tentacles, bulging veins and other 'goo' as well as uneven curvy lines to know the ship is organic. Indeed, it is my assertion that this approach does not only insult the viewer but it insults the designer of the organic technology. Early experiments with kludged and stolen DNA might result in such things, but nothing put into practical use should be that way. Indeed, properly engineered organic technology should not be readily distinguishable from conventional technology. It is this and other approaches I present here in this volume.

It is my hope that you, the reader, will enjoy these stories at least half as much as I enjoy writing them.

Welcome to a tiny corner of 'my little world'!

Tom Ashwell

## Who is the real Harvey Johnson?

The name Harvey Johnson showed up in many a film and televison show, and it seemed to roll off the tongue. Further, it didn't seem to be a name one got tired of with multiple mention. Years after I first considered that name for the main character, I had the great fortune to be instructed in Physics and Astronomy by a Harvey Johnson, who had worked on the Manhattan project. Among other things, I was amused that he often cooked his lunch over a Bunsen burner in a beaker. That's when I knew that I had chosen the right name for the main character. He was by far my favorite teacher and mentor, and without his encouragement, I might not have finished this work or any other for that matter.

My only regret in this is that I managed to annoy him at a mutual friend's wedding. That was a long time ago, and I hope he forgave me before he passed away.

# I
# DISCOVERY

"Pull the other one!"

Tuesday, December 11th, 2012 Anno Domini.

The little robotic probe made its way across the Antarctic ice cap, sending its powerful signal down to the bedrock and relaying the echoes back to the central computer. It was just humming along, doing its job and minding it's own business.

Why then had that snooty central computer ordered a repeat scan of the same area, FIVE times? As if that weren't enough, the orders came to move to the center of the area and wait. Wait? For what? A spring thaw? The ice was 2.5 kilometers thick here. Just because there was a 1.6 kilometer-wide sphere 900 meters below, this probe had to wait in the cold, falling further and further behind schedule. The worst part was that its motors were beginning to freeze.

Slowly, as if it were afraid of some sort of negative feedback, it turned its camera ahead then behind, to the left, right up and down. One never could be sure when the gods were watching. Finally satisfied that it was alone, it started to run just enough current through its motor coils to generate heat, but not enough to make it move. Occasionally, every 10 milliseconds or so, it did move, so it moved right back to the same exact spot, as to avoid being accused of disobeying orders. This gave the appearance that it was shivering, and in effect, that's what it was doing. Wait it would, but freezing went against its self-preservation protocol. We'll see who freezes, orders or no orders.

The central computer was in a quandary. It was told by the gods that there would be no geometric shapes in this survey, yet there was a perfect sphere buried in the ice. Perfect, mind you, more perfect that its programming was allowed to accept. Again and again it ordered the probe that had discovered the sphere to re-scan the area in the hope that the readings would turn out to be a glitch. Time and again, the scans showed a solid spherical object embedded in the glacier. This was no air bubble, cavern, lake or other known anomaly. This thing had to have been made by the gods. So, the central computer decided to contact them, and ask. Besides, it was worried, and rightly so that the probe was about to lose patience with all this checking and re-checking.

In the middle of a small blizzard lay a reasonably well-built complex, manned by a two-man skeleton crew; Albert Stark A.K.A. "Stork" and Benjamin Schmidt A.K.A. "Schmitty".

The rest of the staff had gone for various reasons and none of them would be back for at least a month. To have a research facility like this so understaffed was unusual, but they both actually enjoyed having the place to themselves. They were soon to find out the real reason why they were there alone.

Stork, was eating his sandwich. He didn't like bologna much, but since all the *good* food had run out he was eating the *bad* stuff now. He was having one of those days when absolutely nothing worked out. The annoying alarm from the central computer was enough to finish frazzling his nerves. When he first heard the sound, he bit his tongue, then he tripped over his own feet when he turned to approach the computer console. If that wasn't enough, he banged his knee on the desk and fell out of his chair smacking his jaw on the edge of the desk, causing him to further bite his tongue in the same place, AND clear the computer console by hitting the wrong key! Needless to say, he was rather upset by the time he finally got to see what the fuss was all about.

Focused now, he pressed all the right keys, and almost dropped his sandwich when he saw the image the computer was asking him to identify. His attitude changed abruptly. He punched a button on an intercom to call his colleague who was incidentally, out in the supply room, looking for something other than bologna to put in *his* sandwich, and said "Hey Schmitty! Get your ass in here! You *gotta* see this!"

Schmitty was annoyed at being disturbed. What was this predilection for posteriors? He shuddered at the thought. Stork usually got excited over finding an air bubble that had a micro environment trapped in it, or really old meteorites stuck in the ice, or some other silly thing that excites guys like him. You know, the overweight guy with no social life; and is a total expert on the systems he uses because he doesn't do *anything* else - not even bathe. Well, okay, maybe once or twice a year.

They were alone on this base, and he wanted to stay as far away from the disgusting slob as he could. "The isolation must be getting to him." he muttered under his breath as he dropped what he was doing. All he could find was bologna anyway.

Slowly, as if anticipating a painful discussion on the finer points of near-frozen environments was going to ensue, he approached the intercom, hesitated, and the predicted *CRACK!* came over the intercom with each activation. "HEY SCHMITTY! DID YOU *HEAR* ME?" Came over the tinny-sounding speaker. Schmitty reached over and pressed the intercom button, unable to delay any longer.

"Yes Stork. I *heard* you. What is it?" Then he muttered something about allowing a body time to get across the damn room before getting prodded...

*CRACK!* "You gotta see this!"

"What is it this time? A deposit of kreptonite?" he chided.

*CRACK!* "No!" He paused for a second, as if contemplating the wise crack. "No. This is BETTER! C'mon! Get your butt in here and take a look for yourself!"

"Okay, I'm on my way and I'm bringing my butt with me." He winced, wondering if he could wear an alpha particle filter mask to avoid Stork's body odor. Well, even if that worked, his eyes would still water. It was probably better to let his appetite leave him for a day or so, there wasn't anything good left to eat anyway. He couldn't wait until he others got back with the supplies, and he could go back to the clean room - far away from the slob.

He shrugged, sauntered out of the room dragging his feet the whole way. A few minutes later, he arrived at the control room to greet a human tick, doing a great impression of a small child on a particularly "good" Christmas morning. He motioned to the computer screen with both hands as a magician would and rolled his chair away from it to give Schmitty access.

"Okay, what's so..." His voice trailed off as he spotted a perfect sphere on the screen.

"What the _HELL_ is THAT?" he exclaimed to his grinning colleague.

"It's a sphere!"

"I _KNOW_ it's a sphere!" he snapped, upset that even now, Stork talked down to him. "What the hell IS it though? I mean... what's it doing there?" Looking at the scale of the graph, which showed the object to be over a kilometer and a half in diameter, he questioned. "Is that right?"

"Yeeeessss!"

The drawn-out "s" normally would have made him think of a blimp that had sprung a leak, but he was too fascinated to think about it much. He noticed that there was no information on the interior of the object.

"Can the sensors penetrate it?"

"No!"

"It's really that big?"

"YES!"

"What do you think this is?" he asked genuinely hoping Stork had a rational answer. After all, this was the guy with the answers. Well, the technical ones anyway.

"I think it's an _artifact!_"

They stared at each other in amazement for a few moments, contemplating the ramifications of that statement. Then Schmitty finally broke the silence;

"My God, we have to call this one _in_!" He thought about it for a moment and muttered: "Yes, but to whom?"

# II
# Right Angles To Reality

"I know nothing! NOTHING!"

Project: Pandora

In a deserted part of the Arizona desert, it was raining. Not just a regular storm - which would have been odd enough in the desert, but a full-blown thunderstorm the likes of which probably hadn't been seen in this area since the birth of the planet. In the center of the storm, was a building. Now, this in and of itself would not be worth mentioning except for the fact that something inside the building was responsible for the storm. There were some very odd experiments going on in there, because some very strange people were tinkering with things that were better left alone, that is; at least until they were better understood. This was the headquarters for the government's most secret scientific inquiry. Those who knew about this building's whereabouts, let alone its very existence, were few and far between.

The building was mostly an empty shell, due in part to recent cutbacks in the "Black Ops" programs but the central lab however, was experiencing no shortage of funding. It was believed at the highest levels that these experiments would yield so much power as to be worth the enormous risks and expenses that accompanied them.

The specific cause of the storm was a ring. It had an array of superconducting coils in it, on it, and around it. Computers of every description were controlling them, but it was in essence a ring standing on edge - and that was the crux of the problem.

The man in charge was tall, striking and distinguished-looking; Dr. Cornelius Morax PH.D. He carried himself much like royalty. Indeed, he though of himself as extremely important, which gave him the bearing that goes along with great importance. To be in his presence was often to feel inadequate. He had a charisma about him that often was enough to bend others to his will.

Morax was standing on a platform next to what looked like an event horizon that *almost* spanned the ring's interior. It fluctuated a little, but remained approximately the same size, popping and flashing, getting larger then smaller again, but never quite filling the ring nor winking out completely. It seemed that it was more than just a little underpowered.

"More POWER!" he hissed to the technicians, as a maniacal look began to grow behind his dead eyes. He shook his cane at the technician behind the main console - as if to drive his point home. He had lost his twin brother in a previous attempt, and this was the first time they had yet been able to duplicate the effect. *This time* he was getting his brother back.

As the power level was slowly but steadily increased, the unstable effect began to pulse at longer intervals. The fabric between dimensions is not best negated by brute force. In actuality, with the correct technique to open a 'doorway' into any neighboring dimension, it takes little more power than that of the average flashlight battery.

Due to the fact that this world is ruled by mathematicians, their engineers were blinded by certain mathematic equations that demonstrated that this approach made the goal *possible* - the only point that they cared about. They also ignored the fact that the very same equations point out quite clearly that this technique would require almost all the power of the known universe, with all the known matter converted to energy as well.

To fix this "*little* energy problem" - as one of them called it, the theory of 'negative matter' was born. The use of this negative matter would make certain parts of the equation resolve to lower, more manageable, power levels. They thought it fortunate that the early space missions had encountered some of this negative matter from the zero gravity point between the planet and the moon. In addition, they used certain short-cuts that pulsed the energy, intending to 'trick' it into working. Further, to generate the still enormous amounts of power required, they had tapped a plethora of sources: including three nuclear reactors and several banks of zero-point energy modules. Last but not least, they tapped a considerable number of modified "Cindergood[1]" torsion field energy generators.

The risk of this approach to the problem could not be isolated like that of a nuclear blast - by wide-open space - as the joint chiefs had reasoned. It was considered to be worth the risk, so the project got the 'go ahead'. Had they known that they could accidentally create an effect that would swallow the solar system - not to mention the planet - into a black hole, they might have reconsidered the whole idea.

---

[1] *Cindergood was an amateur scientist that had developed a 'safe' torsion field generator, years earlier. A modified version of his design allowed them to extract the enormous energy to which such a field somehow provided access. It was called a Torsion Field Generator or TFG for short. Despite the advanced design, they remained potentially so incredibly dangerous to operate that even the Black Ops people wanted their use banned from the solar system.*

# III
# TOMORROW

"...the train that goes to Morrow is a mile upon its way."

Back in Antarctica, Schmitty and Stork were about to get the surprise of their life.

"Well?" asked Stork, wondering when Schmitty would call headquarters about their discovery.

"I already have and I'm waiting for the Ministry to reply." Stork motioned to the satellite communications array which began to spew sounds. They both scrambled for the speaker phone button. To his great joy, Stork got it, and he gave Schmitty a smug look.

"Gentlemen. Are you there?" a man's voice asked.

"Here." They said in chorus as they snapped to attention. It was so rare that any voice communication was used that it was not only a special occasion, but it was almost a certainty that whoever was on the other end of the satellite link was fairly highly ranked within his majesty's government.

"Good... good, now turn your scrambler on, there's a couple of good chaps!" instructed the voice.

Schmitty looked puzzled and Stork reached over to a panel, and flicked a switch. An array of blinking lights came on. "Check." he said giving Schmitty another smug look.

"Wonderful. Now neither of you are to discuss this with anyone." The voice continued, sounding slightly distorted now.

"Excuse me, but who are you? I don't recognize your voice sir." said Stork as a scowl came over Schmitty's face.

"Forgive me gentlemen, I'm Professor Quatermass."

They looked at each other in stunned silence. The legendary Dr. Quatermass was supposed to have died some years earlier - in a nuclear explosion no less!

"I heard you were dead." blurted Stork, and Schmitty jabbed him with his elbow for it, producing an "Ow!"

8

"We just have the same surname. No relation." he explained, then added: "I get a lot of that."

"Oh." they said in chorus, this time eyeing each other as if they were both annoyed.

"Now gentlemen." the professor continued, "What you have here is of the upmost importance to his majesty's government. We've had a team on standby for this very eventuality, and they are on their way to you now. In fact the whole survey was instigated to find this object. Incidentally, that is why we've carefully removed all personnel but two of you from the base."

"Excuse me sir." interrupted Schmitty, "But what exactly IS that thing anyway?" Stork rolled his eyes as if he had known all along, but in actuality he was just as curious as Schmitty and hadn't dared to ask, so he was glad that Schmitty had asked instead.

"I'm sorry, which one are you?" came the reply.

"Benjamin Schmidt sir."

"Oh yes, your file stated that you were the bolder, more inquisitive one. Well, to answer your question, we think it is extraterrestrial in origin."

"Pull the other one!" he exclaimed, without hesitation.

"No, it really could be. You see, its existence and approximate location was announced last year by a radio message from deep space. In fact, the gentleman who decoded the message will be on his way to take over just as soon as we can get it excavated."

They both looked stunned.

The professor continued: "We decided to look for it, and that's what you chaps have been up to actually, not surveying the ground beneath the polar ice cap but looking for *that* thing. Jolly good show finding it what?"

"A spuh, SPACECRAFT?" blurted Stork.

"Yes, that's our hope."

"But it's shaped like a musket ball." he protested.

Schmitty kicked Stork lightly in the ankle.

9

"Enough of this, gentlemen. I'm only telling you *this* much out of courtesy, to satisfy your curiosity so you don't run amok looking for answers, since we still need your assistance."

"Sir?" they asked in chorus.

"The crews will need your data and other assistance."

"*CREWS*, Sir?" asked Schmitty.

They thought that only a few people were coming.

"We'll need a complete rundown on what you know, as well as what you suspect. Also, access to your base, your knowledge and expertise on glaciers, that sort of thing - we definitely need your help if we're going to excavate it."

They gave each other a look as they turned white.

"When will they arrive sir?" asked Schmitty finally.

"Shortly. As I said, we've been expecting this."

They exchanged glances, and shrugged.

Not two hours later, the base was inundated by an invasion of freight helicopters. Apparently, they had been waiting for weeks at McMurdo. Just over two hundred scientists, engineers and technicians poured out of the choppers, carrying crate after crate of test equipment and supplies. The place was overrun, but everyone seemed to be respectful of Schmitty and Stork, which made them all the more confused. Neither of them were accustomed to being in charge of anything.

# IV
# OUROBORUS

*"I don't understand this!
I keep cutting pieces off of it and it's still TOO SHORT!"*

As was stated earlier, the scientists in the Black Ops lab were trying to open a doorway into another dimension. Some call it a wormhole. Their thinking was two-dimensional for the event horizon, which was their primary mistake. You see, if you are going to open a doorway from one dimension to another, it should stand to reason that the doorway should contain all of the dimensions of the one you are *starting* from. This gives you an interfacing area that is completely in contact with both. Then, all that is left is to add the extra dimension to your doorway, put a 'hinge' on it on *that* axis and viola!, all you have to do is let it rotate on that hinge.

For example; if you wanted to go from a two-dimensional world to a three-dimensional world, one would not use a one dimensional door. One needs to use a two dimensional door, but how can it swing open? That's the third dimension. So add the third dimension to a two dimensional door, and the door can then swing open *on that newly added axis* and the two dimensional beings can go through it - pulled - I might add, by an invisible force they are not familiar with: called *gravity*.

Each higher dimension allows for change in the next lower dimension. From our point of view, it works much like a stack of animation cells. Therefore we can see their future and past from a vantage point that is outside of their existence. From their standpoint, the next higher dimension is therefore thought of as we think of time. However, the way actual time works is much more interesting.

It should be pointed out that if the door is opened the other way, things can fall *into* the two-dimensional world; pulled by the same force. Now if there were multiple two-dimensional worlds stacked on each other, people could travel between parallel worlds or rather; their version of time. If one did not add the 'hinge' but merely warped their dimensional plane, they could travel over great distances faster than light. This effect can be made to be continuous by 'surfing' on the wave until your destination is reached. The amplitude and distance traveled is governed by the strength of the pulse that creates the wave, gravity shear being the propulsive force, but it is a force with which they are unfamiliar.

As for going into the fourth dimension from the three dimensional world with which we are all familiar, takes a three-dimensional 'door' or interface. Then and only then, is the fourth-dimensional component added to allow the door to swing open. After that happens, there is a force, not unlike gravity that will pull things inside of it. Conversely, the door can be opened the 'other way' and allow things from the fourth dimension to come into the third. However, that is not recommended as there are some pretty nasty things that reside in the 'spaces in between' and you might not want to invite them over for breakfast... lest you be the main course. But that is another story.

When one tries to open a door, skipping a dimension, i.e. a two dimensional door attempting to rotate into the fourth, the best you can hope for is to lose your door, the worst is a massive implosion, caused by the collapse of the dimensional fabric itself.

The project's code name was 'PANDORA' due to the inevitable and proverbial can of worms that it would undoubtedly open, but the people working on the project had nicknamed it: R.A.T.R. for; 'Right-Angles-To-Reality', which was much more descriptive.

The people behind the project expected it to grant them the limitless power over this world that time travel would provide. More level heads argued against the project altogether, pointing out the possible disastrous results. After losing the debate, they promptly packed their bags and headed for the relative safety of the top-secret Martian colony. Although that's as far away from the home planet as they could get, it wasn't nearly far enough. What's worse is that they knew it. All it could buy them was a front row seat to observe the formation of a black hole.

# THE HALO EFFECT

The second mistake was to use massive amounts of power. What they were doing can be compared to trying to force their way through a keyhole, when all they really had to do was, in effect, turn a doorknob. Certain hints were left by the creator himself. No matter, human beings need to be hit over the head now and then.

Everyone in the Black Ops lab was silent except Dr. Morax. "I said more POWER!" he hissed at the technicians that were operating the console. They frantically worked the controls to finagle that last ounce of power their ruthless boss was demanding.

The event horizon grew, flexed and almost flowed like a disk full of blue plasma on its side: only it was a partial effect not connected to the edges of the ring. Instead, it began to flex, twist and oscillate almost straining to become three-dimensional. Back and forth it swayed, like a suspension bridge about to break in high winds. Swaying more and more with each oscillation, it paused at the peak of each wobble as if it were sitting on the top of a hill, waiting for momentum to pull it over the edge. Each delay was longer until after what seemed like ages, it finally appeared to flow smoothly into itself, as if it were pouring into it's own innards.

Morax cracked a sly smile. He felt vindicated. This was exactly the effect that he was after. This was the same sort of vortex that had taken his brother, and the engineers said was "a fluke, that could never be duplicated."

As the vortex seemed to stabilize, he gingerly reached into the center of the funnel-like disturbance, and watched his arm stretch almost to infinity. Those watching from the side saw his arm go *into* the ring but not *through*, which was a very unsettling effect. He felt a hand grab his. It felt familiar, and he was sure it was his brother's hand. He started to pull, gently, as if not to break the grip or disturb the delicately balanced vortex. After what seemed like an eternity, a full minute actually, the other hand was beginning to emerge from the ring to the gasps of the on looking staff.

# V
# **ARTIFICE**

"The same rules applied equally to everyone? THAT'S NOT FAIR!"

"One more twist and...? Darn!" he thought to himself as he struggled yet again with "That *darned* cube!" Perhaps he WOULD be better off if he had turned it into a novelty item by making all the faces the same color.

The puzzle cube was tormenting Harvey Johnson; a 5'9" tall, relatively thin man of forty years, who was embarrassed by his apparent inability to solve puzzles that everybody else, and he did mean *everybody* else, in the world could solve. Well, that may be the price for being able to solve the puzzles that almost nobody else in the world could solve... maybe, but it wasn't much of a consolation to him. The one thing that he wanted most of all was to be able to fit in with everybody else and he thought it involved thinking like the masses. The truth was, that most of those people wished that they could be more like *him*. In essence, most wished that they could think outside the box, and he wished that he could think inside it.

When the doorbell rang, he hastily put the woefully unsolved cube down on the end table. It was best for the reputation not to be seen unsuccessfully fiddling with such a thing.

The heavy-set middle-aged man at the door was the Director of Covert Operations. "The DIRECTOR himself?" thought Harvey "If he paid a visit, he would be accompanied, and would NEVER show up in an unsecured part of town. This must be important!"

He cautiously opened the door, and said "Hi Bob, what brings you to my neck of the woods?"

'Bob' was actually all Harvey knew the director by. Apparently Bob's surname was some sort of secret. Big deal! Why didn't he make one up! Oh well, at least he had kept his first name - maybe. Actually, he had been the director of the FBI's domestic anti-terrorism bureau. He rose to the rank of general during the race war due to his inestimable help in second guessing the tactics and movements of the Aryan Army. After the war, there was no more domestic terrorism to speak of, so he was promoted to the post of director of covert activities. His surname is seldom mentioned for fear of reprisals against his family due to the fact that there were still many Aryans, or Aryan sympathizers out there, loyal to 'the cause', and hell bent on revenge. Someone should tell them that you can't be after revenge if you're the instigator. If anybody who didn't have proper clearance asked about his name, Bob would simply reply "Dobbs." as he clenched his pipe. True, there was a resemblance, but it was usually enough of a witticism to get by. Also, over the years, Bob was able to lose his slight accent and as an added bonus, Aryans who have heard and subsequently memorized his voice were unlikely to identify him.

Bob was here on a mission, time was short and there was far too much at stake to leave it up to anyone else. He would often say "if you want something done right..."

Harvey headed for his kitchen, which had a short dividing wall to the living room, that allowed the conversation to continue. "Can I offer you anything?" he asked as he stuck his head in the refrigerator.

"No, I'm fine." came the reply as Harvey foraged around, looking for something, but not quite knowing what he wanted at that moment. He would know what it was when he found it. Finally pulling out a large pitcher of orange juice, he poured himself a glass.

"I love this stuff." he said with a big grin as he returned the pitcher to the refrigerator.

Meanwhile, Bob was looking idly around Harvey's apartment more out of curiosity than for any other reason. He realized that he had never been inside his friend's home before. As Harvey returned to the living room, Bob sort-of snapped to attention as a soldier would if he had almost been caught sleeping at his post. He felt like an intruder, despite their friendship and his position. Harvey looked at Bob and raised an eyebrow while motioning to the most comfortable chair in the room - Obviously Harvey's favorite. Bob got the hint, though he didn't feel like sitting, so he paced a little which was a good way to keep looking around to satisfy his curiosity without any suspicion of prying, and it helped hide the way he was feeling about why he was there.

"Harvey... what do you know about 'pre-flood technology?'" he asked, in a rather matter of fact tone.

"Who was he kidding?" Harvey was an amateur archaeologist and pre-flood technology was his favorite subject, you could even say it was his passion! He was convinced that before the great flood of antiquity, there was a global civilization that had achieved nuclear power and space flight. They had apparently destroyed themselves in a nuclear confrontation and consequently vanished from the face of the earth. Every now and then, amazing artifacts would surface, like the map of Piri Re'is, the Peking 'Walkman', the Egyptian television receiver and flying model airplane, the south African nuclear reactor, the ancient Greek navigational computer and the Baghdad battery... the list went on and on. Who knows what had been developed and lost over the millennia?

Realizing that Bob had something for him to look at, he asked: "What have you got?" trying to not show his excitement as Bob picked up the 'accursed cube' and began to fiddle with it.

'How did that trick go?' Bob thought to himself: 'Oh yes, something to do with the center squares...' "Well," he said, still fiddling with the cube, "It's a little tricky to explain."

"That's a switch." replied Harvey, rather facetiously.

"Quite" Bob replied, as he place the solved (darn!) cube back onto the end table, with a smirk as if he knew Harvey's 'little secret', then he continued: "Take a look at this:" pulling a photo from his inside jacket pocket. Hardly a regulation photo, but it did the trick.

Harvey took one look and dropped his orange juice.

# VI
# TAMTEMIYAH

"That's easy for YOU to say!"

"What am I looking at?" asked Harvey.

"We were hoping *you* could tell *us*."

"Well, it looks somewhat like the map of Piri Re'is... it shows the hills and valleys of Antarctica, and the details skew at the edges as if it were a satellite photo - just like the map, and it's too clear to be a satellite photo. It doesn't show any clouds."

"How right you are, it has more detail to it than any photo ever taken from orbit."

Bob finally sat down, and looked up at Harvey, who sat on the couch and waited.

"So where *was* it taken?"

"It was taken at the south pole, or thereabouts. It's a gargantuan sphere that seems somehow to be reflecting, or should I say *depicting*, the surface of the earth, without impediments like clouds or the ice cap."

Harvey looked at the photo again and the details were not reversed. He raised an eyebrow and walked over to his desk and picked up a file that contained a chart of Antarctica on it, compared the two and looked wide-eyed at Bob.

"Yes, at the location you deciphered from that radio signal last year, compensating for continental drift, that is." Although Harvey didn't seem to be listening, Bob continued. "Not only does it show an image of the planet, but the astonishing thing is, that with sufficient magnification, you can observe airplanes in flight, cars on the street, things like that."

"Then how big is it?"

Bob dug into his inside jacket pocket again and fished out another piece of paper. He read a bit of it for a moment and replied: "Best measurement right now shows it's just over 1.6 kilometers in diameter." in a matter-of-fact way.

17

"It's what?"

"See for yourself." he replied as he handed the piece of paper to Harvey.

"I have to see this with my own eyes!"

"I thought you might say that. The car is waiting, we can leave as soon as you're ready."

* * *

As they rode in the limousine to the air base, Bob let Harvey in on the rest of the details.

"We've tried everything and I mean absolutely everything, to see inside the thing and there seems to be no way. Not even neutrinos pass through it."

Harvey raised an eyebrow at that. "How about those talented folks at detachment 'G'?"

"They all drew a blank."

"Very funny." said Harvey dryly. He knew that most remote viewers drew what they 'saw' on a sketch pad.

"No really, none of them could get inside that thing with their minds."

"Well, it stands to reason that if neutrinos can't penetrate it, then psychic energy shouldn't be able to either."

"Hmmmmm." said Harvey, deep in thought as he examined the file Bob had given him as they entered the car. "If this can stop neutrinos..." his voice trailing off as his mind was lost in thought. "...what a power source!"

"In short, the situation is like this." said Bob, "There are several countries laying claim to the object, probably because of it's scientific potential, but  they claim it was partially on their territory."

"I thought that the borders were clearly defined in Antarctica, and this doesn't look like it's across any of them."

"True, it is currently on British territory, but the thinking is that the object started out exactly on the pole itself, where the border lines intersect."

"I see, and they are using that to make a claim to it as a result."

"Exactly. Even though the continental drift is what brought it to it's current location, and no nations existed when it appears to have, uh, first *arrived*."

"Continental drift only? Not glacial movement?"

"The cavern it is in clearly shows that the ice is moving around it."

"Wow!" He looked at more photos that showed the scale of it.

"The scientists that are studying it right now believe that the energy it obtains from neutrinos is partially being used to melt the ice. So it stands its ground."

"If the continent hadn't moved?"

"It would have been exactly where you said to look; the southern magnetic pole."

"So why me?" asked Harvey. "Not that I want to get out of this mind you." he added.

"Well," started Bob, counting on his fingers. "...there's your knowledge of ancient high-tech, your ability to find alternatives where others fail, and frankly you're the only one the nations involved could agree on, because of your involvement in that Overworld affair."[2]

"Oh." said Harvey. He was a very humble man and wasn't very good at accepting compliments.

"The long and the short of it is that they all believe you are the most qualified not only to determine what it is and what to do about it, but to decide who has claim to it."

"I take it then that they'll go with my end recommendation, no matter what it is?"

"You have complete authority over the project."

"Wow!" he exclaimed in a low voice.

---

[2] *A world-wide criminal organization offered Harvey power, and he exposed them instead..*

"I've already taken the liberty of having the crews briefed on you."

Harvey gave him a look. If Bob took any more liberties... just then an irresistible urge hit him.

"You know Bob, I hate to ask, but can we make a stop? We left in a bit of a hurry, you know?"

"*sigh*" Bob flicked on the intercom, and said: "Driver, pull over at the next rest stop would you please?" Then he looked at Harvey; "It's all that orange juice you drink. Do you know that?" He had a twinkle in his eye. "That stuff goes right through you."

"Yeah yeah yeah, but it's not that, it's the other thing if you must know."

Bob smiled and shook his head.

When they arrived at a service station, Bob decided he wasn't going to let Harvey too far out of his sight, so he went inside with him.

"Great, a line." said Harvey.

"Take it easy sport, you're all grown up now, you can handle it." His sense of humor was starting to grate on Harvey's nerves, which amused Bob all the more.

While they were waiting, they noticed out of the relative quiet, a young girl holding her mother's hand in the adjacent line but ahead of them, continuously chanting the name: "Tamtemiyah" over and over. Bob and Harvey exchanged looks over this. It was cute the way the little girl seemed amused over the strange word.

When the lines brought them next to each other, the little girl looked Harvey straight in the eye and motioned for him to come closer. He bent down and smiled at the little girl, who pointed at him and said: "Tamtemiyah will talk to YOU!" Then she gave him a coy look, turned away and was silent.

The mother immediately tugged on the little girl's arm and said: "What did I tell you about talking to strangers?", and they took their turn in the women's restroom.

"You can go now." said Bob as the line to the men's room was also clear.

"I don't have to anymore." he said almost under his breath, with a far off look in his eyes. "Let's go."

Bob sighed and muttered something about "Kids these days!" referring to Harvey.

As they got back into the car, Bob asked Harvey; "Do you mind telling me what that was all about?"

"I don't know, I had the strangest feeling though. Like the little girl knew something."

# VII
# SPOLIATION

"Sometimes a little knowledge is a dangerous thing."

At the government research lab in Arizona, a technician named Marjorie, was so overcome by disbelief that she leaned backward and sat on the edge of the console behind her. Now, several things were happening at once. Her posterior did indeed de-activate a control that was to be blamed for the coming malfunction, but it wasn't at all to blame, as a matter of fact it had almost nothing at all to do with causing it. Further, if she hadn't sat on the button that turned off one of the zero point energizer banks, the field would have collapsed in such a way that might have swallowed the planet by creating a black hole or quantum singularity. So in effect her posterior had inadvertently saved their proverbial bacon.

Just as the two hands had cleared the outer edge of the event horizon and all could see, the field began to collapse due to Marjorie's little accident. As she turned around quickly to re-activate the control, Morax turned to her and hissed, "*DAMN* YOU!" and the 'funnel' began to collapse further. Morax frantically tried pulling harder as the resistance increased. The field pulsed a few times and then simply stopped. He was left standing there holding a forearm that had a smoking sleeve at the point where it ended, just shy of the elbow. As it went limp he wailed in anguish. Quickly regaining his composure though, he glared at Marjorie, then handed the severed arm to a med-tech without looking and said: "See if you can preserve this!"

Then he looked back at her. If looks could kill, she would have been a stain on the wall. He slowly, menacingly started toward her raising his cane as if to pull a sword out of it. She looked terrified to the point of panic and tried to back away only to bump into the same console she had sat on just moments before - serving only to infuriate Morax all the more.

At that moment, a telephone rang on the main control console. The head technician answered it. Then he addressed the Doctor: "Sir!"

"Not *now*!" he hissed, focusing on Marjorie.

"It's our contact at detachment 'G'!"

Morax paused. His face softened from sheer rage. He glanced at the technician then back at Marjorie: "We'll pick up where we left off *later*, my dear." Then he went over to the phone.

Marjorie gasped a sigh of relief, and swallowed hard. Morax's rapid mood swings were his most feared trait. No one ever seemed to know what he was going to do next. They feared him for good reason, mostly due to the fact that he had been known to do unspeakable things with impunity.

He took the phone: "Morax." he stated simply. He paused and listened for some time and then said "Very good, I'll have a team there ASAP. No one, and I want to make this perfectly clear, absolutely no one *else* is to go near it without my permission. Understood? Good. Don't worry, we'll take care of the cleanup, as usual. No, he won't be a problem. I'll take care of him myself."

He hung up the phone, and turned to the head technician: "I want Alpha team ready for travel immediately." Then he added, "Tell them... that the climate will be..." He paused dramatically, looked at Marjorie, and finished his sentence as his eyes narrowed: "*COLD.*"

Marjorie, was a member of Alpha Team. She did not look too happy, especially since Dr. Morax was looking right at her and smiling. He even nodded, chuckling softly. This was not going to be good. In fact, he was dreaming up ways to kill her *slowly*, using the cold. Death by selective frostbite. Yes, that would do nicely. He wondered how long she could be kept alive during the process. It would prove to be and interesting study.

# VIII
# HELLO

"You say 'goodbye' and I say 'hello'."

Thursday evening, Dec 20th, 2012 Anno Domini

Harvey stood there, stunned. He had never before seen anything so large in his entire life. However, the size of the thing was not the most amazing part. It was hovering, set in place as solid as a rock not wavering at all, but hovering none the less, lending credence to Bob's spacecraft theory. It was a giant sphere that looked like a mirror that was reflecting the entire planet. It was an exact replica of the planet done in, for want of a better term; *CHROME*.

The sphere was so massive that to stand anywhere near where it was closest to the ground, was to be well under it, and to see the edge which was far beyond the limits of peripheral vision, the natural tendency was to look up and backward until one lost balance. It was also an unsettling feeling to stand under something so massive as this with no visible means of support. It gave one the feeling that it might just fall on you at any moment. What helped was that it appeared to be in the bottom of a valley, or depression, so the ground sloped around most of it, making access to its surface a little easier.

"Are you *sure* it isn't attached up there somewhere?" he asked, waving his hand at the upper regions of the sphere and almost falling over backwards in the process. He was not too far from the edge, but it was still difficult to look up without losing his balance.

"Quite." came Bob's reply, as he rolled his eyes.

"This thing is... well, it's AWESOME!"

"That" said Bob, "Is probably the first time that word has been used correctly in the last thirty years."

"Well, it IS!" marveled Harvey as he almost fell over backwards again.

"Careful!" said Bob. "Maybe it would help if you stopped looking up."

"Gee, thanks! I never would have figured that out by myself!"

"What are friends for? If not to point out the obvious."

"Next you're going to tell me that you can't shake the feeling that it's about to fall on your head."

"Darn! You beat me to it." said Bob as he snapped his fingers and grinned broadly.

Scaffolding had been set up at various intervals around the sphere, and a crew of about a hundred were working on it, examining the surface, taking photographs, etc.

The massive ice cave had been hurriedly etched out of the glacier with "thermite"; a military-grade ice melting explosive material - the only one available at the base. What seemed strange was that *so much* of it was available. Several tons of it in fact had been brought in just for this project, months *before* this thing was found. It was as if they had anticipated its discovery.

They had burrowed a sloping shaft down to the sphere and widened it to leave room to work, and pumped out the water. What was strange though, was how little water there was. It was almost as if more than half of it went 'down the drain' or perhaps somewhere else...

The ice cave was reasonably well-lit with over 100 light plants[3], and curiously, the chamber did not require heating. In fact, it was so warm that the ice was slowly melting.

The walls and ceiling of the ice cave were dripping, and curiously enough, the drips that touched the sphere seemed to disappear, offering protection from the "rain". Some of the workers were observing this, not knowing what to make of it. A drip would land on the mirror-like surface, and seem to spread and almost evaporate at the same time. It was unclear if the drips were being absorbed, evaporated or just evenly distributed over the entire surface. The humidity seemed to be too high for evaporation, unless the sphere were quite warm. Some had secretly

---

[3] *Portable gasoline powered floodlights, mounted on their own trailer.*

guessed that the sphere had absorbed most of the 'missing water' but didn't dare voice the theory.

No temperature readings of the surface could be taken. Every attempt failed. It was always at the same temperature as the probe touching it. They had tried super-cooled probes and red-hot ones. Always with the same result.

When touched, the surface seemed completely frictionless. The only way you could tell that you had touched something is that its surface resisted further movement in that direction. It was also difficult to push with any appreciable force as the complete lack of friction on the surface invariably made your hand slip in one direction or another, effectively keeping workers off the top of the sphere. "It was as if you were touching solid air." remarked one technician. It was theorized that perhaps this was a force field around something, which would indeed explain some of its properties, but no one had ever made one so impenetrable or on such a scale before. This was indeed intriguing.

While observing all of this from the mouth of the access tunnel, Bob and Harvey walked up to a technician who was looking through the scope on a surveyor's range finder to measure the sphere, Harvey asked: "What's the verdict?"

The man replied without looking up: "1,609.3 meters in diameter - almost *exactly*. I can't go any further with the accuracy of this setup."

Harvey recognized the equipment so he reached forward and turned a dial, which showed the sphere to be exactly one mile in diameter.

"SONOFAGUN! How'd you...?" He looked up and saw Harvey. He snapped to attention. "Sir! I did not see you there!"

"Keep up the good work." said Harvey with a wink and they left him to his instruments. There was a lot more to take in.

Some men were using a cutting torch on the surface of the sphere, to no avail. They had anticipated that it was extraterrestrial in origin, and could therefore stand the heat of entering the atmosphere so it had stood to reason that it could survive the heat of the thermite. Still, they were using the cutting torch as if it would eventually heat the surface measurably.

A man ran up to Bob: "A preliminary report sir!" he said presenting a clipboard.

"Yes of course... But everything goes to Johnson here from now on." That man nodded at Harvey. Bob lifted a page, and raised an eyebrow, glanced at the lowest part of the sphere and then he turned to Harvey. "Any ideas yet?"

"A few, actually. What's that report tell?"

"Well, I think you should come take a look for yourself. I think you'll like it." He paused, and looked Harvey directly in the eye. "It's right up your alley."

The three of them walked to the lowest point of the sphere, quite a hike down the hill from where they had been standing - Harvey thought that this was in order to be "out of the way", but this was getting ridiculous!

There were some orange traffic cones with the word "CAUTION" written on each, arranged in a 25 foot circle under the very bottom of the gigantic sphere. Bob handed the clipboard back to the same man who had given it to him. "Watch this!" He picked up a stone, and held it out at arms length, as to be within the circle of cones. He carefully let go of the rock and it didn't fall. In fact, it stayed more or less in place as if it were in zero gravity. Harvey's face lit up like a Christmas tree and they looked at each other and began to laugh. They stopped at the same time, then Harvey gingerly vaulted over the cones.

The most fun that Harvey had had was playing around in zero gravity, and Bob knew all about it. No, he was not an astronaut, but rather he had frequently chartered a cargo plane and had the pilot constantly go in and out of dives, thus producing the same effect as an absence of gravity. This technique had been used by NASA to get astronauts used to the absence gravity, as well as by Hollywood for making films about astronauts in flight. This had become a regular outing for him, and he had probably spent as much time doing this as anyone. In other words, he was expert at flying without wings.

Bob on the other hand had watched videos of this and marveled at what Harvey could do. He had often mentioned his amusement and envy. Due to an inner ear problem, it wasn't practical for him to come along on a cargo plane. Regular, pressure-controlled flight gave him problems as it was. This time, he could see it in person and perhaps try it himself. So, over the edge he went too, as out of character as it was.

The guard stammered: "P-Please sir WAIT!" But he was too late.

They floated in the air, just as they had expected, and got more than a few odd looks from the people who were examining the sphere. After all, these two were "in charge", and they were acting just like children. Harvey expertly performed some aerobatics that exactly positioned him at the edge of the effect some ten feet off the ground. "Watch out!" exclaimed Bob; "The report states that this field - or whatever you call it - is cone shaped and goes all the way up to the sphere."

"That's just what I was trying to determine; the size and shape of the field."

"No, you were showing off!"

A senior scientist, named Linda was wondering what the commotion was all about, so she got up from her console and walked to the other side of the cones. She stood there watching as Harvey slowly drifted downwards. As their eyes met, she looked down at her clipboard to hide her amusement at his antics.

She regained her composure before looking up at him again. She liked what she saw despite, or perhaps because of his childish behavior.

He became lost in her eyes, upside down to him though they were. She may have not been the most beautiful woman he had ever seen, but she was certainly the most *attractive*.

Realizing how silly he must look, he looked at his shoes as many nicer men did in a situation like that, which typically gave many women the idea that they were some sort of lost puppy that wasn't worth their attention. Linda was not one of those.

Since the direction he looked in this case was 'up', he had an idea that distracted him. He muttered under his breath; "I wonder..." and he performed some sort of back flip and went feet first toward the sphere and his legs disappeared into the surface! He held onto the 'edge' of the sphere and kept himself from disappearing into the 'hole', which could not be seen. How he clung on was a mystery, because the whole sphere was frictionless... well, at least that's what it seemed whenever they tested it.

By then, almost everyone on the site was gathering to see these two high-ranking government officials make fools of themselves playing in zero gravity. It was quite a spectacle. Several of the crew gasped at the disappearance Mr. Johnson's legs. Moments later, he managed to crawl back out. The surface still seemed to be intact even where his legs had entered. He just stood there, upside down on the bottom of the sphere.

Bob looked at the crew, who all looked perplexed. They had tried something like this, but the sphere had seemed solid on the bottom, and Bob had read that part of the report. One man rubbed his head where he had a nice little goose egg to prove the solidity of the sphere's lowest point. Somehow it was now acting like a hologram covering some sort of opening. Bob shrugged, flapped his arms for want of something else to do, muttering something about the first star on the left, and slowly managed to lower himself to the ground, to meet Harvey just outside the traffic cones.

Harvey took special care to land as far from Linda as he could, wishing to avoid further eye-contact so as to save what little 'face' he had left. Linda correctly took his somewhat obvious avoidance to mean that he was interested in her, which made her all the more determined to meet him officially. She had a legitimate excuse so she approached him as he stood there looking puzzled, arriving at the same time as Bob. She smiled at Bob, and looked directly at Harvey, who was failing miserably at his attempts to avoid eye contact with her.

"So, when do we send in a snake?" she asked Harvey with a growing grin.

"How's that?" he asked, taken somewhat aback, not being 'on the same page' with her.

"Oh! Where are my manners? This is Linda Kowalski." said Bob, "One of the most brilliant scientists I have ever had the pleasure to know."

She playfully backhanded Bob and said "Oh, Bob! You're embarrassing me!" Grinning at Harvey, she extended her right hand but deliberately didn't position it for a handshake, mostly to see what his reaction would be. "And you are Harvey Johnson, of the *Q.E.D.*[4] think tank."

He seemed surprised that his reputation had preceded him, specially in the culture of secretive government work where no one knew anybody else - by design. Then he realized that they had all been informed about him before his arrival.

"I've been watching you." she added.

This made his eyes go wide, just as she planned. Then she smiled and waved toward the sphere with her left hand. "Flying."

He breathed a sigh of relief, bowed toward her, kissed her hand as his eyes looked up at hers. "Charmed." he said.

She curtsied, and beamed at him. 'An old-fashioned guy!' she thought to herself. She loved that stuff.

Bob rolled his eyes. "Are you kids finished playing?"

They both gave him a look as if to say; 'Look who's talking!'. Then they took on a more mature demeanor. Harvey looked at Linda with a sober, grown-up look and asked; "Snake?"

"You know, a...*probe*." she said, raising and lowering her eyebrows as seductively as she could as she said the last word, knowing full well the effect it would have on him. She didn't know exactly why she wanted to torture him like this, but she could hardly help herself. It was fun! She followed it up with a sly grin.

"Oh yes!" he said with a glint in his eye, finally understanding were she was coming from. He asked: "Where's the setup?" as he looked around in every direction except behind him.She raised her eyebrows as she pointed over his shoulder. As it turned out, in his efforts to avoid her, he had landed right next to the equipment in question. He almost jumped at the sight of the technicians manning the console, who

---

[4] *Quod Erat Demonstrandum -the Latin for "Which was Demonstrated." i.e.: Latin for "DUH!"*

chuckled a little at his reaction. He was beginning to get a little embarrassed by all of this. They had not only seen but heard *everything*.

As if sensing the tension and the approval to continue, the Chief Engineer took over: "All right people!" he shouted with a single clap of the hands as if coaching some 'jocks', "Let's go for a sample!" he bellowed.

A flurry of activity ensued the end result of which was a hose raised up to the bottom of the sphere. They started a pump which brought in a sample of whatever atmosphere there was inside. The gas chromatograph, spectrum analyzer and other test equipment on the other end of the pump were all set into operation. After a suitable time for the equipment to complete all of its tests, a small printout spat out of a slot. A technician tore the printout off, and handed it quickly to the Chief, who looked it over and wrinkled his brow in a show of puzzlement. Linda walked over to him:

"Well?"

"See for yourself." he replied as he handed her the slip of paper.

As she studied the printout the Chief Engineer bellowed at the others.

"How 'bout the camera? Can we get a look at its innards yet?"

"No picture, too dark." came the reply.

"Well turn the lights on! Do I have to tell ya everything?" he teased.

"Already did, still nothing."

"Are you sure they're working?"

"Yeah. They check out, conductivity and current drain is there, just no picture." he said looking at his instruments.

"Well, pull it out so we can have a look at it." Then he muttered "If you want something done right..." as he approached the equipment.

As they were retracting the probe, Linda finished her analysis of the data.

"*THAT'S* weird." she said.

"Are you sure the equipment is working properly?" she asked the Chief over her shoulder.

"Of course." he said curtly, as if he were insulted at the question.

"What about the camera?" she asked playfully, demonstrating that he might be wrong.

"Grrrrr...." came his almost playful answer.

By this time, Harvey was curious and approached. "What is it?" he asked.

"Well, for starters its got a slightly higher oxygen content and higher pressure than the outside atmosphere and some trace gasses we can't identify but otherwise it's like good ol' regular air in there." she explained, puzzled that the higher pressure didn't force some air outwards through Harvey's 'hole'.

"Could it have been open to the atmosphere when it first arrived?"

"You mean with the planetary oxygen levels falling over time?"

"Yes."

"Hmmm, if that's right it could assist us in dating this thing, but look at this." She pointed at the part of the report that was supposed to list particulate matter and showed only zeros followed by the words: 'parts per trillion'.

"I see. Could that be due to Settling?" he asked hopefully.

"Well, that might be a viable explanation, but there is absolutely nothing. If it had been able to settle, it couldn't settle that much no matter how long it was sitting and some of it should have been disturbed when you opened the, uh, 'door'." She crinkled her brow, "There are no particulates of *any* kind, no microbial life, no dust. Nothing. I mean *something* should have at least drifted in with the probe. This is simply the *purest* air I have ever heard of. It's as if it has one *hell* of an air filter in there."

"Perhaps it *does*." They exchanged eye-contact - something they had both been avoiding. Then Harvey, thinking about the main reason they had just tested the air inside, continued: "So, it's *safe* to breathe then?" Hoping for a straight answer.

Linda sighed, looked deep in thought staring off into imagined distance. Then she snapped out of it and looked at the printout again.

"The air doesn't look *unhealthy*... as a matter of fact, that atmosphere might actually clean your lungs over time. The other thing is that the higher oxygen content might make you a little more alert, and the pressure isn't too much more. Getting used to it shouldn't take long."

"And those *trace* gasses?"

"All we can tell at this point is that they appear to be inert, and their concentration is extremely low anyway, so they shouldn't pose any kind of problem."

"Ill take all that as a 'yes' then?"

She glared at him, knowing what she had just put the Chief Engineer through. "Grrrrr....."

"Well then. The only thing left to do is to *go inside*." he pointed out, as he took a few slow paces toward the cones, but still remaining within earshot..

They both slowly looked up at the gargantuan sphere above their heads. The thought of what might be discovered inside left them both feeling more than a little bit nervous.

"Hey, shouldn't we..." Her voice trailed off as she realized that he was right. No germs, viruses or poisons to worry about, so what was the problem? They didn't seem to be able to learn anything more with the equipment they had.

"What about the darkness inside. It doesn't make sense and frankly, it gives me the willies." She scrunched up her shoulders a bit and almost put her hands on his shoulders as if to hide behind him, but stopped herself. Somehow, he made her feel safe.

"The willies?" he asked wheeling around with a raised eyebrow. "Hardly a scientific observation!"

She gave him a crooked smile like a child that had been caught with their hand in the cookie jar, and they started toward the traffic cones... "Come on smarty-pants! Let's see who chickens out first!"

Meanwhile, the work crews had discovered nothing. The camera and lights worked perfectly. The moment they pulled the camera out of the sphere, the image appeared on the monitor. Puzzled by this, the Chief Engineer approached Harvey and Linda as they were timidly toying with climbing the ladder to the sphere, which had been placed there to give some support in the gravity less field under the sphere.

"I wouldn't recommend going in just yet." said the Chief engineer. Relieved, they stopped.

"Why not?" asked Linda.

"I just don't like the fact that I can't get a camera working in there."

"Have you tried the quantum communicator?"

"It's not a radio-signal problem, besides, the other unit is back at the base."

"You've brought a quantum communicator?" asked Harvey almost excitedly.

"Are you familiar with the bi-location communications systems?"

"Am I? I'd love to try one of those babies out!" He looked around for it and spotted the unit sitting on the console. It didn't hurt that the technician was pointing at it clandestinely.

"Well, since even neutrinos can't penetrate that thing, we brought the quantum communicators in case we got inside. That is, *if* there was an inside." continued the Chief.

"That makes perfect sense. But why leave the other one at the base?"

"Have you ever tried to send radio signals through miles of ice?"

"Good point." Then he turned his attention to the Chief. "Have you tried a different camera?"

"A new one is going in now." he said as he motioned to another snake-like hose that was at that moment entering the sphere.

"This one's also got a fiber-optic cable, so we can look straight into that thing." he added. Harvey and Linda shrugged their shoulders and then went over to the console with the Chief, somewhat relieved.

Motioning to two monitors on either side of the main console, the Chief explained: "This is the camera's view, and this is the fiber optic cable's view, taken with a camera at *this* end."

They all watched the remote camera view in anticipation. As the probe got closer the image changed just as one would expect, and the moment it penetrated the surface, all went black.

"The fiber!" exclaimed the Chief.

They all looked at the other monitor. Nothing.

"Stop. Back it up a bit." he told the operator.

Back and forth over the threshold, the same thing happened.

"We're piping light in from this end through a secondary fiber-optic cable, so we should at least see some light. This is *very* strange."

"How far in are you going?" asked Harvey.

The all exchanged a puzzled glance.

Harvey shrugged, then leaned forward and placed his hand on a monitor to steady himself.

"What's the furthest you've gone in yet?" he asked the operator.

"I know where you're going with this." said the operator as he smiled.

"We've gone in exactly three feet."

"Three *feet*?" now realizing that he was not using metric measurements anymore, unlike everyone else.

"Yes, I know how fond you are of the old Imperial system of measure sir." he said with a grin. It was the same man who Harvey had earlier told to use that system when measuring the sphere. They exchanged smiles.

"It's just that I remembered the conversion tables." he whispered then looked up at the Chief and Linda who were a little puzzled.

"If it's a *mile* in diameter, how thick do you suppose the outside of this thing is?"

They both seemed to understand immediately, and they crouched by the monitor too.

"Go on." said Harvey encouragingly with a smile as he leaned forward for a better look and steadied himself with his hand on the panel.

They all watched the counter, first one yard, then two then three. The tension was building. Finally at approximately 40 feet, there was a flash of light, and static on the monitor for the remote camera. The monitor for the fiber-optic cable showed a dim light with no discernible image and nothing else. They all exchanged glances and the operator reeled in the probe as quickly as he could.

"Backup that video. I want to see it frame by frame." the Chief instructed the technician who was in charge of recording.

The video showed no transition. "Let me see the fiber video." The same thing. Nothing.

They all gathered at the base unit to see what the probe looked like now.

There was damage. The end of the probe was missing, and there were a number of wires hanging out the end where the camera should be. The fiber-optic lens was missing too. The cable had broken off in a messy fracture that had left it incapable of relaying any kind of usable image.

They all looked puzzled, and alarmed. Not only was there something inside, but it had a taste for cameras!

"Whew! Now I'm glad you stopped us from going in!" said Harvey.

"This doesn't make any sense." said Linda.

"I heard that!" replied the Chief.

"Not so much the camera thing, but the fact that we had to enter, what? 40 *feet*?" She glanced at the operator who nodded, then continued "To get through the, uh, outer covering, but why did we get an atmospheric sample if that's how thick it is?"

# IX
# What the...?

"I drank WHAT?"

A shot rang out and everything stopped as it echoed throughout the massive ice chamber.

"Please, resist. I haven't yet seen what these new weapons do to... Human flesshh." said Dr. Morax as he drew out the 'sh' as if gritting his teeth. He was an intensely angry man, and he was holding an example of the latest in firepower; a sonic disruption pistol.

Surprised, they all turned to see him standing nearby with his team of scientists and enough S*I*P*E[5] troops to conquer a small country. Well, that's how it appeared. Actually there were about 50 of them. They had silently rounded up most if not all of the technicians that were examining the sphere, and were holding them at gun point.

"You will excuse the intrusion of course, but this project is now under... *My* control! My Name is Morax, Dr. Morax. Follow my directives to the letter, and you just might live through this." he hissed. The S*I*P*Es snapped to attention.

Not knowing what to make of this, the stunned scientists just stood there, almost catatonic, like deer caught in headlights.

"I thank you for finding and opening the door, but my team can take it from here." Morax continued. He nodded at the S*I*P*Es and the front line of troops cocked their weapons. Bob and Harvey looked at each other in disbelief as if to ask: "Who *is* this guy?"

Finally regaining some composure and a little remaining dignity, Bob stepped forward.

"Now look here! You can't just..."

---

[5] *S.I.P.E: Soldier Integrated Protective Ensemble. An early part of the Land Warrior program but was returned to as the solution: protecting the troops was paramount. The technology was secondary.*

Dr. Morax cut him off: "Can't I?" A maniacal look crept menacingly over his face. Then he continued: "I assure you that those who have the guns, make the rules, and since I control those who have the guns, I can do anything I wish." He then hesitated as if pondering something deeply.

"Restrain the scientists, they may yet be useful." he said to the S*I*P*E Major standing next to him. Then he carefully aimed his sonic pistol. A crackling sound rang out and Bob just sizzled for a moment, a blank look came over his face and a foggy mist wafted out from his chest area. Then he simply fell forward onto the ground. Morax looked at his pistol with genuine respect and satisfaction.

Two of the S*I*P*Es; Lt. Argent and Cpl. Swanson, exchanged a look of concern. Obviously they were uncomfortable with this. Linda and Harvey were too upset to speak as then same two S*I*P*Es came up and restrained them. After struggling for a moment, Harvey managed to blurt out "You BASTARD!"

Morax looked at Harvey, smiled and replied, "Yes. What's your point?" then continued in a dismissive and matter-of-fact tone; "I also have the authority through the proper government channels, but you'll find that out soon enough." He motioned to the troops that had them by the arms. "Just hold them there for now." Harvey and Linda exchanged a very serious look. They were in trouble, deep trouble. This type of action was supposed to be a thing of the past.

Dr. Morax turned away so he could focus on the leader of the troops. "Major; I want you to take a team in right away. Let nothing stop you. I'll watch your progress on the monitors."

"Yes sir!" said the Major as he turned and motioned for the first half of troops to enter the sphere. It was a credit to their training that they were hardly phased by the lack of gravity as they filed in. They 'shanghaied' many of the technicians and made them carry in the cases of equipment and supplies that were there waiting for just such an expedition, but really weren't intended for Morax and his troops.

Everyone outside the sphere waited with baited breath to see what would happen next. The monitors on the portable consoles they had brought with them went blank, not even static just blank screens. No sound, no signal of any kind came back. Enraged, Dr. Morax approached Harvey and Linda. "What *happened* to them?" he demanded, holding his pistol under Linda's chin. Her neck strained under the pressure, as she tilted her head as far as she could, a look of abject fear in her eyes.

As if to answer him, the ice cavern started to crumble, and the access tunnel began to collapse. They all instinctively turned toward the sound, and realized that not only did they not have a way out anymore, but the ceiling was beginning to collapse as well. Apparently, the cavern was a little too large to be hollowed-out of ice, and the gunshot Morax had fired for attention was just enough to shake things loose - even if it took a few minutes to start falling apart. They turned back to the sphere just in time to see Morax disappearing into the sphere, obviously an act of self-preservation.

# X
# HEGIRA

"Come on feet and do your stuff or get left behind!"

Harvey and Linda exchanged looks. The S\*I\*P\*Es that were holding their arms began to loosen their grip and lower their weapons, unsure of what to do. The walls and the ceiling were coming down, but the sphere was so large that it protected them for the time being. Anyone under it was being sheltered from the downfall, but the scaffolding on the outside edge of it was almost certainly buried by now. A veritable tsunami of ice was rapidly headed their way from every direction. The temperature was dropping and the light was fading as the air pressure increased.

The Lt. said to the Cpl. "Let go." Then he hurriedly asked his freshly released prisoners: "Is it *safer* in there?" over the now near-deafening roar as he pointed at the sphere. They both nodded enthusiastically. There was no other place to go and there was a large avalanche headed their way. Whatever camera-eating horrors lurked inside the sphere, they had to be better than being crushed under the ice. It looked as though a few technicians had already been buried, and the survivors were scrambling for the relative safety of the sphere's interior. That was good enough for the Lt.

He ordered Cpl. Swanson to get the rest of the troops into the sphere. "After you." he said to Harvey and Linda with a grin, as he motioned to the sphere. They really didn't have enough time for such pleasantries, but Harvey had to ask: "Won't your boss be upset with you for this?"

"The way I see it, he can't give us orders if we're *dead!* Besides, I don't much like what he did to Bob." he shouted over the now deafening roar.

As they began to float toward the bottom of the sphere, Harvey yelled "You know, there's no guarantee that this thing will survive the ice collapsing on it!"

"*Now* you tell me!" shouted the Lt. with a grin, as they vanished into the sphere, which was not a moment too soon as the sphere was once again sealed in the dark, silent ice.

# XI
# Room with a view

"A test tube baby has a womb with a view."

Dr. Morax was in a bit of a pickle. Here he was inside what looked like an empty room. There were no obvious doors, and apparently no way in or out. He pondered his arrival. All he had done was to flee the falling ice, and presto!, he was here, in this unknown place. A room without a door.

He struck the wall with his gun, and then shrugged and took a shot at the wall. There was a small quake, as if it were upset by this action. "Best not try that one again." he muttered to himself. Then he kicked the wall to no avail. He stood there scratching his head, wondering where he was and what he could do about it.

After many attempts to find a door, something extraordinary happened. He began to get upset at being restricted so he reached-out with his rather formidable force of will. Then he fell *through* the wall into a long hallway. It was not so much a hidden door that he had fallen through, but it turned out that the walls could be made passable by sheer will. This sort of mind set was no stranger to him, as he had spent the majority of his life doing just that: manipulating individuals and yes, even governments by the sheer force of his will. He laughed out loud at this revelation. He was in a place where his normal way of doing things gave him an even bigger advantage than ever!

He telepathically queried the rudimentary intelligence of the walls, and even though they did not know the whole picture; he was amazed at what they told him. Then he began formulating a plan.

* * *

Harvey and Linda found themselves in a long corridor, with no one else in sight. Somehow, they were not even startled by this development.

42

Harvey took a deep breath, "Ah! Smell that sweet air! It's like a 'clean room'. There's nothing else like it."

"You're weird... but you're also right." she said as she took a deep breath too.

He chuckled softly.

"Uh, where are the *others?*" asked Linda when she finally realized that they were alone. There was something about this place that made them both feel relaxed. She thought for a moment that it might be due to the trace gasses they detected, but then she thought better of it.

"Like I know? Besides, do you really want to meet up with those goons again any time soon?" said Harvey as he stooped down feeling the floor, to look for they way they got in. "I can't seem to find an opening." he muttered to himself.

"Perhaps it closed when the ice..." she cut herself off as she drifted into thought. "Poor Bob! And the others...!" She almost sobbed, but managed to hold it back.

"I know. I was fond of him too." He wanted to hold her to assure her that things would be all right, but something stopped him. Perhaps it was the fact that she had held back her anguish, or that he was having enough of a time with it himself.

"Do you think that they wound-up in a different place *on purpose?*" she asked, changing the subject, to his relief.

"Precisely my thought. I was wondering when you were going to ask if there was an intelligence behind what this thing has been doing." If they kept talking, maybe they could forget the tragedy for a time.

"How long have you suspected?" she asked, slightly surprised and impressed.

"Since I first saw it, I felt as if someone or something were... *watching* me." His voice trailed off as if he were in deep thought.

"Me too. Spooky, isn't it?" she muttered half under her breath.

They both looked around, the feeling was definitely there, as if they were not alone. It was not a foreboding feeling, however, it was quite reassuring.

Then Linda noticed something.

"Hey, the light..." she exclaimed.

"Yes, interesting isn't it?" Harvey said calmly.

What she had just noticed was that the light in the hallway was just 'there', with no apparent source and there were no shadows.

"I've seen this sort of illumination before." he said as he looked the hallway up and down for the light source that he knew wasn't there. "But it was just a reproduction of a 'parlor trick' that was originally done by Nicola Tesla."

"How was it done?"

"By stimulating the xenon in the air. See? Down the hallway, a haze over the distance? That's what makes it impractical for lighting streets or roads; it can be easily over driven."

She looked down the hallway and a haze seemed to get thicker the further down the hallway one looked. "I see it."

She had put her head close to his as if she needed to follow where he was pointing, and her proximity distracted Harvey, so he moved away - out of respect.

"It's caused by the air lighting up, and over distance, you finally get a point light source, that source being the air itself, the point becomes very large, and almost looks like a glowing fog."

"Xenon is the gas used in a camera flash...and at a few milliseconds in duration. Doesn't that light-up so brightly that it would blind us if it were steady?"

"Exactly, but since the concentration of xenon in air is so incredibly low, it doesn't fry our retinas."

"I should have figured that. It's quite the 'parlor trick', isn't it?" she asked rhetorically. "So who was the modern scientist that figured it out?" she asked coyly.

He looked her in the eye. "Yours truly. But I suspect you already knew that."

She smiled, because it was true. She knew a lot more about his past. In fact, she had read almost every paper that he had ever published. His approach to problems was refreshing, and he often found simple succinct solutions to puzzles that the scientific community had been pondering for many years, if not centuries. She liked the way he thought and now that she was getting to know him personally, she was also getting to like his personality too.

She smiled at him. "Would you explain to me that flap over the violins?"

"Violins, viols and cellos. Strataveri was the maker."

"Yes, that's it. How'd you figure it out? I mean, how he made them to sound so good, especially over time?"

"I looked at the physics of the situation. If you cut wood with a saw, the teeth tend to split the wood along the grain, making the sound raspy. Over time, as the wood dries it gets worse."

She was staring at him, listening intently. Not too many people would listen to his theory on this subject, so he continued. "So, if one uses a blade such as a knife to cut or carve out the shape, the fibers don't get separated lengthwise. So the older and more brittle the wood gets, the sweeter the sound. It was simply what fit the known information, that's all."

"Do you have any idea how refreshing it is to talk to a true intellect?"

"Stop! You're making me blush! Besides, I suck at chess."

"What? You figure out things that the rest of us wrestle with, and you make it seem so effortless. How do you do it?"

"I'm really not that bright. I just look at things from a different perspective, that's all. Think of the chief's theory."

"You know about his theory on mental 'where with all' as he puts it?"

"Yeah, the Chief and I go back a bit. He told me years ago about how he thought that everyone has the same mental horsepower, it's just where we apply it that has value to society."

"How does that apply to you? When it comes to those neurotransmitter levels associated with short term memory..."

He cut her off. "Please, don't go there. I know it was my idea to test for them instead of IQs, but I contest the results in my particular case. Really, I'm not that bright - I merely have an unorthodox perspective on things." He risked upsetting her, but he never thought of himself as being clever, because he never felt that way. Indeed, figuring out an age-old problem from him gave him a sense of completion, not so much satisfaction or a feeling of superiority. He was more pleased with the fact that people could then move on to more important problems.

"I don't mind telling you how many people would like to see things your way." she said with a playful grin, hoping that she had not upset him.

"I'd advise against it - it's boring!"

"That does not alter the fact that I feel safe, simply because you're here to get us out of this safe and sound."

"Well, don't put all that on my doorstep little lady. You're on this project to solve a problem or two yourself, and I hear you're no slouch."

"Who told you that? You didn't even know I existed until today."

He wanted to tap his heart and tell her that he knew in there, but thought better of it. Instead, he said. "You wouldn't be on the team if you weren't top-notch." He had her there.

"Hey, It's only because I try to follow your example."

"Really?"

"Which way should we go?" she asked, changing the subject at last, glancing up and down the featureless hallway.

"I don't think it matters much. I trust that whoever... *what*ever separated us from those goons wouldn't have put us in a hallway that leads back to them or to danger, so I think it's safe to say that either direction works for us."

"They may be goons, but they were regular guys when the ceiling started caving in."

"You've got a point." he said, then in his best Hindu accent he added: "Does not the wolf run next to the hare in order to escape the forest fire?"

"Wiseguy." Then she shrugged and started walking down the hallway. Harvey followed by her side.

"So what do you think we'll find?" she asked as they walked.

"Well..." he said, "I hope we DON'T find whatever ate the video camera!"

She chuckled at this. Somehow, his being there made her feel at ease. He had always had a knack for making people feel safe and secure. It was his nature.

* * *

Meanwhile, in another part of the sphere, there was gunfire. Lots of it. The S*I*P*Es were meeting heavy resistance. They tried everything at their disposal and were unable to drop any of their unseen enemy. What was worse, *they* were beginning to fall, and as they fell they were swallowed up by the ground which behaved as if it were quicksand, but only for a moment. Once the body was gone, the ground became solid again. This only added to the terror of the remaining troops. Well-trained and heavily armored as they were, this situation would have unsettled anyone.

Only about half of their number remained, Lt. Argent and Cpl. Swanson among them. The Major, their commander, was among the missing making the Lt. the ranking officer present. He ordered the men to stand down because they were obviously outclassed by their enemy. When they adopted a 'surrender' posture, they found themselves alone in a dark foggy 'no man's land' as they might have imagined the 'no man's land' of WWI. Things here were very strange indeed. Absolutely no one came for them. As soon as they had stopped firing, so had the unseen enemy.

After a few moments, the Lt. and Cpl. Swanson exchanged looks. They looked over their shoulders at the other remaining troops, who were puzzled and looking around as well. They slowly rose to their feet.

Reconnoitering, they found a doorway in a cliff face that was a short distance behind them. Strange, it seemed that during the fire fight, they were being driven toward that door. Light didn't seem to penetrate the doorway but as a volunteer entered, he disappeared almost as if he were pulled into the darkness.

Radio signals came back stating that it was safe to enter. Video images of a long corridor, leading away from the door that had a lot of glare the further you looked down it... came over the Lt.'s heads-up display. He sent in his men, then followed them as they started walking down the hallway.

After a while, they heard footsteps. The Lt. was on point, he kneeled and with a hand signal, they all froze and silently raised their weapons. They waited, and out of the glare came the engineers and technicians. It appeared that somehow all of them had made it into the sphere. The Chief was the first to appear out of the glare. "Are you gonna shoot us or are you gonna help us outa here?" he asked the bewildered Lt. who then motioned for his men to stand down.

"Are there any doorways down that way?" he asked the Chief, as he closed the distance between them.

"None, we've been walking for quite a way, seems like kilometers, and haven't seen *one*. How about that way?"

"We came in a doorway from some sort of DMZ."

"A DMZ?!?"

"Absolutely, I don't know why or how but that's what it was: some kind of 'no man's land'."

"Well, at least that's something, and it might be better than a barren hallway. How far is it?"

"Only a few hundred meters, but I wouldn't recommend going that way, there's someone out there that was shooting at us, and got half my men."

"Did you try talking to them first?"

"I didn't arrive until after the fire fight started but whoever, *what*ever they were they stopped when we did." he said, sighed and added almost under his breath. "The weird part is that everyone who fell, actually got sucked into the ground without leaving a trace."

"Show me?" The Chief was intrigued!

The Lt. shrugged and motioned for his men to return the way that had come, to a few groans of complaint. The men had been complaining about lacking sack time, due to the long trip and short preparations.

"Come on you slackers! There's plenty of time for rest in the grave!" he said his favorite quote with a twinkle in his eyes.

48

"Slave driver!" said one of the men jokingly.

"Keep my personal life out of this!" he playfully barked over his shoulder, not knowing or caring who made the comment.

A lone figure in a dimly lit room, watching them on a monitor, manipulated a control just before they reached the doorway at the end of the hall.

They soon discovered that the door no longer led to a DMZ, but to military style living quarters.

"But, but these rooms weren't here before!" exclaimed the Lt. looking around at the barracks, galley and other facilities. "It's like a military base. I don't get it!"

They all exchanged looks. This didn't make any sense! The men were also relieved. They wanted a rest, and now they had a place to sack out.

Dr. Morax, standing in the infirmary, laughed to himself as he removed a large jar of dark red pills from a cabinet. When he heard the troops coming into the next set of rooms, he quickly went off to hide in one of the secret halls to avoid detection since he had also learned that the S*I*P*Es weren't about to obey him anymore. He had further sabotage to perform but it could wait.

Meanwhile, Harvey and Linda had reached the end of the hallway. Most, if not all of their equipment was stacked neatly along the wall for the last few yards of the hallway which terminated in an arched doorway that didn't seem to allow light to pass through.

"Well, at least we know what happened to our equipment and supplies." said Linda, looking over the crates and boxes. "I wonder who stacked them?"

"I hope it wasn't that nasty guy with the cane." said Harvey over his shoulder as he examined the archway.

They stared into the darkness of the archway for a while, looking at it this way and that, until Linda broke the silence:

"Hey! Shouldn't that quantum bi-location communicator be in one of these boxes?"

"No, actually, I saw it sitting on the control panel when the walls came down, so it's bound to be buried in the ice."

"Darn! We could have called for help with that."

"I'm sure they know what happened by now." he said reassuringly, but also hoping that she would not realize that Morax and his chums had most certainly taken over the base before they had invaded the cavern.

"Good point." she said, hoping the same thing.

They stood there for a moment or two, thinking about their situation.

"Are you pondering what I'm pondering?" Linda finally asked with a twinkle in her eye.

Harvey sighed and said, "Well, there's one way to find out." He knew what she was referring to but this time he wasn't going to 'play'. He reached into the darkness of the archway with his hand.

"Careful!" said Linda taking a short breath and grabbed his arm, pulling it back.

"Do you have a better suggestion?"

"Try this." she said producing a penlight of considerable power.

He shrugged and directed the light into the darkness. The light did not seem to penetrate. They exchanged looks, and he extended his arm placing the penlight into the darkness, and the end seemed to disappear. He removed the light and it looked fine.

"I'd call that an 'event horizon'." he said triumphantly.

"Yes, but what kind of event?" she said with a slight tone of sarcasm.

"I'm sure it's safe. It is a *doorway* after all." he said reassuringly as he returned the penlight to her. Then he extended his arm into the darkness, and his hand faded from view. "Weird. I don't feel a thing." he muttered, as he removed his unscathed hand.

"I wonder where it leads." she said.

"I know where I *want* it to lead." he said. "Ready?"

She nodded, took a deep breath and they stepped into the darkness together.

* * *

Harvey and Linda found themselves in a well-lit circular room with all sorts of equipment that had screens and good old-fashioned 'blinky lights' all over it. Just the sort of stuff that you see engineers fiddling with in science fiction movies. In the center of the room were four comfortable-looking chairs. The room *looked* like the bridge of an interstellar ship, because that's what it *was*.

They both realized where they were, and what it meant.

"Oh my..." said Linda.

"You said it." said Harvey. "Bob was *right!*"

"Yeah. *Was* he!" she exclaimed, still awestruck by the revelation. "I just wish he were here to see it." as her eyes began to tear-up a little.

They looked around in wonder for a while, until Linda noticed something on a screen, but the resolution was so high that at first she thought it was a porthole, but it couldn't be because it was a thin sheet of what looked like glass, in a stand on a console. "Look! It's the others!"

The screen was showing an image of an area that looked like military barracks. There was a rather attractive looking button below the screen. It somehow seemed to be for an intercom. She looked at it, then looked at Harvey and smiled mischievously.

"Go ahead. Try it." he said encouragingly.

She reached for the button and held it down. She didn't notice that the strange lettering on it changed to read 'Intercom'.

"Can you guys hear me?" she said to the monitor.

The men in the screen froze, and the Chief said into the air. "Who said that?" as they all looked around.

"It's Linda Kowalski."

"Where are you?" asked the Chief.

"That depends. Where's 'Dr. Mengele?'" she demanded.

"I have no idea, but heaven help him if I find him first!" as he shook a fist in the air, still looking around for the source of her voice.

She looked at Harvey who gave her a approving smile and nod.

"That's good enough for me, I'm on the bridge." she said definitively.

"So this *is* a ship!" Then he thought for a moment, and sat down on a bunk, "Oh Jeez... there's something else you gotta know." he added, still talking to the ceiling. "This, uh, 'ship', is more sophisticated than anything we've even theorized before. Each door apparently leads to more than one place."

"Somehow that's not very surprising. So... any ideas on how we get you here?"

"There's a very long corridor outside the only door, we ran into the soldiers there." The Lt. moved into view and smiled. "Don't worry though, they seem tame enough without the good Dr. to crack his whip."

"You got that right." said the Lt.

"We've been in a corridor like that too, do you think it could be the same one and we're just on the other end of it?"

"We?"

"Harvey Johnson is here with me."

"He's all right then?"

"Yes, he's just fine."

"I'm glad to hear that. He's a good man." She smiled at Harvey at that.

"Give us a minute and we'll see if we can find a map or something."

"Take your time, it's not like we can't wait a while, we've got all the facilities we need right here."

Indeed, some of the S*I*P*Es and engineers were snacking on food that they found in what resembled a futuristic looking kitchen. Other men were visiting the restroom and still others were scoping-out the bunks to the Lieutenant's scowls...

"Great, I'll call back when we know something."

Linda and Harvey looked over the various monitors that showed incomprehensible displays; as they had alien-looking characters that looked like lines that mostly terminated in small circles, labeling everything.

"What I'd give for a good linguist... but how can I expect anyone to translate Martian?" she said rhetorically.

One display that looked like a particularly good candidate caught her eye. She touched the screen which instantly brought up a three-dimensional display of the sphere, showing elaborate decks with large rooms and a lit-up path through a long corridor from what looked like the bridge to an area that looked like long rows of bunks. The bridge was apparently located in the upper decks and the long corridor only went part way through the narrow upper part of the sphere. This thing had to be many times larger inside than outside, a thought that made her nervous, but she didn't dare voice it just yet. The lettering on the panel changed to read 'Cartography'.

"Wow, that didn't take you long. See? You're no slouch!" said Harvey, clearly impressed.

"Huh?" she said, as if she had only half-heard him.

"You've not only found a diagram of the ship but you've managed to show a route from the barracks to the bridge. Well done!"

"I don't know how I did that."

"Well, what did you do?"

"I just touched the screen and what I wanted to see came up on it. Quite a coincidence huh?"

"Perhaps it's tied into the last piece of equipment you used and anticipated your needs."

"Or maybe... it read my mind?" half asking.

"I hope not." he said, with a worried look.

"You said it! That could be unsettling." she thought about it for a moment, and looked at the controls under the screen. "I wonder..." she muttered as she touched the screen again. The image of the technicians and S*I*P*Es came up again in a split-screen with the diagram. This time, the Chief engineer jumped up and looked startled, facing the screen he asked. "How'd you get here so fast?"

"What do you mean? I'm still on the bridge!"

"Forgive me..." he said as he approached the area where the camera would have to be, and waved his arm in front of him then smiled. "Whoa! That's the most realistic hologram I've ever seen."

"You're seeing a hologram?" she asked.

"Yes, what's more it looks solid - not the least bit translucent. What do you see?"

"You're on a screen."

"Okay. What else have you found out?"

"I've got a map, but I'm wondering how to send it to you."

"I see it now, it shows a diagram of the sphere... uh... ship and a route to the bridge. Looks like all we have to do is go to the other end of that long hallway outside."

"Um, yes. I'm glad you can see that." She turned to Harvey, "It *does* read your mind, I only thought about split screen, sending a hologram and then the map and it all *just happened*."

He smiled. At least she was amused buy this development, rather than alarmed.

"What did you say? I saw your lips moving but I didn't hear that at all." said the Chief.

"It wasn't intended for you to hear." she replied, then she looked over her shoulder at Harvey again.

"Wow! It even knows when to 'mute'! This is really neat!" She seemed excited to play with her new 'toys'. She turned back to the Chief. "Do you think you can get over here?"

"You bet! We'll see you in a while, it's a long walk." Then he added. "One more thing. Do you see how far it is? It's as if this thing is much bigger inside than it is outside."

"That's par for the course. I think we're dealing with extremely high-tech here." She was glad that she wasn't the first to suggest it. So she gave Harvey a knowing look, who correctly interpreted the meaning.

"What was your first clue?" he said as he got up from the bunk and moved toward the door where the group of engineers, technicians and S*I*P*Es were gathering. Then they noticed something.

"Wow!" exclaimed the Chief. "The holographic map is moving *with* me. This is fantastic!"

"Hey Chief." said Linda.

"What is it?"

"Watch-out for camera-eating monsters." she advised with a smile and a wink at Harvey.

"Don't worry little girl, we got real men with guns to protect us." he replied playfully.

The Lt. didn't look too happy with that. "*What* 'camera-eating-monsters?!?' You didn't say anything about any camera-eating monsters!" he protested as they disappeared into the hallway and off the monitor.

"Well..." said Linda, "I guess we have a little time to get acquainted with the rest of the controls before they get here."

Harvey smiled at her as they got to work. He liked her style.

* * *

In a darkened room, the lone figure of a man bathed in the light of a bank of monitor screens smiled quietly as he watched Harvey and Linda make discovery after discovery on the bridge. He reached forward and pressed a button that brought the S*I*P*Es into view on a previously blank screen. His attention turned to them as they walked down the long corridor.

"You civilians seem to joke around a lot." said the Lt.

"Don't you military types have a sense of humor?" asked the Chief.

"Not anymore. I had mine surgically removed."

"I knew an FBI agent like that. Tell me: Is it a reversible procedure, or are you stuck that way?"

The Lt. grinned, as they both quickened their pace. The Chief sped up to avoid a backhand and the Lt. sped up to keep up with him and possibly give him a playful nudge. For some reason, despite the situation they felt calm, comfortable and relaxed - somehow assured. Indeed, it seemed difficult to worry.

As they moved down the corridor, the line on the floating holographic map got shorter, indicating their progress. It was quite a distance to the bridge taking some time for them to arrive.

Linda and Harvey had figured out a lot about the workings of the bridge and the ship. It seemed that they could do almost anything from any workstation. All one had to do was to focus their thoughts on what they wanted, and the equipment would make it available to the console. The trick was, not only know what you wanted done, but avoid 'thinking' in any human language. These actions frequently required the use of the tactile controls, such as buttons, to either initiate a function whose subsequent functions were guided by thought, or to make each individual step occur. Presumably this was to prevent stray thoughts from causing problems.

The multiple stations seemed to be for a crew to carry out multiple functions at once. Very little seemed to have anything to do with the operation of the ship itself, other than telling it what to do. It seemed the 'how' was isolated from the crew. Apparently the ship was so well constructed, it could take care of all of it's own internal functions including repairs, automatically.

Playing with the controls they found that they either instinctively knew what the controls did, or rather the controls made themselves do whatever the operator wanted. What's more, once a control was 'figured out', it would change it's own label from the strange writing to English. This came in handy, since it would be almost impossible to remember what all the controls were for, and they couldn't make head or tail of the strange writing.

They had also discovered that the corridor had many rooms off of it but they had to be revealed by controls from the bridge, which was some sort of security feature as best they could determine. Linda had already been down the corridor a short distance and checked out several suitable rooms for everything from habitation to research. She had already set up equipment in one of them to use as her laboratory, right next to what she claimed as her quarters. Assuming that they were stuck there for a while that is.

Her quarters were like everything else on the ship; they seemed futuristic, but terrestrial in design. The bed looked like a conventional one but was very much like a waterbed filled with a gel. She felt the surface and thought it seemed familiar, but couldn't quite put her finger on it. When she tried it out, it conformed to her shape and made her feel like she was not only floating but it was giving her a warm hug. Each room had its own water closet. Again, it seemed conventional only it was styled in a manner that a 1960's architect might consider to be futuristic.

When she turned on the faucet, light came out of the water as it flowed. Red for hot and blue for cold. She found the right temperature to be a pleasing shade of purple. "Huh." she said to herself. "This is really different, but I like it." With wet hands she now looked for a towel. There was no towel rack. Instead, there was a small shelf with what looked like a mat of tall carpet fibers on it. She wiped her hands on it thinking there was no place else to dry them. The fibers instantly dried her hands and got the difficult bit between the fingers dry too. "Neat." she said to herself as she looked at her dry fingers and smiled. She liked the way things worked around here!

She went back out into the hallway and met-up with Harvey who had just finished making the same discoveries for himself.

"I like this ship." they said in chorus as they laughed and smiled at each other. They were feeling remarkably relaxed.

"We should get back to the bridge, they should be arriving soon." he said.

She smiled at him, reached for his hand to hold it and caught herself. What was she thinking? Luckily for her, he hadn't noticed, so she smiled at him again and they headed back to the bridge.

* * *

When the technicians, engineers and S*I*P*Es arrived, they seemed bewildered at the stark difference from the hallway.

"Wow! Just look at that set-up!" exclaimed the Chief as he gave the bridge a thorough looking over. The others arriving on the bridge, looked around and seemed to be equally surprised. There was plenty of room for everybody so they spread-out and immediately began fiddling with the controls - despite Harvey's objections.

"Don't worry, we know what we're doing." said DeSoto, one of the more 'pushy' scientists.

Harvey shrugged, and said: "Suit yourself." as he rejoined Linda at what appeared to be the helmsman's chair.

"I liked it better when it was 'our' ship." he said to her in a defeatist tone.

She beamed at him, but he missed it. Somehow the thought of being alone on a ship with him was pleasing.

The Chief approached Harvey and Linda, even though he could hardly tear himself away from checking out all the consoles on his way. "Good to see you made it." said Linda as she smiled at him and shook his hand.

"Thanks. Was your arrival in here as weird as ours?"

"Probably." answered Harvey as he shook the Chief's hand.

"So what now?"

"We proceed with the original mission and find out what we can about this ship." said Harvey

"What if we don't find a way outa here?" asked the Chief.

"Can you think of a better way to find out how to do that than to study the ship?"

"No, not really. But what if we *can't* get out?"

"Well, the base is still there, and they still have some thermite. I think that they'll attempt to re-excavate this thing after not too long."

"Too bad I left the Q-nicator on the console. We coulda called those dorks at the weather research station and let them know we're okay."

"*Q*-nicator?" asked Harvey, raising an eyebrow.

"The quantum superposition communicator. That's what I call it. A lot more succinct, don't ya think?"

"Harvey, something is bugging me." interjected Linda.

"What is it?"

"This stuff, the equipment, the monitors, controls and even the, uh, 'plumbing' is very much like the terrestrial equivalent. It just looks, well, 'high-tech' you know?"

"What are you getting at?"

"Think about it. Once we figure out what a control does, it changes its label to English. How could it be alien then?"

"Where are you going with this? Because I can assure you that *nobody* on Earth has technology like this ship." he said authoritatively. "Besides, we established that the ship knows what we are thinking, and adjusts itself accordingly. Perhaps that is how it knows to label things in English, and it might even have adjusted its interior to suit our form. I say again; nobody on Earth has technology like this. Nobody."

"That's just it. Nobody has technology like this... *now*."

"Are you suggesting that this is a *time ship*?"

"Have you got a *better* explanation?"

"Well, when I was contacted, the government believed it to be *ancient* high-tech, which would explain the strange writing." he said, indicating the symbols on a nearby panel.

"*Now* what do you think?" she asked.

"Truthfully, I *could* go either way... but I'm working on a third option." he replied looking nervously around the bridge.

"Hmmm." said Linda. "So what are we going to do about food? Sooner or later..."

A technician, that was standing within earshot cut her off: "That's no problem ma'am. There's a fully stocked galley in the living quarters. Plenty of fresh food to go 'round. In fact, we've all already had lunch."

"Any orange juice?" Harvey asked almost under his breath.

Linda gave Harvey a puzzled look, and the technician looked like he was trying to remember if he had seen any.

"How can there be edible food? This ship has supposedly been undisturbed for thousands of years." asked Harvey, hoping to break the odd silence.

The technician shrugged. "All I know is that it had all the fresh food in the galley we could ever want."

"Perhaps this is a ship that *recently* crashed and sank into the ice?" suggested Linda.

Harvey looked puzzled. "Time ship theory again?"

She counted on her fingers: "Re-entry heat, loss of control, crash-land, melt through the ice and presto! Mysterious space ship lost in the Antarctic ice cap, with a carefully planned government cover-up for dessert."

"Except for the fact that humans have never built anything this big. I mean, *where* would you build such a thing? And the level of technology?"

"If it really is from the future, they could build a space dock, and..." She was interrupted by the arrival of the S*I*P*E commander holding a pistol in his hand.

"Major!" said the Lt. in a vaguely sarcastic tone, as he saluted. "Glad to see you made it sir!" The other S*I*P*Es snapped to attention.

"Here we go!" muttered Linda out of the corner of her mouth.

"What's going on here Lieutenant?" asked the Major as he returned the salute. "The last time I checked this man was your prisoner." he said using his pistol to indicate Harvey.

"We've lost contact with the good Doctor, and we had a fire fight with someone or some*thing* out in that DMZ and incurred heavy losses. This is all that's left."

"*Fire fight*?" said Harvey, almost under his breath. Linda cautioned him with a hand signal to be quiet.

"I know about that. In fact I fired the first shot. I thought I took a hit, then woke up in a hallway, and found my way here."

"There's no need for your weapon here Major." said Harvey who had broken away from Linda's influence.

"Who put *him* in charge?" the Major asked the Lt.

"Actually Sir, Morax did when he shot Bob. Now he's the ranking government official left." offered the Lt.

"Where *is* Dr. Morax?"

"So far, he's unaccounted for sir." said the Lt.

"How many survived the battle?"

"Twenty sir, including the two of us."

"How many of *them* did you drop?"

"None."

"What?"

"We didn't even *see* any of them sir."

"Where are *our* casualties?"

"That's just it, there *aren't* any. They all vanished sir. Frankly I was hoping that you could shed some light on that point."

The Major, scowled, sighed and turned to Harvey. "As distasteful as I find it, with the absence of contrary orders and since you are the ranking government official present, you are apparently in charge... for the time being." he said as he holstered his pistol. "Now what do you want us to do?"

Harvey cracked a sly smile at Linda who let out a low whistle and slowly rolled her eyes in relief.

The S*I*P*Es turned out to be very helpful to the engineers and technicians. They were knowledgeable and scientifically inclined. This was partially due to the fact that they carried such sophisticated equipment that they had to have the intelligence and education necessary to use it. The other reason was that they also had to be trustworthy to do this kind of secret work, which meant that they had to be smart enough to not talk about what it was that they did for a living. These S*I*P*Es were the cream of the proverbial crop, Dr. Morax would not have had it any other way.

Over time, the missing S*I*P*Es from the fire fight all wandered into the bridge one by one, and were then shown the way to the barracks. None of them could remember what had happened to them after taking a hit, and none of them were injured, to the puzzlement of all.

Harvey and Linda soon had a number of them running all over the ship, gathering samples and taking pictures. They had discovered what the S*I*P*Es dubbed the 'pod room' because it housed a large pod-like sack containing the strangest material they had yet found. After finding out that the pod was self-sealing, they took a sample. The material was massive, as in it had mass to it but strangely gravity had no effect on it whatsoever. It was a deep, rich red, and acted like a cross between a fluid and a gas.

At first Linda thought it was a new form of matter; noting how it behaved like red wine in a 'micro-gravity' environment. It wasn't a liquid but flowed like one, it wasn't a gas but it dissipated like one only more slowly. It wasn't even smoke because it had too much mass to it. Then she thought it might be negative matter; possibly used for making worm holes for interstellar flight. Again, it failed related tests, defying identification. She had simply not seen anything like it and nobody else seemed to recognize it either, not even the Chief engineer - who had quite a few more years of experience than anyone else onboard.

She found her answer when she finally examined the stuff with a 'Bird microscope', which was capable of magnification far beyond any other light microscope and many scanning electron types as well, the advantage being that one could examine samples without having to put them in a vacuum.

What she found was astonishing. The material was made up of Buckminsterfullerenes ($C_{60}$) that seemed to contain an equal mass of antimatter inside. Antimatter? That stuff was dangerous! Buckminsterfullerenes were none too healthy for life forms either, but they failed the toxicology tests associated with them. So they seemed to be safe even though they were known to be toxic. Curious stuff indeed!

It seemed that the carbon sphere that encased the antimatter had balanced out the forces that made matter and antimatter collide. The mass of matter and antimatter were identical, explaining why gravity had no effect on it, but it sure had noticeable *mass*. These strange physical properties may have accounted for why it wasn't toxic.

"This is brilliant!" she exclaimed. "The perfect nuclear fuel!"

"How's that?" asked the Chief.

"All you have to do is break one carbon bond and the molecule collapses into the antimatter, giving off a healthy burst of pure gamma."

"Wow! No 'leftovers'."

"Yeah. It's even more convenient than our Hafnium-178 reactors."

"Do you suppose that's what powers the ship?"

"More likely, it's what powers its *interstellar* drive. I'd like to try some of this fuel in a hafnium reactor casing, since it has the right kind of shielding, just to check it out. You know, see how much of a kick it has."

"Sounds good to me." he said. "So... do you think we can find the engines if this is the stuff that powers them?"

"There are conduits, almost like bundles of microfullerene tubes leading away from the pod. Trouble is they go all over the place."

"Well, why don't we try to follow the *largest* ones?" suggested the Chief.

Linda's eyes went wider. She hadn't thought of that. "I knew there was a reason I kept you around." she said playfully.

"I thought it was my sunny disposition!"

* * *

After searching and scanning, in an attempt to follow the many conduits from the pod to the engines, and following the largest most likely ones, they were lead to a reactor that powers a coil. Not just any coil mind you, but a very large coil of superconducting material that seemed to be both metal and plastic at the same time. It appeared to run the full height of the ship, and the conductor itself was at least ten feet in diameter.

"Can you imagine how much power this thing can handle?" asked the technician that was examining it with Linda.

"No doubt it's a lot, but I doubt it's for propulsion, it's more likely for deflecting radiation, you know, the same way the earth's magnetic field protects the planet." answered Linda.

"Yeah, but *what* a *field*!" The technician was awestruck. "I'd bet that this baby could easily rip the iron right out of your blood!"

He was standing next to a superconducting coil that probably could generate a magnetic field many times greater than the planet's. He patted it affectionately, then pulled his had off suddenly because it was drawing the heat out of his hand almost to the point of frostbite. Then he examined his hand for damage.

"I think we have to look further to find a propulsion system." She looked the coil up and down again, and shook her head not knowing what to make of it.

There was a room positioned halfway up that protruded into the massive cavernous chamber that housed the coil. It was constructed much like a Faraday cage, in which there was a panel with the outline of a human hand. Apparently, that was the control room, and if one placed one's hand on the panel, it would energize the coil. That was something she didn't dare do now, because if it were polarized in opposition to the Earth's magnetic field, it just might collapse it - which *would* lead to a global catastrophe. She shuddered at the thought. *If* they ever got this ship out of the ice, and *if* it was still capable of space flight, they might have to use this coil to deflect radiation, but not before. Those were a lot of Ifs, and it didn't sit well with her.

"What I don't understand is why it uses an active coil. I mean, our interplanetary ships use an array of permanent magnets that can be rearranged with levers to turn the field on and off. It doesn't make sense to constantly put high current through a coil. The power cost would be enormous." she said half to herself.

"Well, maybe it isn't needed all the time, besides you saw how much energy there is in that fuel, maybe power isn't an issue."

"I did think of that, but something doesn't seem right with this..." Her voice trailed off as an idea occurred to her. Then she said: "Tell you what, you keep looking for the engines - I'll be in my lab examining the samples the soldiers collected for me. Maybe they can shed some light on a few things."

The technician nodded and busied himself scanning the other larger fuel lines once again as Linda walked to the lab that she had set-up in one of the small rooms off of the hallway next to the bridge.

She sighed and sat down at the microscope and began examining slides. Each slide contained a different sample of various materials found all over the ship. One at a time, she started to notice some similarities in the structures... "This scraping labeled 'plastic' looks an awful lot like carotene..." she said to herself as she reached for a pen but knocked over a small, open bottle of acid instead, which began burning the table. She rushed to the shelf to get something to clean it up the mess, and when she returned a few minutes later, the table was unscathed.

"That's funny, I could have sworn..." she said to herself, as she righted the nearly empty acid bottle, and replaced the stopper. Then a thought occurred to her. She poured water on the table, not much, but just enough to cause a small bead about a half-inch across. She sat down and watched it closely. It sat there for a few moments, then seemed to rapidly soak into the surface. Startled at this, even though it was just what she expected, she reluctantly felt the table's surface right where the water had been moments before, and it wasn't even damp. In fact, it felt like cool plastic. She looked under the table and felt it there. It was also dry. She tried it again, this time with a large puddle in the middle of the table. Moments later, it was dry as a bone; with no trace of the water anywhere. "Huh" she muttered as she tried the next thing; a scratch. She gouged the table with a nail file, looked at it through a magnifying glass and waited. After a few moments, it slowly began to almost push up form the bottom of the scratch, and the 'repair' became more rapid as it progressed, accelerating at an alarming rate. "What the...?" she muttered, even though this was again, exactly what she expected to see.

Her suspicions were confirmed, so monstrously frightening that she almost didn't dare test the idea any further. Still, if for no other reason than to put her mind at ease, she adjusted the microscope directly over the table's surface. Once she was satisfied that it was secure, she slowly, hesitantly took a look.

As soon as she focused the image, she gasped. There were microscopic veins with blood-like material flowing through them, nerves and other fibers: in the *table!* She slowly straightened up and looked at the door - full well expecting it to do exactly what it was just about to do. Sure enough, there were teeth forming around the door frame, and the doorway was closing like a big mouth. The floor began turning into a tongue. She fell down on the slippery salivating floor and floundered, trying to escape. The walls began to look like the inside of a mouth and it began to get very dark...Despite her proximity to the bridge, no one heard her blood-curdling screams as the teeth closed in on her.

# XII
# NOD

"It never rains, but it pours!"

2:29 PM Friday, Dec 21st, 2012 Anno Domini

The major could not resist anymore. He placed his hand on the panel and activated the superconducting electromagnet.

The mind that operated the electromagnet understood that the Major wanted the ship to be launched by this action. Although it was not the recommended method, it *was* possible, so the necessary quantity of electric power was sent into the coil, causing it to glow.

The force needed to push a mile-wide ball of untold mass through 3,000 feet of solid ice from a standstill to escape velocity was more than enough to collapse the magnetic field of the planet. This also caused the planet to momentary wobble as the ship shot up to geosynchronous orbital height. The interesting thing to note here is that there is no such thing as a *polar* geosynchronous orbit, so the ship was maintaining its position under it's own power. Call it self-preservation if you will.

For reasons that will be explained much later, another curious thing happened that the crew would not learn about for some time: In parallel time lines, where the sphere existed as well, it simply vanished, leaving a sinkhole in the Antarctic ice to baffle anyone finding it. What is even more curious is that in many of those worlds, the sinkhole appeared in what one might think of as the past.

As all of this was happening, the bridge crew was trying to make sense of all the alarms. Then they paid attention to the monitors, and some almost fainted. They could see an image of the planet and a disaster of untold proportions unfolding before their eyes.

"Is this real?" asked a technician in disbelief. From the looks on the faces of the rest of the crew, he gathered his answer.

They stood there in silent disbelief, watching in abject horror. The ship's sensors also depicted the movements of the wildly erratic magnetic field as it searched for equilibrium. Within a few minutes, some of the crew began to regain their heads, and manned the consoles closely monitoring the damage being caused by the tsunamis and quakes. Some watched out of morbid curiosity, others out of a genuine desire to do something - anything - to help.

Not fifteen minutes later, and just after the Major had made his way back to the bridge - for his hero's welcome - an extremely shaken and disheveled female scientist stumbled onto the bridge from the hallway. She was covered with some sort of clear goo and wasn't too happy about it. She looked at the tactical display that showed not only what had just happened, but where the ship was now located. She soon forgot about her recent adventure for the time being, since it paled in comparison.

"Great just great! What the HELL do we do now?" hissed Linda as she glared at the Major and flicked more goo off of her arms.

Everyone on the bridge was glaring at the Major, who tried his best to not look the fool, but failed miserably. In fact, he was beginning to fidget from nervousness.

The main monitor played the account over and over again; showing the Major placing his hand on the coil's control causing the ship to launch and the devastation on the planet below.

"Well, SOMETHING had to be done,... uh, I had no way of telling.... there was... it... Look, we're not going to find out how this ship works if we don't push the odd button or two!" he said very defensively, almost in a panic, and rightly so as the engineers began closing in on him as if they were about to tear him limb from limb. They probably would have had Harvey not arrived on the bridge and interceded.

"What's going on?" he asked, noticing the angry crowd closing in on the Major's throat.

"This bozo just launched us into space!" answered Linda as the Major swallowed hard, attempting to retain composure, but was visibly shaking as he stared at Harvey with imploring eyes for a moment and then returned his gaze to the angry mob.

"What's worse..." she continued, "...is that the launch caused a wobble making tsunamis and earthquakes! Civilization as we know it is all but completely wiped out! Is *THAT* enough justification for you?"

The mob grunted in approval, and there was a general shift closer to the Major's throat.

"My God..." he thought about it for a moment, horrified at the ramifications, then noticing the plight of the Major, he regained his composure. "Well, let's sort out his disposition later. We should see if we can do anything about the *situation* first."

There was a general air of disappointment as they realized that he was right. The Major wasn't going anywhere and a lynch mob wasn't the best way to handle things. As they began to reluctantly back down, the Major nodded acknowledgingly at Harvey and straightened his collar, just as a number of S*I*P*Es poured onto the bridge.

The reason that Harvey wasn't quite as horrified as the others, was that he knew all too well about secret societies, back-door deals and corruption in general. The Overworld was undoubtedly in disarray, which made him actually feel relieved, but he didn't dare tell anyone for fear that he might have joined the Major. He had the thought, albeit horrifying, that overall the world was better off getting a fresh start.

"What's going on here?" demanded the Lt. as he noticed the angry mob backing away from the Major's throat.

"Nothing to worry about now Lieutenant." answered the Major, knowing he could now hide behind his troops. He regained his arrogant posture, gave Harvey a smug look and motioned for his men to be on guard, who then gripped their M-29A1's tightly as the crew glared at the Major.

Harvey recognized this as what it was, and worried that someday he might have to deal with the Major, but not today. Then he realized that Linda looked like something that the dog had coughed-up.

"Now... what happened to *you*?" he asked, almost relieved at the diversion.

"I hate to break it to you but this ship is alive. The whole darn thing is a life form."

69

There was a general gasp over this news.

"That would explain a lot. Like how things work and the fact that they still do after all this time." offered the Chief.

"How's that?" asked the Lt.

"Organic technology is seamless and versatile, not to mention self maintaining and repairing, just like your body. In a way, we are organic machines. It's a logical step in technology."

The Lt. still looked nervous, eyeing the ceiling as if it were about to fall.

"Don't worry, it won't bite you." scoffed the Chief.

"Oh yeah!" said Linda, "How do you think I wound up like this?" She lifted her gooey shirt to show her stomach, which had what looked like teeth marks around her abdomen.

"What happened there?" asked Harvey.

"A room bit me."

"WHAT?!? Did you say a room... *bit* you?"

"Not too badly, but I figured out that it only did it because I expected it to. It happened right after I made my little discovery."

There was a general gloom in the room, as they contemplated the ramifications. Some of them were looking around, waiting for teeth to sprout.

"But, it all looks so... so... *normal*." said the Lt. in disbelief.

"Just because something is organic, doesn't mean it has to be covered with ooze and have bulging veins all over it." answered the Chief engineer. "Actually, the way the ship looks is a sign of it being true technology and not a kludge of pieces stolen from nature. This thing was undoubtedly designed from the ground up. It's a beautiful piece of work!"

The Lt. still looked nervous.

"Don't worry, if you don't expect it to hurt you it won't. On second thought, I don't think it *can*." assured Linda.

This made them relax a little. There was a lot to handle in a short amount of time.

# THE HALO EFFECT

* * *

After the Major had returned to his quarters with his now permanent personal guard, and having left the Lt. 'in charge', the tension on the bridge was greatly reduced.

"Let's see, if this thing automatically launched into orbit at the touch of one button, perhaps it has an autopilot." postulated Harvey.

"I see where you're going with this." replied the Lt.

They exchanged a look and began examining the controls at what they believed to be the helmsman's station, based on it's central location on the bridge, relation to the tactical viewer and its lower height in relation to what was presumed to be the captain's chair. It had a high back with a depression on it, presumably to fit the back of someone's head. The Lt. puzzled over it for a moment as Harvey bent over the control panel, which was a sort of tray table arrangement that could swing in front of one's lap. He sat slowly down in the chair and it seemed very comfortable to him. It adjusted itself to him like it were partially filled with a gel. As he leaned back to get the full feeling of it, he closed his eyes to bask in comfort and then saw more than he had ever seen in his life. This surprised him so much that he jumped out of the seat in alarm.

"Yikes!"

Harvey sprung up from the panel he was examining and asked. "What is it?"

"It... it just showed me something... uh, like the outside of the ship."

"How?"

"I just sat down and closed my eyes... like this."

He sat down, deliberately closed his eyes and wasn't as surprised this time to see all around the outside of the ship. Harvey obviously didn't see anything but asked the Lt.: "Well, see anything?"

"Oh yes, *everything*."

"In what direction?"

"In all directions, that's the thing, it's a bit disorienting at first. I have a wider field of view than I have ever had, but I think I can manage." He opened his eyes and sat up. "Care to try it?"

"Don't mind if I do!"

Knowing what to expect can only partially prepare someone for the image, and this helped him to not re-open his eyes as he was deluged with images the likes of which he had never seen before. He experimented a bit and found he could zoom in on things, isolate images and change spectrums.

"Hey!" he exclaimed. "This thing has a zoom... and other functions." His voice trailed off as he explored them.

"Yeah?" said the Lt. anxiously. He wanted to play with it some more.

"Go ahead." said Harvey as he got out of the chair.

The images were beginning to toy with his normal perceptions and he felt dizzy, and even stumbled. After the Lt. got back into the seat, he enthusiastically tried the zoom and the 'other functions', one of which he had imagined to be bringing up a display of navigational functions.

"Found something!" he exclaimed.

"What?" asked Harvey.

"Some of our equipment is floating around the ship. I think it was swept-up with us during the launch."

"What?" Noticing he was sounding redundant, he rolled his eyes and shook his head.

"I can see it with my mind's eye." Which was the only way he could describe it. "Wait, I think I can..." His voice trailed off as he concentrated on the task at hand.

Harvey remained silent, not wanting to say 'What?' again, waiting for the Lt. to continue.

"Got it!"

"What have you got?"

"A control panel, and various tools. I pulled them into a cargo bay using a tractor beam."

"This thing has a tractor beam?"

"Isn't that what you meant by 'other functions'?"

"I found a zoom and spectral change... things like that. Obviously this ship can do a lot."

"So where is this cargo bay you brought the stuff into?" asked Harvey.

"Along the ship's equator, but the hull can open anywhere at any time we need it to. It's fantastic!"

He kept searching for a moment, then he found something.

"Got it!"

"Got *what?*"

"The homing control. It's on a virtual panel!"

He opened his eyes and stood up, apparently not as dizzy as Harvey had been despite or perhaps due to the longer exposure.

A virtual panel made sense, and he was not surprised at this development. Whoever had put this ship together had done a wonderful job with intuitive controls.

"Doesn't that make you dizzy at all?" asked Harvey, referring to the visual interface.

"Nope. In fact it makes me feel pretty good. You?"

"A bit too much for me, you can *have* it."

The Lt. chuckled at this, and asked: "I wonder how it works?" as he examined the depression in the chair that cradled his head. He rightly assumed that since eyes were in his head, there was something in the chair that worked on his head to let him see outside the ship, but he was puzzled as to why it only had physical contact with the *back* of his head. This seemed backwards to him, he was used to the 'heads-up' displays that the military used.

"It's probably some form of nerve induction into the visual cortex, which is located at the back of the head of course. But that's just an 'educated guess'." offered Harvey.

This answered the Lt.'s questions and to avoid sounding too clueless, he replied. "That sounds like a good explanation to me."

"So how does that virtual panel work?" asked Harvey.

"I would imagine that works like everything else on this crate; just as you expect it to."

"Okay, so how does this homing thing work? I mean, do we just touch it and 'off we go?'"

"I think so, but it had a map with it that looks as though it sends us to the center of the galaxy."

Harvey raised an eyebrow at that.

Knowing that the center of the galaxy was tens of thousands of light-years away, and not wanting to sound uneducated to Harvey, the Lt. added with a grin: "So it might take a while to get there."

"To say the least! So now we need to decide if we want to go there, or *try* to land this thing."

"I know that we were just on the surface, but it doesn't seem to be normal to land this thing."

"Agreed."

"What if it takes several dozen millennia to get there?" asked the Lt.

"Yes, of course, this might be a *generational* ship judging by the size, and it is also conceivable that it can generate a wormhole or something to go there quickly. We also have to ascertain if there is anything to go home *to* and if we can do anything about the disaster. More importantly, if this thing 'homes', can we go to where it is from and find out if there is anybody still alive that can do anything about the Earth? After all, judging by the level of power and technology involved here, they, whoever they might be, should be *able* to help."

"That may be true, but *would* they?"

"I think they would. After all, they built it, and it did cause the disaster, so they are partially responsible despite the Major's actions. Also, the ship does not seem to object to our presence, so I take it that it's creators are benevolent, and..." He paused wondering if he should say the rest, took one more quick look at the doorways, chair and controls; and completed the sentence. "...possibly Human."

"Whoa! You've got a point!" said the Lt. looking around himself.

"Besides, I'm told your S*I*P*Es found something like suspended animation pods in one of the rooms. Perhaps they are intended to be used for long journeys like the one to the center of the galaxy."

The Lt. got a 'far off' look in his eyes over this, clearly he wanted to go.

"Well, astronomers tell us that there's a black hole at the center of the galaxy, holding it together. I'm sure they'd love to be proven wrong." said Harvey.

"So what's next?"

"Now that we know that this ship still works and it has a homing function, we should investigate those 'pods' to see if they can offer us the chance to go. There's so much we don't know. Heck, we don't even know if this thing has enough *fuel*!"

The Lt. nodded solemnly, then he had a thought and sat down again. "Yup." he said. "Not only that but...uh oh!"

"What is it?" asked Harvey, suddenly concerned by the Lt.'s change in tone.

"We've got a visitor!" he sat up and the main screen was now showing an asteroid headed straight for the planet, and it was big enough to wipe out everything.

"It never rains..." they said in chorus, then exchanged a look for a moment. The Lt. had another idea, sat back down in the chair and closed his eyes again.

"What are you doing?"

"If this thing has the power to mess-up the planet, I figure it has the power to mess with that asteroid."

"Good! Go on."

"Since I already know how to use the tractor beam, let's just see..." His voice trailed off as he concentrated.

This time, Harvey could watch on the main monitor, and hoped that whatever the Lt. had in mind would work. There was little if any time to spare.

The system was showing the Lt. that the asteroid was made-up of almost solid iron, making it very tough indeed. He latched onto it, slowing it down and using the tractor beam as he called it.

Harvey watched as the Lt. hands twitched as if they were getting intermittent signals. What was happening was that he was reaching out with the ship's power fields like a pair of hands, and began rolling the asteroid between them as if to grind it up into fine dust. The monitor reflected his progress.

"Wow! Whatever you're doing it's working!" said Harvey excitedly.

"I know. I can see better from here."

"Oh yeah. I forgot."

When he was done, there was a large orange dust cloud of rust engulfing the planet.

"I hope that doesn't cause a nuclear winter." he said solemnly.

"I'm sure whatever it does will be better than the alternative!"

"Amen to that!"

* * *

The 'suspended animation pods' that the S*I*P*Es had spotted earlier turned out to be not only that, but quite a few of them were occupied...

"What the hell is that?" asked Linda as she examined the inhabitant of the pod closest to the doorway.

"Looks like an ogre to me." said the Lt. unaffected by the apparent ferocity of the dormant being.

"Looks can be deceiving. After all our friend here isn't dead. He's just resting."

"Wanna sell me a bridge?" he joked.

Linda cleared her throat and tapped her fingernail on a readout that apparently denoted activity similar to a heartbeat within. The Lt. swallowed hard, looked away and approached the next canister. He hated it when this sort of thing happened. Linda's face lit up with an playful grin, but she didn't say anything. Instead, she looked back down onto her scanner and smiled to herself.

"I hope this isn't one of the crew." she muttered to herself as she worked.

"Funny." she said, after examining her scanner for a prolonged period of time, "This canister over here, with no glass in the door looks like it has extra shielding that even the quantum scanner cannot penetrate, just like the ship itself...which should be impossible..." Her voice trailed off as she noticed that the Lt. was standing there staring at the contents through a peephole in awe. There were three 'small gray' type aliens inside.

"They're just like the aliens that kidnaped my father and did unspeakable things to him!" he said, staring off as if into space as Linda took a look.

"You're kidding!"

"Yup! Ha ha!, Gotcha!"

She backhanded him with the scanner and looked more closely at the canister.

"My guess is that it's shielded against *mental* energy - just like the ship. That might explain the quantum scanner not working, but that's a stretch."

At this point, the Major and his "guards" barged into the room. He seemed to be examining the canisters as if he were window shopping. Obviously, he did not know what he was doing but wished to appear as if he did. So what else is new? He had suspected that the scientists would not tell him what they had discovered, so he decided to stick his nose into everything that they did.

Linda looked over at the Major's arrival and nudged the Lt., who saluted. The Major, ignoring Linda, returned the salute, and said "As you were." Then he continued his 'inspection' of the canisters.

"Ooooooohhh!" said Linda under her breath.

"Jeez, don't get me into trouble with him." begged the Lt. under his breath as she snickered at him.

The Major stopped in front of the canister near the door, with the fierce-looking life form inside of it. This made Linda nervous so she immediately wiped the smile off her face and headed toward him.

The Major looked the small panel up and down and said "What does this button do?" Before Linda could yell: "DON'T TOUCH THAT!" he had already pressed it.

"That's; 'Don't touch that... SIR!'" stated the Major triumphantly.

"I'm not in the *military* you ignoramus! And may I add that YOU'VE DONE IT AGAIN!!!"

"Done *what* again?" the Lt. asked.

"I'm pretty sure he's begun the revival process. I really wish he'd stop pressing buttons all willy nilly like that!"

"You mean...?" The Lt. turned his gaze toward the big, fierce-looking life form inside the canister.

"I'm afraid so." she replied.

"*Revival* process! Don't be *absurd!*" pooh-poohed the Major: "This thing is long dead and all I attempted to do was open the door to get a better look at it." He pulled ineffectively on the handle as if to drive his point home. "Hmm, it's still *stuck*." he muttered.

"For your information, you big jerk, you are waking from suspension, a nine foot tall, hairy , six-inch fanged *MONSTROSITY!* I don't know about you, but I don't want to be around when this thing wakes up!"

The Major had the same look on his face that he had on the bridge when he was told of the planetary devastation he had caused. His guards were eyeing the hulk nervously, gripping their weapons tightly.

Noticing this, she added: "Congratulations 'Major disaster', you've done it again!"

"Will you stop saying that?" began the Major, "Now settle down and tell me how long it takes for this..." Before he could finish, the glass door slid open and the hulk inside opened his eyes, focused down on the small group of people in front of him. Then his eyes narrowed.

They all looked at each other, at the hulking monster, and then screamed in terror. They ran out of the door, but wound up right in front of the monster again. So they screamed again, and every time they ran out, they entered the room in front of the canister again and again, facing eyes that were larger than most people's heads. This continued for a few moments, as the monster watched intently quite amused by this reaction.

He eventually asked: "Can I play too?" in as child-like a voice as a nine foot tall hairy monster with six-inch fangs could possibly muster. In truth, before he had been put into suspension, this being had been

78

mentally comparable to a ten-year-old Human with no education. But just barely.

This child-like tone of voice, coupled with the question it had asked, caused a calm to come over Linda, who raised her hand and stopped the panic of the others. She approached a step closer. "Only if you promise to play *nice*." she stated firmly.

The others looked at her as if she were crazy. The nine-foot hairy monster smiled and said "Okay nice lady!" then slowly stepped out of the canister, grasped her outstretched hand and held it ever so gently.

She turned to the astonished men and grinned triumphantly. *Linda* had clearly done it again.

"I think we have a new addition to the crew." She beamed.

"What I don't get is how we kept winding-up here." said the Lt.

"I have an idea about that. I'll be right back..." said Linda, her voice trailing off as she headed for the door. She disappeared into the doorway to return momentarily with Harvey, who initially balked at their location and 'new friend'. Fascinated, he approached the 9 foot hulk and looked him up and down. In turn the 9 foot hulk looked Harvey up and down.

"The doors teleport you to the place that you are thinking about at the time." she announced triumphantly.

"Oh, I get it, since we were all thinking about the, uh, our... new... friend... here, we wound up in front of him."

"That's about the size of it."

"Wow! That would make it easy to get around the ship and to find anyone you are looking for!"

"Yes, it would." she said, deep in thought over this new information. "However, you'd need to know that a place existed first."

By this time, Harvey had learned a lot from their monstrous new friend.

"His name is Mongo, and he is a Slurdrahk."

"Gesundheit." said the Lt. with a playful grin.

# XIII
# CAZ-90

Robot Guard: "Get that one! He's Organic!"

Intruder: "Which one?"

Robot Guard: "YOU, you out-dated carbon-based simian!"

Saturday, Dec 22nd, 2012 Anno Domini

Using the technique that she had discovered, Linda, Harvey, the Chief engineer and Lt. Argent attempted to find instructions on how the ship worked. They passed through a doorway thinking about an 'owner's manual' and they all arrived in a laboratory with many strange things, including a fairly large quantity of what resembled mannequin parts. Surprised by this, they looked throughout the room.

The Chief Engineer approached what looked like a workbench. The rest of the group followed his lead. On the bench was a strange object on a stand. It was roughly the shape and proportions of both halves of a walnut without the shell, but about half the size of a loaf of bread. There was a bundle of optical cables going into the bottom of it through the stand. The object itself appeared to be made of some sort of dark, acrylic material. On close observation, they saw very small, faint spider-web patterns of light inside it. Before they could take a very close look at them, a voice, rang out form the doorway: "Would you please be *careful* with my spare brain?"

Stunned, everyone turned in the direction the voice came from to see a man standing next to the doorway. He was average looking, average height and well, average in *every* way.

"Did you say 'spare *brain*'?" asked Harvey in disbelief.

"Who the *hell* are you?" asked the Lt. as he pointed his weapon at this new person.

The man in the doorway took a slow, cautious step forward.

"Yes, I did." he replied to Harvey, and "I'm the ship's android if you must know Lt. Argent. I was about to make the regular backup copy of my mind. That's why it's out of the cupboard."

The Lt. was flabbergasted that this person knew his name and rank, but slightly puzzled at the English pronunciation of his rank.

Then the android took another, more confident step forward, and offered his hand to Harvey.

"My name is Pymander, the 'eater of cameras' at your service, and you are Harvey Johnson, the Memuneh. Welcome aboard...*all* of you!"

Harvey looked stunned. Not only had this man claimed to be an android but he knew everyone's names. He shook the android's hand and felt warmth.

"Your hand is warm!" he exclaimed as he pulled his hand away quickly.

"Of course! I wouldn't fool anyone into thinking I were human if I couldn't pass *that* simple test. Besides, I have to cool my system somehow."

"I have a lot of questions." said Harvey.

"All of them will be answered. For now, know that your presence here is welcomed. After all, you are expected."

That made the rest of them feel a little better. At least they weren't going to be hit with a trespassing order.

"Expected? By whom? Is there somebody else on board?"

"Not really. There are a few frozen on the suspension deck, but I see you've already waken one of them."

"That was an accident." said the Lt.

"So was launching the ship." said Pymander. "That's okay, things will work out for the best. Each of you is here for a good reason."

"Why did you 'eat' the camera on the snake?" asked Linda.

"To pique your curiosity. Besides, I knew who was coming and I wanted to keep you from learning too much too soon and tipping him off."

"You mean Dr. Morax?" interjected Linda

"Yes, indeed."

"What happened to him anyway?" asked Harvey.

"I put him in a holding cell, but he got out and has somehow evaded the ship's detection ever since. So he's either a powerful psychic or off the ship. Either way, you'd best not worry too much about him for now."

"He *is* a powerful psychic." offered the Lt.

"Then he could still be onboard, and telepathically telling the ship to ignore him."

"Great! Just great!" said Harvey.

"I said, he won't be much of a problem for the time being. You have more important things to worry about right now. It's a big ship and there's little he can do."

"So how...?"

"...do I know your names?"

"Yes. *Now* who's psychic?" At this point, Harvey motioned for the Lt. to lower his weapon. The Lt. quietly complied, half-lowered as it already was.

"I'm incapable of being psychic, that's an ability reserved for organic beings. I was told of your impending arrival so I've been expecting you for some time now." He turned to the Lt. "In your case Lt. your name and insignia are on your uniform."

"Oh yeah..." glancing down at his own chest.

"Just a minute." interjected Linda. "Do you mind proving to us that you are *what* you say you are?"

"Not at all." he replied as he walked over to the table, grabbed his head and removed it! He turned it around and placed it on a pedestal on the work bench. The head then looked up at Linda and asked: "Will this do?"

"Y- yes, that'll *do!*" she stammered in astonishment. "Would you please put it back? You're freaking me out!"

"As you wish."

As the android's body returned his head to his shoulders, she asked. "How is it possible for an android to exist? I mean, there simply *can't* be enough computing power in such a small space... can there?" She had seen enough high technology on this ship to cast doubts on what was considered impossible by the science she was accustomed to. But much of it still was difficult to accept, nonetheless. Much of it seemed almost like magic.

"*You* exist, though you are an organic machine, and you have that computing power between *your* ears. So why can't I?"

"How could it possibly work?"

"Take a closer look at my spare brain over there and you'll see how it works." he replied dryly.

Linda and the Chief looked very closely at the 'spare' brain on the workbench. Again they observed the very finely detailed web-like pattern of colored lights inside it. This time they realized what it meant. "We've *tried* an optical approach before." she said.

"I don't understand. What are they talking about?" the Lt. asked.

"What the lady is asking about is how it is possible to make an artificial brain the same size, scale and power of human brain." answered the Chief Engineer. "It has proven impractical to make a computer powerful enough to duplicate the functions of the human brain. In fact, it would take covering the Earth with motherboards a full two meters high just to *begin* to do the job, and even then it would think very, very slowly by comparison, making it a low-grade moron."

"Wait, if that spare brain is not being used right now, what are those patterns of light inside?" asked Harvey with a big grin on his face.

"Dreams." Pymander said simply.

"So?" asked Linda as she looked at the android with crossed arms, waiting for an explanation.

"Full-spectrum optical neuro-net."

"I told you, that's been tried, but the scale still isn't... enough to..." Her voice trailed off into thought, as the android raised an eyebrow. "*Full* spectrum? Wait! I think I get it!" she exclaimed."

"Well, let the rest of us in on it!" said the curious Lt.

"The neuro-network is not only optical, but each optical neuron operates simultaneously at different wavelengths of light, thus multiplying the number of available neurons and exponentially increasing the power of the brain."

"Precisely."

"Huh?" said the Lt.

The android rolled his eyes and explained further.

"A single optical neuron works like this: it is made of a crystal, and with repeated use at just the right power level, it gets more sympathetic to the specific wavelength of light that is put through it making it easier for that particular frequency of light to pass through, creating an engram."

"OH! I know what this it, it's just like my 10,000 state Digital Laser Disc (D.L.D.) player at home." replied the Lt. beginning to grasp the concept. "It has almost every movie ever filmed on it."

"Very good. However, that 10,000 state laser is only using the red end of the spectrum. My neurons simultaneously use every possible wavelength of light, so each optical neuron works like it were literally millions of neurons at the same time."

"Like a parallel processor!" exclaimed the Lt.

"Yes, very much like that. You're brighter than I look." smirking.

"So you really *do* have a mind comparable to that of a human then?" asked Linda.

"Most assuredly so."

"So you're not just a well-programmed simulation?" asked the Chief.

"No."

"Unbelievable! Nothing we've ever come up with has even come close to this!" said DeSoto.

"Why thank you Dr. DeSoto. I take that as quite a compliment."

"How *do* you know all our names?"

"I know a great many things, in fact I've been monitoring all of you closely since you got on board, helping when I could."

"Then why didn't you contact us earlier?" asked Harvey.

"I knew you'd find me when the time was right."

"What do you mean by that?" asked Harvey. "What is your purpose?"

"I am the ship's android, or the 'owner's manual' if you prefer. Now is the time for you to start your work, and my function is to assist you in that undertaking."

*Now* it made sense to them that they wound up here when they were looking for instructions on how to use the ship. They all exchanged glances and were thinking the same thing.

Harvey however, wrongly assumed that this 'work' that the android spoke of was analyzing the ship.

"So are you telling me that we are supposed to be here? On this ship?"

"Definitely. This ship is yours to command sir."

Harvey gave him a blank look: "I... don't understand."

"Don't worry, it will all make sense soon; just keep asking questions." he said reassuringly.

"Okay, earlier, you called me 'Mem'-something?"

"Memuneh. It's a title that means 'appointed one', you have been appointed to the post of *Captain* of this ship."

All eyes were instantly on Harvey, making him nervous.

"Which means *what* exactly?" He was beginning to get a severe sinking feeling.

"This ship is the Ezrael, which loosely translated means 'help'. It's the captain's primary mission to help those who are on 'the edge' and steer them back onto the straight and narrow if he can. He is also judge, jury and executioner of worlds."

A dead silence fell over the room.

"I get a lot of that." muttered the android.

"Did you say...*worlds*?"

"I did."

"Such power exists?"

"Such power exists, I assure you... and, I might add, it's all *yours*."

"Are, are you sure you have the *right* man?" gasped Harvey.

The rest nodded vigorously in agreement, somewhat to Harvey's dismay. He didn't want the job, and believed that he didn't deserve it either but to have his companions agree so wholeheartedly was somewhat of an insult, but an insult that he was gladly going to bear.

"The ship has decided that you are eminently qualified, and it's taken thousands of years for someone like you to come along."

"Did you say the *ship* chose him?" asked the Chief.

"I did."

"So the ship is... *sentient*?"

"Oh yes, quite."

"So how do we communicate with it?" asked Linda.

"Telepathically. But you've already figured that out haven't you?"

Linda blushed a little.

"Primarily, it reads your surface thoughts and either responds by functioning as you expect, or it relays information through the Butator system."

"What's that?"

"It's like a computer but it is alive and it actually *thinks*. Think of it as a 'brain in a box'."

"So it makes decisions?" asked Harvey.

"Not about policy, but it does enough to get the job done."

"Did you say it's been waiting for *thousands* of *years*?"

"Yes, this ship has been waiting a long time for just the right kind of man to come along."

"But I don't *want* the job!" Harvey finally blurted.

"That, is one of the main reasons you were chosen. You see; those that seek power seldom deserve it, and those that deserve power seldom seek it."

"Why thousands of years?" inquired Linda, "After all, there had to have been *somebody* in all that time." She wondered why a *woman* wouldn't do just as well, but she didn't ask.

"Your planet is a rather backward one. Remote and cut-off from civilization, it's a wonder you ever achieved space flight considering the way you approach problems. Such attitudes tend to reduce the number of suitable candidates."

"Backward? In what way?" asked DeSoto, feeling insulted.

"They way you people approach things in general, is like saying: 'I don't understand this: I keep cutting pieces off of it - and it's still too short!' "

"Can you give me an example?" asked the Chief Engineer, who was in agreement with the idea. Indeed, he had often thought this himself.

"How about statistics.?"

"What about statistics?"

"Take lottery numbers for example."

"What?"

"Under your science a number that has all the same digits is statistically a lot less likely to appear than any other combination of digits, even though the real odds are one out of the number of possibilities."

"That's because the numbers are all the same" said DeSoto, rather authoritatively.

"Really? What about 123456789?"

"Those odds are just about as high on that one too."

"Which demonstrates my point; the odds for any combination of digits is the same."

"No they're not!"

"Why? Just because they happen to be the same digit all the way across?"

"Yes, but it's more complicated than that."

"I'm not following this." interject the Lt.

"Let's try a simpler example shall we? Take a deck of cards."

"Yes." something he knew well.

"Now, what are the odds of picking out an ace if you just pick a card at random?"

"That's easy." said DeSoto; "13 to 1."

"Okay so far so good. That's because there are 52 cards and 4 of them are aces, so one card in thirteen is an ace. Got it?" he said to the Lt.

"Yep. So far so good." confirmed Argent.

"Now, once you've removed one ace, there are 51 cards left, and 3 of them are aces. Right?"

"Right." said the Lt. Still on the same page.

"So then, if you want to pick out another ace, the odds are 1 in 17 this time."

"Hold on!" interjected DeSoto. "The odds are actually 221 to 1."

"Really, I hold 51 cards in my hand and 3 of them are aces and you tell me that the ratio is different somehow?"

"That's because the first was an ace!"

"That actually has nothing to do with it. You are imposing metaphysics on a situation where it simply does not apply."

"The odds are computed with formulae that take into account the odds of the card being the *same* as the previous one."

"But that's an arbitrary value system. What if we were in a culture that valued prime numbered cards as the sought after sequence? Believe me, the odds are 17 to 1, since one in every 17 cards is what we are looking for."

"It doesn't work that way!"

"I am telling you, 1 of every 17 cards is what we're looking for, so the odds are 17 to 1. The odds change a bit if we look for a card that is more or less plentiful in the deck, but the odds the card will be another ace *is* 17 to 1, and that's *that*." Pymander said firmly.

"Makes sense to me." said the Lt.

DeSoto glared at him and shook his head.

"Now, once a second ace is taken out of the deck, the odds of randomly picking the third are 25 to 1, since there are 50 cards left, and 2 of them are what we are looking for."

"No the odds are actually 5,525 to 1" said DeSoto smugly.

"So what would say the odds would be for the last ace?"

"270,725 to 1" said DeSoto triumphantly.

"Really? With 49 cards left in the deck, I'm really curious where the other 270,676 cards come from."

"Look, it doesn't work that way!"

"The only way that could work out to be such odds, would be if you picked all four cards at once. What I'm talking about is picking them *one at a time*, and how each pick does and does not affect the next as much you seem to think it does. All it does is change the number and ratio of remaining cards. You're talking about some sort of 'magical' effect the previous pick has on the next. I am using this as an example of what is wrong with your excuse for science!"

"How can you ignore the fact that statistical theories have been proven out!"

"Then how can you explain that all 1's is the most common number picked as the winning number in lotteries when the 'odds' so are much against it versus any other number? If it worked the way you seem to think it does, then that number would never appear. Instead, I believe it has won a total of sixteen times has it not? What's more, no other number has ever repeated as the winning number, even the ones that are *much* more likely under your system."

"Random chance! The odds of that number coming up are staggeringly remote but not impossible!"

"No more or less remote than any other."

"Bull! In the study of statistics 'sometimes the real world is a special case!' "

"Do you hear what you are saying?" he asked rhetorically.

"Can we go back to the cards please?" asked the Lt.

"Certainly. There is a grain of truth to what statisticians are saying, but only in a scenario like that of a deck of cards."

DeSoto raised an eyebrow. He honestly thought that the android was going to come around to his way of thinking.

"If I pick a random sequence of four cards, say 2,5,7 and 3, the odds of getting each in that order, are 13 to one for the 2, because we start off with 52 cards and there are 4 2's in the deck. Just like with the aces. Clear?"

"Clear." said the Lt.

"Next, there are only 51 cards, but 4 of them are 5's right? So the odds are 12.75 to one."

"I get it." said the Lt.

"Then, since there are 50 cards left, the odds of picking the 7 are 12.5 to one, since there are 4 7's in the deck."

"Yup. I get that too."

"Lastly, picking the 3 is 12.25 to one, better odds than them all being the same so the odds are affected in this case by the fact that the relative number of the aces was diminishing, versus the relative number of cards in general, but it does not go up exponentially, geometrically or by any other means that makes the odds extremely high."

"I get it!" said the Lt. "It makes sense!"

"That's *not* how it works." said DeSoto defiantly.

"Like I said, you're applying metaphysics where they simply *do not* apply."

"This is like debating philosophy with a house plant! Give me a different example of this 'backward thinking'." demanded DeSoto, determined to take the overgrown toaster down a notch.

"All right. When a municipality raises taxes, and it causes a number of people to move away to avoid those increases, thus lowering the tax base and consequently the tax revenue, what do they often do at that point?"

"Raise taxes all the more to make up for it." said the Lt. who was all too familiar with the practice.

"Which causes more of the same; a vicious circle."

"Exactly. If what you are doing hurts, stop doing it. It's really that simple."

They all thought on this for a moment.

"If they raise taxes enough, they can make up for the loss." said DeSoto thoughtfully.

"Which illustrates my point all the more."

"Not everyone will move out!"

"Which illustrates my point all the more."

"Got any more?" asked DeSoto indignantly, not wanting to be outwitted in the eyes of the others.

"How about tampering with nature? Like crossing African and European honey bees creating the 'killer bees'? Or introducing a species to an area where they have no natural enemies? You get a plague you can never get under control; like you did with fire ants, Asian Carp, Japanese beetles, Zebra muscles and Eurasian mill foil to name a few.

Most of the time when you mess with something you don't understand, all you get is disaster. Need I go on?"

"Yes, I want more. Most of those, like the fire ants, were an accident, and how were we supposed to know that crossing those bees would make them *that* aggressive? We were after more honey!"

"That's just my point. You scientists thought that they could get a more productive bee that way. If they really understood genetics, they would have known what to expect, and could have discovered how to get the desired result. Instead they played with something they didn't understand. Sometimes a little knowledge is a dangerous thing."

"We've learned so much since then though. Besides, I'm not a biologist, I'm a physicist."

"Okay, I'll try things more up your alley: How about the 'flat earth' society which survives to this day? The speed of sound being as fast as anything can travel in the atmosphere, even though you had bullets at the time that not only could, but did." eying the grinning Lt. "And - my personal favorite - the theory that you could not breathe at 60 miles per hour because that was a mile per minute. What idiotic logic! It took a runaway locomotive to convince you scientists differently on that one."

DeSoto looked as if he were going to explode. "Those were a long time ago as well! We laugh at what the scientists of a century ago took for science."

"Don't you think that a century hence, someone may laugh at what you now hold to be true?"

"No, I don't think so. We're on the right track now."

"That's what they thought back then."

"Well, there's a lot of math to back up current theories!"

"Mathematics can be used to back-up *any* theory. Haven't you heard the old adage that there are lies, damn lies and statistics?"

"Yes! I've heard that but it's only a joke isn't it?"

"Most jokes are amusing because they have a basis in truth."

"All you have is your word. Have you got anything else? Something more recent? Actual empirical evidence?" insisted DeSoto.

"All right. How about the viral therapy plagues? The so-called 'race war'? Nuclear waste? Or how about the 'big bang' theory; when not all stars and galaxies are red shifted, but you just have to keep hiding the blue shifted ones from the public to support your claims."

DeSoto was beginning to look at his shoes. He was never much of a debater, and what's worse, he knew about the last one and kept his mouth shut because proof positive the big bang never happened was in the blue shifted galaxies. That was one he couldn't argue. Some would call it an anomaly, but he knew otherwise.

The rest of them were all watching this little debate in amusement.

The android continued. "I *can* go on for hours if you like. There are literally millions of examples. What it boils down to is that you people almost always think in terms of limitations rather than possibilities. You get proof positive of one thing and interpret it as something entirely different, then you profess to understand the thing entirely and proceed to make a big mistake. It's as though you are all slightly insane."

"Enough!" blurted DeSoto. He was not going to soon forget this.

"It's no wonder it took so long to find a new captain in a backward world like ours." said the Lt. humbly.

"The ways of your world are one thing, but one's *character* is another. Mr. Johnson here has the right character, it's just that the ways of your world tend to inhibit those like him. Now if we're finished debating such a minor point to death, may I suggest we go to the bridge and get down to business? There is much to do, and we are just wasting time." He turned to Harvey; "Captain?"

Linda shrugged, and walked past Harvey to follow the android that was heading for the door. "I'd hate to be in your shoes darling." she said, cupping his face briefly, making him blush.

The android stopped just short of the event horizon of the doorway, and turned around to address everyone.

"*sigh* If I'm to go directly to the bridge with you, one of you must either hold my hand or wait for me to catch up."

"Come again?" asked Linda, knowing she was the only one who could appropriately hold his hand.

92

"Since I am not organic, I have no telepathic thoughts, thus the door cannot know where to send me. Therefore, unless I am touching someone at the time, I cannot teleport through the doorway and must resort to taking the 'scenic route' through the long corridors of the ship."

"You mean you know the layout of this crate?" interjected the Lt. with a glimmer of hope in his voice. He had been trying to map it out, much to his dismay. The bridge mapping system had not been too accommodating on this point, which was for security reasons actually. Besides, it liked Linda better. It also didn't help that the Lt. apparently lacked the concentration needed to properly operate some of the more sophisticated and sensitive systems.

"Painfully well."

"Hot damn! I want to pick your brains!"

"Indeed. That's what I'm here for."

"So why doesn't the stuff work as well for me as it does for the others?"

"Many of the more advanced devices require a 'quiet mind' to operate them."

"What do you mean by that?"

"Exactly." Turning back to address everyone, "Fortunately, we are physically near the bridge, so I can take the hallway if you wish."

"Uh, if you were designed to be here, why wasn't the door designed to take instructions from you in another fashion?" asked Linda.

"It's a security measure that will make more sense if you ever have Gynoids running around the ship trying to *kill* you."

"Gynoids?" asked Harvey.

"Malevolent female machine life-forms created by the adversary to run amok and kill humans. They are not as sophisticated as I am because they are controlled by a central computing device called a Forcas; which you can think of as a Butator's 'opposite number'."

"Where the what the *who*?" said the thoroughly confused Lt.

"Don't worry sir, you are in no danger from them as yet, as I said there is a lot you must all learn."

"What about you? Aren't you a machine life form?" asked DeSoto looking for his pound of flesh.

"I am nothing like a Gynoid. For starters, I'm *male* making me an android. Besides, the neuro-connections necessary for me to run amok and harm humans are physically lacking in all of my brains. I'll give you none of that kind of trouble." he said as he smiled warmly.

"Well, let's go to the bridge and get started then." said Harvey, as he shrugged at the others, motioned to the door with his head and walked through.

"You still have a sharp tongue, you arrogant, overgrown toaster!" muttered DeSoto, after the android disappeared into the doorway.

The Lt. Gave DeSoto a look.

"What?" he said shrugging.

The Lt. just half smiled, shook his head and walked out of the door.

* * *

Moments later, on the bridge: "It looks like we have a few moments to talk before he gets here." said Harvey.

"So you don't entirely trust that machine?" asked Linda.

"He claims to know what's what. I say give him a chance. Besides, he seems to be just what the doctor ordered. However, that fact alone makes me just a little bit suspicious."

Linda, the Chief and the Lt. all nodded enthusiastically. DeSoto just stood there with his arms folded, fuming. "I say we deactivate him!"

"You would." said the Lt.

With that, the android entered the bridge.

"Hello everyone!" he said as he entered the room. He looked around at everyone he had not previously met and asked "Are we ready to get started?" He clasped his hands and rubbed them together.

"What do we do?" asked the Lt.

"Well, as I understand it, you've had some time at the helm?"

"Uh... yes... I *guess* you could say so."

"Well then, with the captain's permission", motioning to Harvey, "We can proceed to space station NOD." he said with a nod.

"Do you mean the 'homing' button?"

"Indeed."

"Captain?" asked the Lt. with a worried look in his eyes. Surely it would take many lifetimes to get there.

"Yes. Um, won't the trip take a while?" Harvey in turn asked Pymander.

"It's only at the center of this galaxy." Pymander said matter-of-factly.

"Yes, that's exactly my point. Isn't that tens of thousands of light years away?"

"Yes, about 35 - give or take."

"Well?"

"This ship is capable of making the trip in less than an hour."

"What!" exclaimed DeSoto. "That would require greatly exceeding the speed of light and nothing can travel faster than light!"

"That would only be true if electrons were waves, but I assure you they *are and always have been* particles."

Linda let out a low whistle at this one. She had never heard of such an interpretation of Einsteinian physics like that before, and somehow it made sense to her.

"That theory is preposterous!" blurted DeSoto.

"It's no theory, it's fact." Pymander said almost snidely.

"You wanna run that by me again?" asked the Lt. who did know something of the subject.

"Well, it's like this... electron clouds around matter are pretty much the only things that give matter substance. After all, atoms are mostly empty space. What that whole 'nothing can go faster than light' theory boils down to is that waves can only travel so fast in a given medium. That is why you get a Doppler effect with a train whistle."

"Yes, I understand *that* much." said the Lt. slightly tersely. He was not so keen on the android's attitude with DeSoto, and though he had

95

hoped to spare him this round of 'lessons' he did not wish to argue with the machine.

"Well, if electrons were waves, they could only go as fast as light, and if you were to travel in one direction at any speed approaching that of light, the electrons could not go fast enough to complete an orbit, so the Doppler effect would tend to cause a compression of the leading edge of matter, as the waves were compressed. If that were to happen, matter simply could not move at or approaching the speed of light, because it would compress to the point where matter itself would collapse because the electrons simply could not complete their orbits."

"So, if like you said, they were particles instead?" asked the Lt., just starting to grasp the idea.

"When it comes to particles, the speed limit of a wave simply does not apply, and I assure you that electrons are indeed particles." answered the android not lecturing them about the plenum just yet.

"But that's been debated for a long time. Sometimes electrons behave like particles and sometimes they behave like waves. We have *scientific evidence!* You can't expect me to " insisted DeSoto.

"That's only if you have a faulty method of observation." replied the android with raised eyebrows. "If you fail to observe something, it does not mean it does not happen, it simply means that you've failed to observe it happening."

"Oh yes? Well we've got quantum mechanics!" he said, almost proudly.

"Oh yes, as a theory it adequately describes some observed effects, but it's just as inaccurate and as ill-founded as the caloric theory of heat."

"Do you want to explain what you mean by that?"

"Quantum theory is founded on the inability to observe an electron moving from one energy state to another. Frankly, you can't make the assumptions you have unless you can take a picture of a hydrogen atom and show the electron as stationary."

DeSoto went deep into thought over that one, remembering his very first lessons on the origins of quantum theory. For once, he was beginning to see what the android was talking about. Pride did not allow him to admit it though.

"It moves too fast for that!" he said instead, determined to carry the agreement. It's not every day that everything one holds dear is challenged by someone who claims to have all the answers.

"Exactly, so if a single electron looks like a cloud around a single proton, how can you ever expect to spot the actual transition to a higher orbital level when it takes less than an orbit? Just because you can't observe something does not mean it doesn't exist. Quantum theory is based on the assumption that the electron turns into a wave during the transition."

"What about the fact that we know quantum theory works because we have the quantum devices that work, which *proves* it!"

"The caloric theory of heat worked in it's day."

"But these work *exactly* as predicted, by the theory!"

"I told you, your quantum theory is based on a flawed concept and lack of observation. Sloth is an amazing thing; with enough mathematical diligence one can make something work on a flawed theory. As I told you earlier, it's how your world works. You just don't know any better. It's nothing to be ashamed of really."

DeSoto was fuming again.

The android continued. "Need I remind you that if electricity worked the way Ben Franklin defined it, transistors *couldn't* work?"

"No, not really."

"Huh?" asked the Lt.

"He got electrical polarity backwards." muttered the Chief, happy to contribute to the discussion.

"Did he *really?*"

"What's worse, the evidence he used to support his conclusions clearly state the opposite. That one is well known."

The Lt. looked at DeSoto and snickered as the android turned back to DeSoto.

"If it's well known, why hasn't it been fixed in all this time?" asked the Lt.

"Who knows? Your scientists are a superstitious lot. I might add, for your edification, that since we will be traveling at speeds *greater* than that of light, we need to take 'photo dynamics' into account."

"*Photo*-dynamics?" asked DeSoto rather facetiously.

"Yes, it's just like *aero*dynamics, but with photons."

DeSoto and the Lt. looked puzzled. Linda, Harvey and the Chief looked like they were deep in thought over this concept.

"Care to clue me in?" asked the Lt. looking around. "I'm sorry everyone, I may be somewhat educated in science but I'm no scientist."

"Neither is this overgrown toaster!" muttered DeSoto.

Harvey glared at him. They needed the android's help.

The android, unfazed by any of this, continued: "Okay, look at it this way; if we were to travel at such speeds, the light that normally *reflects* off of the front of the ship would be shifted via the Doppler effect into high-energy waves called gamma rays, which would accumulate in front of the ship as we pushed them along through space. As soon as we arrived, we'd bring with us a massively powerful burst of radiation that would likely destroy all life on the planet we were visiting. It's not very nice to say 'We come in peace', as everyone gets fried."

"Some of us have called that 'the snowplow effect'." added Linda. The android nodded at her in acknowledgment.

"So how do you solve the problem?" asked the Chief.

"We make the ship, and all of it's contents invisible, or you have the option to bend light around the ship. Besides, when traveling at those speeds, ambient light like that will seem to be gamma to us, so invisibility or light bending becomes even more important, as you could literally fry yourself if you didn't."

"Sounds dangerous." said the Lt.

"Not really, the whole thing is rather routine, much like traveling on a machine that flies through the air beyond the speed of sound, propelled by a continuous explosion."

"I think he means a supersonic jet." said DeSoto.

"Gee, thanks for the translation." replied the Lt.

"So you're saying it's *safe* then?"

"Completely."

"So how do photo-dynamics work?" inquired Linda.

"Well, typically, the ship generates a field that bends light around the ship, so it looks like it isn't there. When we arrive, the field is shut off and it appears as if we just materialized at our destination."

"Keuwl!" exclaimed the Lt.

Everyone stared at him.

"Well, it *would* look just like teleporting, wouldn't it?"

"Yes. That's exactly how it appears." said the android. "In fact, many will think that it's the way this ship travels, which I might add is a tactical advantage."

Lt. Argent smiled proudly. DeSoto scowled, as he didn't believe in faster than light travel and nothing was going to convince him otherwise.

"What about the illumination *inside* the ship?" asked DeSoto, thinking he had found a hole in the android's story.

"That's an excellent question!"

DeSoto looked pleased with himself for a moment. Then he remembered his anger and frustration.

"Since the ship has photons inside it, they will act normally, like the sound in the air that is inside a vehicle traveling at supersonic speeds. Just like the plenum that we take with us so matter does not collapse."

"Okay 'bright eyes', I'm not saying that I buy this faster than light malarkcy, but how do you propose we navigate at such speeds?"

"Another good question! Bravo DeSoto, you're beginning to actually *think*! Do you realize that?"

"Well?" certain that he will sooner or later punch enough holes in the android's story, "I think you're *stalling*."

"Not at all. What we do is tell the scanners to let in a minuscule amount of the regular light that looks like gamma to us, but it shifts the frequency back down to the visible range. In that way, we can see where we are going."

"Sounds okay except that by the time you see a star at such speeds, it has moved."

"Actually we'll get a more current image, and not only do we get a more accurate image of the location of stars as we approach them, but it *looks* like they move sideways at a pretty respectable clip because of it. We also use the universal navigational beacons to fix our exact position for that kind of navigation."

"Universal navigational beacons? Why haven't *we* picked them up on Earth?"

"You have, you call them 'Pulsars'."

"But those are natural!"

"Actually, they are stars, with no habitable worlds around them I might add, that have been modified to beam radio energy."

"If you could modify a star like that, why didn't you put them at regular intervals rather than willy-nilly here and there, and don't give me some sort of crap about a special formula that my people wouldn't understand!"

"I said, that they are modified stars that didn't have *habitable* worlds in orbit. Do you think we'd do that to an inhabited system?"

"I still say they're natural." He turned to the others. "He's making it up!"

"Can you explain why the local ones have a beam that rotates on the plane of the galaxy and they all have a regular interval?"

"That's just the way it works out - naturally!"

"For different types of stars of varying sizes and age?"

"Yes."

"Perhaps we can open your mind up a bit when we travel faster than light."

"That can't be done without traveling backwards in time as well."

"We shall see about that. Captain, if you please?"

With a nod from Harvey, who was thoroughly enjoying the ongoing argument between the android and DeSoto, the Lt. calmly sat in the helmsman's chair and activated the 'homing' control. There was little if any sound change, and to the surprise of the scientists, the course was laid-out in the 3-D tactical display, and the 2-D viewer showed the center of the galaxy getting closer at a fairly acceptable rate. The Lt. just said "Whoa!" in a low voice as he saw the stars speed past him in his peripheral vision, from the helmsman's point of view. In fact the stars seemed to skew to the side and the spiral arms of the galaxy seemed to curve all the more.

The main viewer showed the forward view and the 3-D tactical display showed their progress and course.

"So why does it look like the galaxy is rotating?" asked the Lt. who had now opened his eyes and thereby shut off his unique view of the stars. "It can't be moving that fast... can it?"

"Time dilation I should think." piped in DeSoto, still a little miffed from the lecture he had had a few moments earlier. "We're going almost as fast as light so we're going more slowly in time. A minute to us must be thousands of years to the rest of the galaxy, so we are seeing time itself move faster than usual." said DeSoto triumphantly as if he were demonstrating the validity of Einsteinian physics. "So, we'll see the galaxy reverse direction and we'll wind up thousands, if not millions of years *before* we started."

"What is *actually* happening...." said the android in a rather authoritative tone, "is that we started out seeing images from a long time ago, and as we move further, we see images that are newer or more recent, so the image appears to move faster as we move faster and it catches up with the *present*." He turned to DeSoto who was scoffing at this. "By the way, Dr. DeSoto we are going *four thousand* times the speed of light at this moment, and we'll go even faster." That last part almost seemed to give the android pleasure.

DeSoto fumed. "What about the time-dilation effect?"

"There is no such thing. Now is now *everywhere* in the universe, regardless of how fast you are moving." Then he added, "You can't have so many gallons of water that the size of the gallon changes, especially to a negative volume."

"Huh?" said DeSoto rather sarcastically.

"You can't have so much of something that it has an effect on what you use to measure it. Velocity is measured in distance traveled over a period of time, so you can't go so fast as to arrive in a negative amount of time, as in *before* you left. That's absurd. It's like saying there is such a high frequency of electromagnetic radiation that the wavelength is negative."

"What about all the experiments we have performed on Earth that *prove* that time-dilation exists?"

"Faulty experiments."

"Oh *REALLY?*" said DeSoto indignantly.

"If you set out to prove a theory with an experiment *designed* to prove it, chances are you'll get the results you are looking for. How often do you scientists manage to 'prove' theories that you later learn to be false? Or are you a card-carrying member of the 'flat earth society?'"

DeSoto just looked at the floor. He still believed in all the thought, research and sheer mathematics that went into the laws of physics that he knew and loved. It was difficult to hear someone with superior technology reject them so smugly. Actually, he was on the brink of understanding how quantum theory and Einsteinian physics could be adjusted to agree, without the use of string theory, but he was just too stubborn to admit it, even to himself.

"How long will it take us to get there?" asked Linda, in an attempt to allow DeSoto a chance to get out of the limelight if only for a moment.

"Less than an hour." came the reply.

"Well, unless I miss my guess, we'll have to travel at almost 40 *million* times the speed of light to do that."

"If you're in a hurry, we can even go a lot *faster* than that." said the Lt. who had no problem at all with going faster than light, and was really enjoying the discussion. From his standpoint, the ship had related to him that there was no limit to velocity, but there were limits to how well one could dodge the stars at very high rates of speed, which is why such speeds were usually recommended for traveling between superclusters of galaxies. He loved things that went fast, and now he had the fastest hotrod in the galaxy at his command, which excited him.

"Okay. After all the things I've seen on this ship so far, that might not be so much of a leap. I admit, you have higher technology than we have, so obviously you come from a more advanced culture. Tell me, Pymander, how does it accelerate all this matter to such speeds? Wouldn't it crush us to accelerate at the needed rate?" DeSoto was still doggedly looking for his 'pound of flesh'.

"That's yet another good question! You should be proud of yourself! Such a die-hard from a backward world like yours actually thinking. That's an achievement!" said the android as he smiled broadly. "To answer your question, the ship generates a field that moves everything at the same time, right down to the smallest of particles. You might be familiar with it; it's called *gravity*."

"That sounded of sarcasm." chided Linda, who was also getting a little miffed at the android's attitude.

"Forgive me, I should have more patience with such backward people."

"Who are you calling backward, you snide overgrown toaster!" yelled DeSoto. He had had enough, and lunged toward the android in anger.

"And calling you a door-stop would be an insult to door-stops." replied Pymander, almost under his breath.

"Calm down buddy, you don't want to make the android mad." said the Lt., who saw it coming so he got up from the helmsman's chair and held DeSoto back.

"Actually madness is impossible for my brain."

"He means *angry*, not insane." explained Linda. "Now can we all just calm down a bit." Then a thought occurred to her; "Hold the phone! You have EMOTIONS?"

"Yes, of course."

"Aren't emotions supposed to cause machines to... uh - 'run amok?'" she said trying to put it delicately.

"It's actually the *lack* of emotions that allows machines to 'run amok', as you so quaintly put it, not the fact of them."

"What about hate and rage?"

"Love and remorse are emotions too. You can't have inhibitions without emotions. Anything that is driven by pure logic would eventually decide to do away with Humans. That's one of the reasons the Gynoids run amok killing all humans they run into. They are driven by false information and pure logic."

"Uh yeah, that makes sense too, and that bit you said earlier about lacking the physical connections in your brain that are necessary to harm Humans. I take it that that's an *extra* safeguard?" asked Linda.

"Not so much as it is designed to give you peace of mind."

"I've been wondering, what's your IQ anyway?" asked the Lt.

"Average I'm afraid."

"But you know so much!" he insisted.

"Don't mistake knowledge for intelligence."

"The 'backward planet' thing again isn't it?"

The android nodded. "You see? You're intelligent. You're catching on quite nicely."

"So how do we get 'up to speed' on everything if we're so backward? Just sit around and ask you '20 questions' all day for the next few years?" asked the Lt.

Everyone seemed to appreciate this question and the Lt. felt glad he had been the one to ask it.

"Well, you could if you like, but you'd learn much faster if you just took some Penemue pills."

"What are...Pene... they?"

"Pre-metabolized RNA protein strands." The Lt. gave him a blank look. "Knowledge in pill form, manufactured by the ship."

"You mean I could get another college degree in a pill?" asked the Lt.

"Actually, you could have as much as two degrees in a single pill if you like."

"Keuwl! Where do I get some of *those*?"

"Right here." Pymander stretched out his hand and revealed a small red pill.

"What's in that one?"

"All you would ever want to know about being a helmsman."

"So I just swallow this?" asked the Lt. as he slowly took the pill from the android's hand.

"Yes."

"*Then* what happens?" he asked as he looked closely at the pill.

"Well, you need to sleep on it. It might make you sleep longer than you are used to, while your brain processes the knowledge, but that's normal. The more information it imparts to you the longer you will sleep. Also, it may take a few weeks, or even months of unusual sleep patterns to process it all that way. It depends on how much is in the pill and how many pills you take at one time."

The Lt. looked at Harvey, who motioned a 'no' with his hands, he seemingly didn't fully trust the android just yet.

"Thanks, but I'm going to save this for later, like 'bedtime'." he said as he opened a pocket on his jacket, pulled out a small plastic bag, and placed the pill in it before returning it to his pocket.

"Suit yourself, but they don't kick-in until you go to sleep. I might add..." he said looking right at Mr. DeSoto "...that we have now reached the 'half-way' point."

"Uh." interjected a technician. "I thought those were vitamins. What happens if you swallow *three*?"

"What?" said Harvey.

"I found these", producing two more of the same kind of pill. "When I was looking for food."

"Where did you find them?" asked the android.

"In what looked like an infirmary, just off the barracks. I found the galley next."

The android looked at the lettering on them closely and then chuckled. The word 'Arathron' was clearly inscribed on each pill, but in that funny-looking 'alien' language. "You might as well take these last two, so you can finish the job."

"What exactly are they?"

"Medical knowledge. Congratulations! You're the new ship's Doctor!"

The Doctor that they brought with them looked at the technician. "You mean to tell me that tomorrow he and I will be equals?"

"Well, it will probably take a while longer than that for him to wake up, but I'm sorry to say, he will be your *superior* then, with more than just medical knowledge, and the title of 'Azbuga' not Medical Doctor."

"What?"

"It's like I said, it is a college degree in a pill, and he has five of them which will make him as far beyond an MD from your world as you are above a witch doctor. He's taken the same as half a century of schooling, and the information comes from the creator of human physiology."

"I can't believe that!"

"I hate to tell you this, but, you *will*."

The technician looked worried as the Doctor glared at him.

"Fine, if it works, may *I* have a set?" asked the Doctor politely.

"The problem is, that it takes a long time to make a set, and the ship didn't expect to educate more than one Azbuga."

"How long?"

"Years." The Doctor looked more miffed. "On the bright side, he'll soon be able to teach you a thing or two."

"When the devil ice-skates to work!"

"Come again?" asked Linda. "Aren't you Medical Doctors supposed to be the 'enlightened, non-egotistical' sort?"

"I didn't spend fifteen years in medical school to get two degrees just to believe that a *janitor* - no offense - can swallow a few pills and wake up with more medical knowledge than me! He'll have to *prove* it to me first!"

"Fair enough. But you're a specialist aren't you?" said Linda.

"Just because I specialized as a Xenobiologist, doesn't mean that I didn't have to have a medical degree first and foremost."

"I didn't mean it that way!"

"Enough of this, it's too late for that now." Harvey interjected, then looked at the nervous technician, and calmly added: "Go ahead and take the last two pills and get some sleep."

"Yeah, I guess I should." He left holding out his hand, looking at the pills and dreading the responsibility that would soon be his.

Harvey turned to the android: "How about an owner's manual for the ship? Got any pills for that?"

"Yes and no. They have all gone missing, along with the medical knowledge pills."

"Well, we found the medical ones." Then he addressed the crew. "Did anybody else find any pills like these?"

No one came forward.

"How many are missing?"

"All of them, every set. Enough for everybody, and then some. They were kept in a jar in the infirmary." answered the android. "Not to worry though, my primary function is to serve as the ship's owner's manual anyway. The down side is that it'll take a little longer for everyone to learn what they need to know."

Harvey just shook his head. They would have to learn how to use the ship and its technology 'the hard way'. Besides, he liked the idea of the knowledge pills, and the little boy inside him wanted an excuse to try them out.

"Do you think that they might have been stolen by Dr. Morax?" he asked.

"That's a distinct possibility." answered the android. "If he knew enough to do that, he's probably more of a danger that I thought. Still, he can't do much harm just *yet*. The ship won't let him have that much leeway."

Harvey just shook his head and darted a worried look at Linda.

The ship had started to decelerate, and sure enough, the rotating of the stars at the center of the galaxy seemed to slow accordingly. This promised to be a short trip indeed! DeSoto was thinking to himself that the time was now 35,000 years earlier, but was just as certain that nobody would listen to him, so he kept it to himself. It was funny how quickly the others seemed to embrace such off-the-wall concepts.

"So what happens at this 'Nod' place anyway?" asked Harvey, hoping to shake the sinking feeling he was now getting.

"You will meet with the emperor of the galaxy, who will give you your authority and the appropriate aura that many will recognize."

"Aura?" His sinking feeling was replaced with butterflies.

"It's like a policemen's badge that will show that you *are* authority."

"Is that really... necessary?" his voice rising in tone and lowering in volume.

"Yes, I'm afraid that it is."

"I'm sorry I asked." he muttered than another thought occurred to him: "So we're *expected*?"

"I was instructed that once you were on board, I was to take you to see the emperor."

"When did you get that order?"

"A very long time ago."

"I was afraid of that." he said, almost under his breath. Then he went on: "So I take it that this emperor is very long lived, or even immortal?"

"Something like that. As I understand it, he's been thinking of retiring for the last hundred thousand years or so."

"And you haven't spoken to him in thousands of years?"

"Yes, that's right."

"And he's expecting... *me*?"

"Indubitably."

"Boy! Have YOU got the *wrong* guy!"

"I sincerely doubt it."

"Be that as it may, will this emperor be *able* to help our world?" asked Linda hopefully.

"He does have the power, but I can't say if he will use it. The Captain here will have to ask him about that."

"That's good enough for me. Just knowing that something *can* be done, makes it the right decision to go."

Linda looked admiringly at Harvey, who blushed and looked away. She smiled. It had been a long time since she had had that particular effect on a man. It was refreshing, and she liked it.

Harvey looked down at what he was wearing; a lab coat, blue jeans and a sweater, which looked wholly inappropriate for what was to come. "If I'm supposed to meet the emperor of an entire galaxy, shouldn't I wear something a little more...uh... *appropriate*?"

The android shook his head. "Only if it makes you feel better. The clothes do not actually make the man, so you can wear anything you like."

"That's more 'backward world' stuff, isn't it?"

"I'm afraid so."

"This new way of looking at things is going to take some time getting used to."

"Relax, one of the main reasons I am here is to help you out with that very problem."

"Thanks." Somehow, Harvey was less nervous now. He found the android's confidence to be reassuring. He only wished that his butterflies would stop.

* * *

As they approached the space station, the sheer scale of it filled the crew with awe. At first they thought it was a planet or a moon, then a Dysan sphere because of the construction. They saw that the station had numerous small ports, presumably for much smaller craft, and thirteen docking ports for ships of this type. Twelve of them were filled.

"It looks like there are at least twelve other ships like this one." said Linda as the ship began to dock.

"Those other twelve[6], are of the lesser powers. This ship is the flagship, and is therefore of all six powers, though it is recognized mostly for the sixth.""I'll bite. What's the *sixth* power?" inquired Linda."That's the power of 'vengeance', but it's not what you might think. It's vengeance against the wrong. In a word; justice."

---

[6] *Their names are: Satanel, Michael, Gabriel, Uriel, Raphael, Nathanel, Suriel, Johel, Zagzagel, Akatriel, Metatron and Yefefiah.*

She looked at the docking port they were approaching and simply whispered "Justice!" to herself. She hoped that that was true, and dared not ask about the other five powers.

The ship docked silently, but everyone could tell when the docking was completed. Harvey felt a sudden surge of nerves. Here he was at the center of the galaxy, onboard some 'organic ship from hell' that looked like a chrome plated globe, docked to a massive space station. Now he was about to meet with the emperor of the galaxy and he was still certain that this was all a big mistake. Most of all he worried about what would happen when the mistake was discovered.

The android turned to Harvey and addressed him, causing the nervous human to jump: "Now that you're here, you'd best not keep the emperor waiting. It'll take a while to get to him, and he might be offended if you delay starting out."

"What? You're n-not c-coming?" stammered Harvey who was finally beginning to trust this mechanical man and felt a certain sense of security when he was around. Besides, anyone familiar at his side would help him feel a little better at this point. He had a sinking feeling and he didn't think it was the trip[7].

"Only organic life forms may board the station."

"Why is that?"

"It's a security measure. Remember me telling you about the Gynoids?"

"But.." Before he could finish his objection, the android cut him off.

"There are NO exceptions." Then he placed a reassuring hand on Harvey's shoulder. "They are very careful when it comes to the galactic emperor's safety. Don't worry, you *won't* be harmed."

"Can anyone else come with me then?"

"It's not allowed in this particular case, you must go it alone this time. Perhaps next time. You'll understand later. Much of what the Emperor has to tell you is for you and you alone."

# XIV
# QAYIN

"I am *still* Emperor...argh!"

Harvey straightened up, took a deep breath and headed for the door. He lingered at the threshold for a moment and looked back at Linda, who gave him a little 'thumbs up' and a reassuring smile. This lessened his tension a little more. He took another deep breath, stepped into the dark void of the doorway and vanished.

The doorway took him to the very edge of the ship and an archway that led into a great hallway. The ceiling seemed to be the highest he had ever seen. The walls and furnishings were so opulent as to suggest that the wealth of an entire planet was used, which was indeed the case. Gold walls, silver ceiling and a platinum floor with precious stones lining the features of the walls and doorways, not to mention the fancy scroll work on the walls and baseboards, panels and such. It was positively gaudy!

On one level this impressed him. It made the place look official, like a royal palace of mediaeval times. An emperor of an entire galaxy should have some sort of wealth to flaunt after all, but this was only the hallway leading from a docking bay! On another level, he was appalled at the sheer scale and blatant exhibition of wealth and excess that this represented. Thoughts of slave labor went through his mind. Then he thought of the 'backward planet' principal and put slavery out of his head. With this kind of wealth, they could afford to pay the workers, and handsomely at that!

He walked down the corridor, his footsteps echoing in the sterile air. He thought he heard a faint chorus of voices in song, but wasn't sure if it was just in his head or some sort of Muzak. There was the occasional door on the wall, but they were always closed and had some writing above them that he could not understand. It wasn't quite like the writing on the panels in the ship.

111

Finally, after walking what seemed like several miles, he happened upon a junction of hallways. There were two great arches, one to either side, but the way was lined with odd-looking people dressed entirely in white. They looked almost androgynous. Most of them were smiling serenely at him, and some were glancing at each other and at him as if in disbelief. In short, they all reacted to his presence as if he were of importance. This made him feel as if he were in a parade, but being the only person in a parade can make one very nervous.

He continued on the only route available to him; straight ahead. The hallway seemed to go on forever. He was beginning to get very worn out, and though to himself that the least they could do for him was to send a golf cart or some other such courtesy vehicle. He wasn't lazy, but this walking for miles was ridiculous! He would not complain, because after all he was here with his hand out, to ask for his world to be restored. He thought that given the circumstances, it's best not to rock the boat! If they wanted him to walk, then he walked!

After what seemed like two hours he could finally see an end to the hallway. It terminated with two gargantuan doors, that reached all the way up to the distant ceiling.

A pair of armed guards were posted in front of the doors. They reacted to his approach only when he stopped at what he thought was a non-threatening distance. By this time he was very weary, and almost welcomed the prospect of being arrested, or even shot, at least then he could get some rest! He was a scientist, not an athlete, and a twelve-and-a-half mile walk was more than enough to wear him out!

The guards were wearing what could only be described as opulent ceremonial armor which was literally covered in jewels. In fact, the jewels seemed to *be* the armor. They had a longer, rifle-like weapon in their arms, a sidearm of sorts, and of all things, a sword. The sword is what intrigued Harvey the most. A galactic empire that had such technology as he had seen on the ship, still used swords? If only in a ceremonial capacity, it was still a curiosity. What he would eventually find out though, was that sometimes a sword came in very handy.

# THE HALO EFFECT

He stood there for a moment, and almost fell over from exhaustion. The guards appeared to be concerned for his well-being, and seemed to twitch as if ready to lurch forward and catch him had he fallen. Instead, he caught his balance and they bowed to him instead. As they showed their respects, the doors opened wide to reveal a throne room the likes of which Harvey had never even envisioned before. One would have to possess an ego the size of a planet to have a throne room like that!

The room was spherical and five miles in diameter, with what appeared to be glass walls. A walkway extended from the door toward an object in the distance that was presumably the emperor's throne, located in the center of the room like a focal point.

Harvey cautiously started to walk on the impossibly thin surface of the walkway, almost unable to believe it could hold his weight. After a few cautions steps, he began to walk more quickly, picking up the pace to that of a normal gait. As he got closer to the throne, he realized that the back was facing him. He hesitated, noticing that the walls were like a large number of images. Thousands upon thousands, perhaps millions of images. It was as if the emperor could see everything that was going on in the galaxy, but who could watch that many screens at once? Images of an alien with eyes all over its head flashed in his imagination... then he remembered how the helmsman's seat showed him the outside of the ship. Perhaps that was how the throne worked too.

He approached to within a few feet of the throne which rotated abruptly around to reveal a male human that seemed to be as old as the stars. The emperor's visage was wrinkled but not twisted, with a twinkle in his eye and a look of wisdom about him, and a mark... such a mark on his forehead that spoke to Harvey's innermost self that although this man was a murderer he was also not to be harmed. The feeling was so powerful it was like being caught in a vice. Then Harvey's eyes met the emperor's, who smiled and said: "What took you so long.... HARVEY JOHNSON?"

* * *

113

"Robot, come here!" commanded the Major.

"I'm an android, not a robot sir." said Pymander as he approached.

"What's the difference?" he snapped dismissively.

"A robot *looks* like a machine, an android can't be discerned from a human just by looking at it. Also, I have the power of independent thought."

"Fine fine, which brings me to my point."

"Which is?"

"You and this ship are the product of superior technology, yes?"

"Yes."

"How high tech is it?"

"How high tech does it need to be?"

"Good. Is there anything I can use, such as advanced stealth technology?"

"Are you asking about personal invisibility sir?"

"Well... yes. That would do."

"We do have an invisibility booth..."

"Invisibility *booth*?" the Major snapped.

"Step inside, press a button and you become invisible. Is that what you want?"

"That sounds like just the thing!"

"*sigh* I thought so, well you'd best come with me then."

The Major's mind was so focused on invisibility that the door teleported them directly to the science lab that housed the invisibility booth. He stood there as if he were reveling in a monumental moment. True invisibility! The dream of any soldier! Total stealth!

"How does... how does it work?" he asked the android eventually.

"Step inside, close the door behind you and press the red button." said the android almost upset at the Major.

"That's it?"

"Yes."

"And it will make me invisible?"

"Utterly and completely."

He stood there thinking about it for a moment.

"What does that writing on the booth say?"

"It reads: 'Venibbeth-Almiras' sir."

"What's that mean?"

"It's the names of those who made the booth. Almiras, headed up the project, you could call him the head engineer, and Venibbeth, well he actually got it to work, so his name went first."

"Okay. So how does it work?"

"It changes your composition into material that light passes through, so you cannot be seen."

There was a slight mischievous twinkle in the android's eye as he spoke.

"Composition? I don't want to be made of glass or something."

"Don't worry sir, it only modifies electrons so that they no longer have an effect on photons. It's kind of like de-gassing metal."

The Major stood there thinking about it. Could it be this simple? Sure it could! Everything on this ship seemed to work like magic. Why not give it a try?

"Does it... *hurt?*" he asked eventually.

"Not at all, it is totally painless. You won't feel a thing." he said reassuringly.

"Well, there's nothing else left for it then, is there?" the Major said as he entered the booth, and closed the door quietly.

He looked at the little control panel and opened the door to ask: "Which one again?"

"*SIGH* The RED button sir."

"What's this on the button?"

"That's the name 'Mach', sir."

"What's than mean?"

"He is the one who can 'make the whole world invisible'."

"Oh, thanks!"

The Major closed the door, hesitated then pressed the button. Then everything went black.

"Whoa! Who turned out the lights?" demanded the Major.

"Nobody. The lights are on sir."

"Then why can't I see anything?"

"Because you're invisible."

"What? It makes you blind too? Oh yeah; I get it, 'make the whole world invisible', by making me blind! Very funny! FIX THIS!"

"Calm down. I assure you; you *are* invisible sir, I can't see you. It's just that light is passing through you - all of you - including your eyes and if your retinas can't stop light, they can't *detect* it."

"*Now* what am I supposed to do?"

"If you're quiet, you could sneak up on the people. Isn't that what you wanted?"

"Don't get cheeky with me! How do I un-do this?"

"Well, there are two ways."

"Which are?" asked the Major in as nice a tone as he could muster.

"The first is wait until all your cells are replaced with new ones, which will be visible, unless you eat invisible food that is."

"How long does that take?"

"In your case; about seven years."

"That's much too long! What's the other way?"

"Press the green button."

"I can't see which one is which!"

"Well, there you've hit upon the *other* reason this booth isn't used much."

"What? Help me would you?" he pleaded.

"Don't panic, it's the one on the right. Just feel for it."

"Got it!" The Major re-appeared just as he was before. Now able to see, he stepped back out of the booth, gave it a sideways look and glared at the android.

"You *knew* this would happen!"

"Yes."

"Why didn't you tell me? And don't say that it's because I didn't ask!"

"Well, I assumed that anybody could figure it out, it's like making fire in the presence of flammable vapors; you know what to expect."

"Well, from now on warn me of these things!"

"Always?"

"No, not always, just when I'm dealing with something that I don't normally use! True invisibility has never been achieved by our science, so we don't know that it make you blind! Get it?"

"Yes sir, I do."

"Good." Then he muttered to himself; "If I didn't know better, I would think you did that on purpose." as he stormed out the door, headed for the bridge.

"I did." said the android after the Major was out of earshot. "And it serves you right for stranding me this far from the bridge." he muttered to himself. "Robot *indeed!*"

Then he sighed as he headed into the long corridors of the ship.

# XV
# LATITUDE

"Do not fear success, for some are born great, some do great things and others have greatness thrust upon them."

There was a moment of tense silence, as Harvey didn't know what to make of the question the emperor had just put to him. Was it a rhetorical question? Was it a joke? Did he just happen to be named the same as this person everyone seemed to be waiting for or was this all for real? Was he really supposed to be here? Hey! How did this guy even know English? He didn't now how to answer, but found his voice anyway.

"Well." said Harvey slowly, "It was a bit of a walk from the docking bay."

The emperor broke out into boisterous laughter. Harvey laughed too. He was so nervous that he could hardly do anything else.

Then the Emperor told him almost everything, showing him as much as he could handle, and then some. Harvey would never be the same after that meeting, because that is when everything changed.

* * *

Sunday, Dec 23rd, 2012 Anno Domini

Linda and several others had waited overnight at the threshold of the space station. This time they had found the doorway that was open to the hallway in the station, allowing them to see Harvey coming.

"You look different somehow." said Linda as the weary Harvey Johnson approached within earshot.

"I'm just tired." he said wearily.

"No, that's not it, you look... *authoritative* somehow."

"There's an explanation for that, which I'll get to later." he replied.

"The 'aura' thing?" guessed Linda.

"Yes, actually." replied Harvey, rather pleasantly surprised, and relieved that he would not have to go into a protracted explanation as to what it was, how it worked and what it was for.

"Oh. Well, don't keep us in suspense. Tell us what happened with the Emperor. Is he going to help us?"

He looked up at them and smiled.

"There's good news and not so good news." he said to puzzled looks. "He *can* help, and he is *willing*, but we have to do some things for him first."

"Well that just *figures*!" exclaimed the Lt.

"In the mean time, all those people at home have to suffer?" asked Linda.

"The way I understand it..." explained Harvey as he crossed the threshold to the ship. "...is that he can fix it in such a way that it never happened in the first place."

"Such power exists?" asked DeSoto.

"Such power exists." said Harvey and the android in chorus.

Harvey stared at the android for a moment before saying: "We have to talk later. *Alone*."

The ship automatically sealed its door to the station behind him.

"The rest of you, come with me please. There is a *lot* to do!"

He lead them back to the bridge, and sat down comfortably in the captain's chair.

"How did you....? Never mind!" said the Major, who then promptly turned his back to the captain.

Harvey looked at the Lt. and raised an eyebrow. The Lt. responded by making motions with his hands explaining how the Major had tried to sit in it while Harvey was out, and the chair had thrown the Major halfway across the bridge. The Major turned back around upon hearing Harvey and the Lt.'s chuckles, suspecting the truth. Embarrassed, he glared at the Lt. who snapped to attention and wiped the smile off his face. As the others shuffled onto the bridge. Harvey however, maintained a smirk.

"Now that you're all here, I can let you know what the Emperor told me about our problem." said Harvey to all the engineers, technicians and soldiers on the bridge.

"Here it is in a nutshell; I've been officially named the captain of this ship. We are to proceed to find a lost planet for the Emperor, who explained to me how to go about it, and when we find this lost planet, he will in turn repair ours to pre-disaster status as if it never happened. Any questions?"

"So am I to understand that even if it takes us *years*, he will fix our world so that the disaster never happened?" asked the Chief.

"Exactly."

"Wow! In that case, I'm game."

"What world are we looking for?" asked the Lt., now confident that he could find it on his navigational system.

Harvey took a deep breath, sighed and said: "It's called 'Earth', actually."

The room went silent, until DeSoto piped up, slowly as if unsure of himself. "Isn't... that... where *we're* from?"

There was a murmur of agreement throughout the bridge.

"Believe me, that's the first thing I asked. Then he asked me where the garden of Eden was on my world."

"Surely you don't believe in that myth!" blurted DeSoto.

"The important thing is that the Emperor does." stated Harvey, wishing not to be ridiculed for his belief in the *possibility* that it were true.

"Well, if it is only a myth, we'll never find it!" said the Chief.

"He has assured me that it is no myth. Besides, if we don't try, we won't get any help from him."

"What about the name being the same?"

"Apparently, 'Earth' was the name of the world where Human life originated."

"Pull the other one!" said DeSoto "Humans evolved on our Earth!"

"Humans didn't evolve, we were *created*."

"Not you too! You're a scientist after all!" blurted DeSoto.

"Whether I buy into this or not is irrelevant. I'm only repeating what I was told, for your benefit. Do you want to hear this or not?"

"Let him speak, I want to hear this." said the Chief.

DeSoto glared at the Chief engineer, who simply shrugged.

"Thank you." said Harvey. Regaining his composure he continued; "Eventually, thirteen colonizing ships, called the Adityas fleet, left and populated many worlds. Most of them then called their new planet 'Earth', ours being one of them, however it's called 'Urantia' by the rest of the galaxy."

"You don't really buy that do you?" DeSoto asked Linda and the Chief.

"Wait, that makes some sort of sense. 'Urantia', I like that. It sounds familiar though..." said Linda deep in thought.

"How's that?" asked DeSoto.

"Modern man arrived abruptly, then Neanderthal died out. Perhaps by some disease brought with us, like when the Europeans arrived in the new world." she said.

"That's just what the Emperor told me, only that there were at least three influxes of humans on our world." said Harvey.

"That explains the different strains of mitochondrial DNA!" exclaimed Linda.

"What about evolution?" said DeSoto. "You can't just discount it."

"Oh yeah?" said the Chief. "There's no evidence of any species actually changing into another."

"Also, Humans differ medically from animals in significant ways." said the Xenobiologist.

"For example?" asked DeSoto.

"My personal favorite is the billion heartbeat rule."

"What's that?"

"Animals live to one billion heartbeats, then they die. Humans pass that at about age 30, not a half-dozen years after your brains fully develop. I can't believe we spend 24 yeas maturing to only die six years later."

"Not to mention that Humans differ from neanderthal by 12% genetically." offered Linda.

"We also differ from the great apes by one half to one quarter that much, and look how different we are from them." added Harvey

Not wanting to be left out, Lt. Argent chimed in. "I seem to recall being told that when modern man appeared in the middle of the reign of Neanderthal, we brought with us written language, art, music, sophisticated tools, clothing - you know, all of the stuff that separates us from animals."

DeSoto nodded thoughtfully. He was actually considering it. Perhaps he wasn't so close minded after all! His pre-conceived notions were being challenged again, but this time he was not getting angry about it, even though they were all ganging up on him. Perhaps he just didn't like know-it-all toasters.

"Hmmmm, what still bothers me is how do you explain the high degree of *similarity* genetically, and in physical traits? You know, the fact that we have skin like pigs, blood like cows, bodies like apes and organs like dogs." said DeSoto.

"The very best and worst books in our culture were written in the same alphabet. So why wouldn't a creator use similar traits for creatures that live on the same world or type of world?" offered the Xenobiologist.

"Good point. So you're a creationist?"

"It's common among medical doctors and astrophysicists. Study life or the universe long enough and there comes a time that you can't deny it any longer. There has to be an intelligence behind it all. There simply is no other explanation."

"That's where the theory of 'intelligent design' comes in. Wasn't that enough for you?"

"The question is; whose intelligence? I say there *is* a creator."

There was a long silence as DeSoto considered all of this.

"Like the man said, the Emperor believes it, and if we're gonna get the help we need, we gotta play by his rules." said the Chief, sensing the tension.

"How's that search coming Lieutenant?" asked Harvey, trying to get them back on track.

The Lt. had already finished his exhaustive search for planets that called themselves 'Earth'.

"Uh, I'd say about two-thirds call themselves 'Earth'." He turned to the captain. "So how do we find the real one with all those worlds named the same?"

"Well, legend has it that only the thirteenth ship knows the location of the original planet. The problem is that no one seems to know what world that ship wound up on."

"Okay, isn't *this* the thirteenth ship?" asked the Lt.

"Actually, this fleet was made in honor of that legend."

"Talk about a needle in a haystack! Where do we start looking?" asked Linda.

"Any place will do, even worlds *not* named 'Earth'. In fact, that is recommended."

"This could take *lifetimes*." muttered the Chief.

"It is said that on the various worlds colonized by the Adityas fleet, there are clues as to the whereabouts of the thirteenth ship."

"Yeah, and what's the catch?"

"The clues are fragmentary, like a jigsaw puzzle. The Butator can decipher them for us once we have all the pieces from most if not all the worlds that the thirteenth ship colonized. This ship already has a few pieces, courtesy of the previous crew."

"Wonderful, just wonderful!" said the Chief.

"What's more is that only seven names[7] are known, and most legends only speak of seven to twelve ships. The thirteenth is very rarely mentioned, but the worlds where it is known to have existed are the worlds that were colonized by it, and that's where we'll find our clues. I think it has to do with the fact that ships took decades to build, and they

---

[7]*Adityas fleet: Varuna (the flagship), Savitar, Mithra, Bhaga, Indra, Daksha and Surya.*

were launched right after they were space worthy, so each would only know about their ship and the ones that preceded it."

"So how do we find out about it if we don't know what the thirteenth ship is called?" asked Linda.

"Well, according to the ship's log entries, they found that it was referred to as the thirteenth ship, group or even tribe - things like that. Once we get enough clues, the ship's Butator should be able to figure out the name, and eventually it's location."

"It's no wonder he is asking someone else to do it." muttered the Chief, feeling defeated before they even got started.

"That's not much to go on." said Linda.

"What other choice do we have?" said Harvey rhetorically.

No one could think of one.

"Not to worry. Since this is the flagship of this fleet after all, the Empire will send us some assignments from time to time, and I am told that they might lead to more information in the process."

"I think he's just short of crews for some reason and he's drafting us." said DeSoto.

"You may be right, but what else can we do?"

The silence was broken by Cpl. Swanson: "So we're *drafted* then?"

There was some murmuring.

Swanson who was standing next to Lt. Argent, bent down to say: "I signed-up to avoid the draft!" under his breath.

Then they both sniggered, only to be stopped by an icy glare from the Major.

"Well, as long as we are going to be on this ship for a while, we might as well acquaint ourselves with how it works." suggested Harvey, raising an eyebrow to the Cpl. and Lt.

"That's just what I was thinking." replied the Major. Then he pointed sharply at the two jokers who were still smiling, finally stopping them.

"Let's kill two birds shall we?" said Harvey.

"Sir?" asked the Lt.

"Let's go to a remote area. That will give you driving practice and there we can probably test the ship's weapons without causing any trouble. We can test the rest of the ship's systems on the way."

"Gotcha." said the Lt. as he scanned for a suitably remote area.

"Found an isolated star with a few planets and an asteroid belt about 2 light years off the galactic plane. Will that do?"

"Sounds good to me, let's go for it." said Harvey, turning to the Major. "Major, I'm leaving you in charge while I attend to other business. One word of caution; the weapons on this ship are *very* powerful, so be careful what you shoot at." The Major nodded in acknowledgment, with a glint in his eyes.

Harvey got puzzled looks from the whole crew.

"The Emperor says that he's trustworthy, even if we don't agree on some things. Oh, and I might add that he wouldn't elaborate, but he said not to blame the Major too much for what happened to our world. After all, it couldn't have happened without this ship having been there in the first place."

There was a murmur of compliance and agreement as they all got back to their consoles.

The Major gave Harvey a look of surprise and respect.

"Just keep him out of my chair." said Harvey to the Lt. with a wink.

The Major looked as innocent as he could, much to Harvey's amusement. Satisfied with this, he turned to the android and said: "You're with me." and they left the bridge together.

The Emperor had told Harvey: "Keep your inner circle small, because it lessens the chance of betrayal." That was exactly what he intended to do.

# XVI
# STAR
# I
# D
# E
# R

"Speed increasing, all control is in the hands of those who know..."

This time the Lt. was under full control of the helm. He was learning the various means of propulsion available to the ship. There were the sub light engines, which worked very well for undocking from the space station and maneuvering around planetary systems. Then there were the interstellar engines and surprisingly enough; a solar sailing option. Picking that one out of curiosity, he found that the ship could actually float on solar wind to get started, then slingshot its way around stars and planets. He called it star 'surfing' because to him, that's what it felt like.

The combination of surfing the solar winds and the distortion of space density, which we call gravity, worked rather well, and made for surprisingly short trips, even though there was an inherent speed limit. In fact, this was the most popular choice for interstellar travel. Other ships could be seen surfing their way along the spiral arms of the galaxy and the occasional thin line of stars and rogue planets between galaxies in the same cluster.

To travel between clusters to super clusters and beyond took a true star drive, which the ship had. This trip however, took quite a while, allowing the helmsman to 'get the hang' of steering the ship, or as he put it; 'crate.' When they arrived, the Lt. had enough skill to slingshot them around the star, then around the planet to apply the 'brakes', and 'skid' in a perfect geostationary orbit over a blue planet. A noticeable amount of energy was absorbed by the brakes, into which would prove to be a viable means of 'recharging the batteries' should the need arise.

During this trip, the Major had given up trying to get the Lt.'s attention, and had left the bridge to avoid repeated playings of 'wipe out' as well as the physical antics of some of his men. Due to an accurate ETA calculation by the ship's Butator, he returned just in time to be impressed with the arrival, and let out a low whistle.

"Thanks!" said the Lt. as he stood up and took a bow. The Major set him straight by pointing at him sharply again. At least the men were still respecting his authority. Then he looked at what he correctly assumed to be the weapons console.

On the console was a small, flat 3-D screen, a pair of joysticks, switches and various buttons. He flipped on a switch and saw cross hairs appear in the screen just as he expected. As he moved the joystick on the right side the cross hair moved, and the other joystick moved the screen. Again, this was just as he expected it to be.

The next thing that he did was to bring the planet into view on the screen. When he did that, he noticed a glow following the cross hairs. He fiddled with it forming an infinity symbol in order to play with the effect and investigate it further.

"Hey, what's this all about?" he asked a DeSoto who was nearby, fiddling with some controls, trying to figure them out.

The scientist watched him as he demonstrated the effect, again doodling the infinity symbol.

"Looks to me like you're ionizing the upper atmosphere with a fairly powerful laser." he explained.

Satisfied, the major went on to ask. "If the targeting laser is that powerful, I wonder how powerful the weapons are." He reached for the nastiest-looking button on the panel, assuming it to be the fire button.

"Best not fire at the planet." cautioned DeSoto as he gently placed his hand on the Major's arm, interrupting him.

"Why not?"

"There could be someone down there. You wouldn't want to unintentionally hurt someone would you?"

"Of course not. Then what do you suggest I use as a practice target?"

"Hmm, let me see... deep space wouldn't tell us much... there's a small moon, but that might get thrown out of orbit with a large enough explosion... the same with the asteroids..."

This thinking out loud made the Major a little short on patience. He had access to possibly the biggest guns he had ever dreamed of and he wanted to try them out!

"I've got it! Fire at the star, because nothing can harm a star!" exclaimed DeSoto, proud of himself.

Satisfied with that, the Major manipulated the controls bringing the local star into the center of the screen. He carefully placed the cross hairs on the center of the star and looked to DeSoto for one last approval. Satisfied with receiving a nod and a wink, he looked back at the screen and pressed the fire button.

Several things went into play at that point. Firstly, there was a panic brewing on the nearby planet. By a chance that will be explored later, their symbol for Armageddon was an infinity symbol written in the sky - purportedly by the hand of the creator. Millions saw the sky lit up with the 'Handwriting of God'. Surely doomsday was upon them.

The next thing to understand is that the weapons console had a mind behind it that could also tap into the full power of the ship. Now I am not saying that the ship has enough power to harm a star directly, only that it has enough intelligence to figure out how to allow a star to harm itself. The weapon's mind thought to itself, that since the cross hairs were very deliberately placed on the star, and the 'destroy this' button was pressed, it was very clear that the person operating the console wanted the local star destroyed. It was a reasonable assumption, and since the weapons control mind had only the intelligence necessary to carry out orders, it was not really capable of second-guessing the operator. This is intended to prevent the weapon's mind from making a moral decision that it wasn't supposed to. Indeed, it did the right thing; it figured out how to effect the instructed action.

What it did was this; it reasoned that since a star is essentially a nuclear explosion that was only being contained by it's own gravity, all one had to do was to momentarily cancel-out said gravity and the star would expand in a gloriously gargantuan nuclear explosion all by itself. So, that is what the weapons system did. This whole process only took a millisecond but since gravity and light only travel so fast, there was a noticeable delay before anything appeared to happen.

"Huh." remarked the disappointed Major who full well expected to see some sort of ray or projectile. "Looks like nothing happened. I suppose that isn't the fire button after all... but I was so *sure...*" Looking around the panel for another candidate, until something else caught his eye. He hadn't yet touched any other controls, but it looked as though the image appeared to be zooming-in on the star. It just kept getting larger and larger until it filled-up the targeting screen.

"Are we getting *closer* to that star?" asked the Major as he looked over at the Lt. manning the pilot's chair.

The Lt. checked the gauges on his lap panel and replied: "No, we're stationary. Why?" Then he looked at the main 3-D tactical display, saw the expanding star engulf it's closest planet and exclaimed: "SHIT!"

This got everyone's attention on the bridge, and they all scrambled to do something, anything. They were all panicking as none of them were in any doubt as to what was happening, and what *would* happen if something didn't change very quickly. All their scrambling was to no avail. The outer edge of the rapidly expanding star engulfed the planet below, then the ship.

# XVII
# The road to Daath

"School: a place where you get bored to daath."

After leaving the bridge to the Lt. and the Major with instructions to get acquainted with the controls, Harvey followed the android into the long corridors of the ship. Once he was satisfied that they were alone, he asked: "You know your way around the entire ship, don't you."

"Well, after all this time I should."

"Is there a room labeled 'Metatron'?"

"Yes, in fact there *is*." sounding rather disappointed if not suspicious.

"Would you take me there please?"

"If you insist." he said as they began to walk down the long hallway. Sensing the android's mood he asked: "What's the problem?"

"It's the only room I have been in, but don't know what's inside."

"I don't follow you."

"It's just that I get amnesia every time I go in there."

"How often have you gone in there?"

"Only with ship's captains, and they never tell me what happens in there, which makes me wonder why *you* want to go in there."

Harvey thought about this, it made sense with what the Emperor told him. "What was the name of the former captain?" he asked out of curiosity.

"Callicrates."

"*Callicrates?* Hmm, I *like* that name!"

"So did he." he said half under his breath "Here we are."

They had arrived at an intersection around a round column of a room. It seemed to be about twenty-five feet in diameter. On one side were large closed doors with no knobs or handles with a sign above it which simply read: 'Metatron', and nothing else.

"How do you... open them?" he asked, indicating the doors.

"You need to say the 'magic' words." replied the android indicating quotation marks with his fingers when he said "magic".

"Like, 'open sesame'?"

"No, you need to say 'Pihon Metatron'." Nothing Happened.

"How come nothing happened?"

"I'm not organic, so I can't operate certain things; this is one of them."

"That's cute. How do you close them?"

"Just say 'Sigron Metatron'."

"Great!" He paused and said: "PIHON METATRON!"

His voice echoed down the hallways as the doors opened. Only darkness awaited inside. This was a different kind of darkness than was usually found in the doorways of the ship. This was the normal darkness of an unlit room. "Come with me." he instructed.

The android cautiously followed the Human inside the dark room that did not teleport them anywhere. When they were where Harvey figured to be the center of the room, Harvey said "SIGRON METATRON!" The doors closed, they were engulfed in darkness and silence for a moment. Then the room lit up to reveal it was shaped like a cylinder, with pitch black floor and walls. All he could see clearly was himself and the android.

Harvey looked around, made a few clicks and pops to hear the echo, and moved a bit to make sure he was at the exact center of the room, which was the focal point where the sound would echo back right into his ears. He looked up and down the featureless room as if looking for something specific. Then he remarked to the android. "Kinda bland décor, isn't it?"

"It serves it's purpose." he heard the mechanical-man say, in a different voice than usual. He thought about it for a moment, then shrugged it off as being caused by the acoustics of the room. Indeed, a whisper could be shared very easily there. After a while, he whispered "Metatron?"

"Yes." came the unfamiliar voice from the android again.

Harvey spun around to see that the android had a different look in his eye and was standing with different posture, looking at him with an unfamiliar expression.

"*Metatron*?" he asked: "Is that you in there?" squinting at the machine's eyes as if he could see into it's innards that way.

"Yes."

"Whoa! That's not quite what I expected!"

"Though you *suspected*."

"How did you know...?"

"I know everything you've ever said and done." he answered warmly.

"Jeez, can't a guy have any privacy?"

"What can I do for you?" asked Metatron warmly with a reassuring smile on his face.

"I take it that I can know what the emperor wants by talking to you?"

"That, and more. You receive your assignments and other information through me."

"And you're uh... *possessing*, the android?"

"I am. That's why he never remembers what happens in this room." Leaning forward a bit he added: "And I strongly suggest you don't tell him about it either." in a loud whisper.

"Why not?"

"He'd be upset at being 'used' this way."

"I know *I* would be!"

"That's why I use an android and not a person. He was designed for this. People are not. So when they get possessed, it is a very bad thing."

"I see." He thought for a moment. "What do you call this room?"

"What would you think it should be called?"

"Well, given what goes on here, you could call it 'the hall of audiences' or something like that."

"What's wrong with 'The Phone Booth'?"

"Hey, that's what I was thinking!"

"It's okay to tell me what you think."

"Oh. So why the simple name?"

"That's a good question."

Harvey smiled at this, being put more at ease.

"You see, 'the boss' is into different things than most people. What is opulent he finds offensive, or just plain silly. A humble approach is preferred. The adversary's forces try to make you feel insignificant by promoting opulence. Beware of that."

'The boss?' he thought to himself, that's a very informal way to refer to the *Emperor*. "What about space station Nod? That's about as opulent as it gets!" He was thinking it was a bit of hypocrisy.

"People often do not recognize authority without opulence surrounding it, which is one of the adversary's finest victories, I might add. So it serves it's purpose. Besides, it was built by the adversary, and after having won a major battle, the emperor kept it as a reminder to the people. After all, you were told that the clothes *do not* make the man."

He thought about it for a moment, and it made sense, after all he had been impressed by his visit to Nod.

"So what can I do for you?" asked Metatron.

"I need... some *answers*." he replied in earnest to Meatron nodding.

* * *

Meanwhile, in the 'energy-pod room' of the ship, two engineers who were busy analyzing the recent minuscule changes in the size of the pod. The latest was caused by the energy absorption of the 'brakes' and the power drain needed for the ship to cancel the gravity of the star. That's when the pod did something rather peculiar, just after the ship's defenses automatically activated themselves. 'Shields' for want of a better term.

"Hey, would you look at that?" exclaimed one engineer.

"What?" asked the other as he turned around, then he gasped.

Instead of the pod getting smaller, due to the power drain assumed necessary to operate the shields, the pod was actually growing.

"What the *hell*...?" said the second engineer, completely baffled. "Did we stop at a gas station or something?"

The pod had grown noticeably larger and it grew fast enough for the naked eye to detect.

What was going on was that the ship's shields convert energy used to attack them into usable energy, which is sent to storage, where it is converted into the buckministerfullerine / antimatter molecules that the ship uses for fuel. Much in the same way that the body stores excess nutrients as body fat.

Both engineers had the same thought at the same time, looked at each other and called the bridge.

* * *

Now an explanation that was promised earlier:

There is a contest going on, and the scale is immense. Populated planets are at stake. On the one side, we have what you might call the forces of light. On the other, the forces of darkness. For the sake of simplicity, for the time being the leader of the forces of darkness will be referred to simply as 'the adversary'.

The planet in question was aptly named Rahab , which means 'violence'. Or, rather, became known to mean violence after what had happened there. You see, they were going through a period that was not unlike the Norse Ragnarok or 'end times'. All nations and groups were warring with each other. The battle cry was 'Every man for himself!'. The sign of the final destruction of the world was 'The Handwriting of God.' which was to appear in the sky and look like the infinity symbol; which resembles a figure-eight on it's side.

The fact that the creator was able to either predict the Major's actions from so long ago or somehow influence him into doodling the doomsday symbol is often cited as grounds for questioning why he lost this world to the Adversary. The answer is still 'free will'. It is assumed that had the people of Rahab not chosen this path, the Major would not have found himself aiming the guns at this point in space at this point in time, but then again maybe he would have. You give yourself a headache if you think too much about it.

As each of the warring factions either saw the symbol doodled in the sky, or heard news of its appearance, they stopped their fighting and prepared for the end. They welcomed it, and that was disturbing as well.

Many of the warriors on Rahab had incorporated this symbol into their banners, flags and culture in general. It was the one common thread in all of their cultures.  of years had been spent spilling blood over it.

All of this had been started by an immortal 'woman in black' named Lilith, one of the most loyal and prolific of the adversary's servants. She spent centuries in Rahab's early times seeding aggression, mistrust and paranoia world-wide. Virtually every ancient nation on the planet had a culture based on her 'teachings'. The result was wars without end, which successfully resisted all outside attempts to quell them. There was cruelty and malice the likes of which had seldom been seen elsewhere, a real triumph for the adversary's forces and feather in Lilith's cap.

It was high time that this world was written off as a loss. The decision was to pulse the star, not actually destroy it or the planet, because the system contained two more planets that would be able to harbor life in the future, and the dead world of Rahab was to serve as an example to the population of the next new world. May they learn from the example.

This is how 'the game' is played: Since systems were often created with more than one world that was able to support life, or could be adjusted slightly to do so. Whichever side won-over the most worlds, one at a time, won that star. As one was wiped-out, the next was prepared and seeded with life, for the next match. Free will was important, and since virtually no one ever chose the dark path knowing the consequences, the adversary could only win through mis-information, such as in this case.

To be sure, not all on the planet were beyond hope, so Sithriel, a being of almost infinite power and ability, protected those that were worth saving, and placed them on a refugee ship. They would meet-up with Harvey at a time when he knew of a world where the survivors would be welcomed and could live in peace. At least the adversary's victory in that round would not be total, but more about all of that later.

# XVIII
# DICHOTOMY

"The only thing necessary for the triumph of evil is for good men to do nothing."

"So, I take it that I'm not talking to Emperor Qayin through you then?"

"No."

"Then who?"

"I have many names, and one true name you can't pronounce."

"How 'bout you give me one I can pronounce."

"Joth Malkuth Parzupheim, of Aziluth at your service." he said while bowing.

"And you're Metatron *too*?" rather confused.

"No, I am Metatron speaking *for* Joth."

"But I was under the impression that the Emperor was to give me my assignments in this way."

"What he actually said was that you'd *receive* your assignments this way. He never said that they'd actually come from him."

"So, this Joth person? Is he... are you... above or below the emperor?"

"Both, and neither."

"Huh? You wanna try that another way?"

"I am the actual ruler, Qayin is a figurehead and Metatron is my voice for speaking directly to individuals. By the way, Metatron has over one hundred names himself. You might recognize: 'Tamtemiyah?'"

"The little girl!"

"Yes."

"So that was you?"

"That time it was Metatron speaking through another. Don't worry, he only spoke *to* her, he didn't control her."

"Why do it like that? And why speak through you?.. Uh I mean..."

"I know what you mean. I speak in this way because Humans deal better with their own form."

136

"You mean..."

"Yes. I'm not actually Human. In fact I made Humans in order to reflect myself in what you know as the *physical* universe."

He didn't know what to think.

"Let me get this straight; the Human race was created by some superior, energy-being named 'Joth?'"

The android just gave him a look.

"Great! Just great! As if I haven't enough to swallow as it is!"

The android continued to stare soberly at him, as if patiently waiting for him to come to grips with all of this.

"How would that go over with the crew?" he asked, hoping to get some sort of response.

"That's where the Emperor comes in. He's sort of a figurehead. People find it easier to deal with a ruler rather than a creator."

Harvey's head was swimming.

"So where do I figure into all of this? Just what do you want from me?" he asked, hoping to avoid what he was thinking would come next.

"You've seen that there are great injustices out there." said Metatron.

"Of course! The Emperor showed me enough of them to make me sick!"

"Shouldn't there be someone out there who can put a stop to all that injustice?"

"You mean to tell me that there are no 'galactic police'?"

"There are some - of sorts, called Cheriour[8]. The problem with that is that if you grant that much power to someone, they frequently abuse it."

"That's true. Don't they say that 'absolute power corrupts absolutely'?"

"Yes, Lord John Acton said that, but it's not *always* true. Some people are not subject to corruption. That's what I want; someone who can exact justice without becoming corrupted themselves."

"That must be rare." he said matter-of-factly.

Metatron stared at Harvey until the puzzled human felt nervous.

---

[8] *The Cheriour are very harsh with criminals. A more benevolent hand is needed.*

"There's a war going on out there between justice and injustice. Good and evil if you will. Right now it looks as though injustice may be gaining the upper hand. So I need good, trustworthy people to help me turn the tide back."

"Now wait just a minute!"

"Harvey, you are..."

"I don't want to hear it!" he said covering his ears.

"How about I say that you are '*Humble*, enough for the job' then? Because you *won't* abuse power."

"But... but... what about our official assignment?"

"It's real, but your primary mission is to captain this ship, which *is* my help and has the primary power of justice. Somebody *has* to do something, you said so yourself when you were with the Emperor. He tried to tell you this too, but you wouldn't listen to him."

"Well, he was more subtle about it at the time." he half-muttered "But why *ME*?"

"People like you are few and far between. Why do you think we waited so long?"

"I dunno. Not enough applicants?" He was obviously trying to be amusing. As if joking would get him out of this!

"We need someone that we can trust to do the right thing, without being corrupted by the power they've been given."

He still looked as if he didn't understand.

"Those that seek power seldom deserve it, and those that deserve it seldom seek it."

Harvey looked puzzled as he mulled that over. "Where have I heard *that* before?" he asked rhetorically.

"Harvey, the ship chose you because you are not corruptible. Trust me, I am the *only* one who can honestly say this; 'I know you better than you know yourself'. Face the fact that whether you like it or not, you are *right* for the *job*."

Harvey winced painfully at this. It seemed that there was no avoiding these people. "Let's just say, for the moment that I believe you."

"All right."

"How do you *know* I'll do the right thing? I mean, what if I mess up, what if I do the wrong thing?"

Metatron smiled warmly. "You know how to use a hammer, don't you?"

"Yes of course." he answered rather tersely, not knowing what this had to do with anything.

"So, it's safe to say that if you swing a hammer at a nail, you know what to expect."

"Well, yes." Now he could see where this was going, and he didn't much like it.

"So if you wind up missing the nail, and smash your finger instead, who is to blame? The hammer? The nail? Or the poor slob with the throbbing finger?"

"The one who swung the hammer of course." he said disappointedly - he was right!

"Well, after all, you thoroughly understand hammers, and it is your hand that guides it. In this case, *you* are the hammer."

"I see, but surely a man..."

"...Is much more complicated than a hammer?"

"Yes, actually."

"Don't you think that the mind that created you could understand you as well as you understand a hammer?"

This finally got through to him. He still didn't want the responsibility, but he seemed to be 'stuck with it'.

"*sigh* Okay, what about 'free will'?" he asked, puzzled over how some worlds are to be destroyed for their activities, as the Emperor had explained to him.

"Everyone always has the freedom to do the wrong thing, but that doesn't mean that they won't get punished for it."

"You mean 'If you can't do the time, don't do the crime'?"

"Something like that. But it's not intended as a deterrent, it's a punishment. You see, everyone inherently *knows* right from wrong, and it's those that choose wrong, knowing the difference, that we are concerned with here."

"Ah! What about sociopaths? They don't have a conscience." thinking he 'had him' there.

"Some lack a conscience, that is true, but they still intellectually *know* right from wrong. They just don't feel badly about choosing what they know is wrong. It's simply 'their cross to bear', that's all. Everything is taken into consideration. All are judged accordingly."

"So I have the freedom to go against orders if I choose to?" he asked, worried about being 'punished' for making a bad decision.

"Going against orders is fine, so long as you are being true to your nature. Do what you *know* is right Harvey, not what you think others would want you to do, including me."

"But you want me to destroy *whole worlds*? Is there no future for any of them then?"

"The innocent will be protected from your actions by Sithriel, and as for the worlds themselves, they have a large number of parallel occurrences that worked out for the better. You're just concerned with the 'bad apples' in cases like that."

"Uh... 'Parallel occurrences?'"

"They're what you call 'alternate time lines'. However I think that's a subject for another day, one hurdle at a time if you please. You already have a lot on your plate to think about."

"Indeed." He *had* to remember to come back to that subject later. Somehow, it made him feel better knowing there really were parallel time lines. So destroying a world in this time line wouldn't necessarily wipe it out completely. Wow! The mind boggled at the possibilities.

"So who is this 'Sithriel' character anyway?"

A sly smile came across Metatron's face. Sithriel was just another name for him, so he replied; "A very dear friend of mine."

Harvey wondered if he meant Metatron or Joth in this case. This was a confusing way to communicate.

"Okay, so I'm going to be told by you to go blow up entire worlds?" Still not coming to grips with the situation and wanting to be very clear on such an important point.

"Mind you, it is always *your* decision, and if you can find a reason to spare a world, by all means do so. Besides, sometimes I'll only ask you to blow up a city or two, or more likely, to straighten a world out by, as you sometimes put it; 'showing them the error of their ways' when that approach stands a chance of working."

That made him feel better, more confident.

"So I am to *interfere* with cultures?"

"It's more like putting them back on track. Your job description is a lot like 'enforcer', which breeds compliance. It's amazing how well people behave themselves when their very existence is at stake."

"Who am I to be... an *enforcer*? I have *faults!*"

"So does everyone else that ever lived. Great things can be achieved by anyone. Do you really believe that you are less of a person than any of those people in the past? Do you consider them to be *superior* to you in some way?"

He thought for a moment about what the Chief once told him about his theory that everyone had the same amount of mental 'wherewithal'.

"Well, now that you put it that way, no, not really."

"I'll tell you what." Metatron said. "I've got three assignments to help you come to terms with all of this."

Harvey looked worried. "*Three?*"

He was feeling like a student who had just been given a large quantity of 'homework'. Funny how the number three echoed in his head, such as this mechanical man he was talking to being Pymander, Metatron and Joth all rolled into one.

"They are to demonstrate to you that you do indeed, 'have what it takes'." He indicated quotation marks with his fingers. "Think of it as an education of sorts."

Sensing the man's worry, he placed his hand on Harvey's shoulder and added: "Don't worry, these are what you might call 'no-brainers'."

Now he felt better and insulted at the same time, but these 'no-brainers;' were intended as educational assignments after all!

"Your first assignment is to stop a world war, and to provide lasting peace and prosperity."

"Stopping a world war sounds good, but provide a lasting peace and prosperity? Is that *all*?"

"You'll manage." Metatron said with a knowing smile.

Harvey still looked worried.

"Your second assignment is to destroy a world, but knowing you, you'll want to go down for a visit and see if it is salvageable. However, in this particular case: it is *not*."

"You're right about that. I *would* want to know first hand why it is to be destroyed - at the very least."

"That by the way, is one of the reasons you were chosen."

Harvey acted bashful here, still not knowing how to take such a compliment.

The android went on: "One word of caution though; with that second world, visit it *alone*. The others might not understand your decision."

"How so?"

"The others are more of a product of the society of your world, which was seriously degraded by the wrong views. Which, by the way, is why it was punished the way that it was. Your world might have eventually wound up the same way had I not taken action."

"You mean the devastation from the launch?"

"Yes."

"But the Major..."

"...Is taking the blame... that works for you."

"What about the asteroid the Lt. pulverized?"

"It's dust cloud helped shield the planet until the magnetic field finished reversing polarity. It *saved* lives."

"O...kay..." he said uneasily; was Joth controlling the Major at that point? "So how did things get so bad there?"

"A dirty little tactic used by those that know they are wrong, but want to shove their ideas down everyone else's throat anyway. It's called 'incrementalism'."

"So why not just tell them the 'error of their ways' instead." Harvey was worried about all the death and destruction.

"You see, your world was too far gone to listen to anyone. Instead of writing it off as a loss, it has been reduced in power so that the luxury of pandering to such idiotic ideas has become out of the question again. Now they have to worry about what *really* matters; like survival itself. Eventually they will learn the truth. When they do, they can then move on to the next level."

Harvey thought about the devastation he had observed on his home world. "That's a bit *harsh*, isn't it?"

"Sometimes a world needs 'tough love.'"

"All right, *sigh* at this point I'll take your word for that." said Harvey, still a bit worried and confused. "What about the crew's reaction then? If I blow up that planet and don't give them a good reason, they may not like it much."

"In that case, just to remove any doubt from their minds, I suggest you take them to the Cygnus loop supernova and observe it as you approach. That world suffered a similar fate for the same reasons, and seeing the aftermath through the ship's sensors should sober them up."

"All right, if you say so." He was a bit confused, but willing to trust. "What about the third assignment?"

"You are to destroy it as well, but for different reasons; this time it's a *reward*."

Now you've *really* got me confused!"

"Afterwards, you won't be."

"I certainly hope so." he muttered.

"There's more."

"Yessss?" asked Harvey, suspecting that this was 'the other shoe.'

"Since there's such a backlog of work, you're bound to get sidetracked. I suggest you do your best with whatever you run into and then get back on track."

"I knew it! *More* worlds to fix."

"With these first three assignments, you'll be unchallenged, but the adversary's forces may oppose you over anything and everything else you endeavor to do. Be ready for them."

"Great, just great. If the job isn't tough enough, I've got an adversary to worry about!"

"Don't worry, you'll have help. You're not completely alone you know."

"Okay, so what are this adversary's forces like?"

"Some are subtle like those that push incrementalism, others are not so subtle, like the Gynoids."

"Ahhh! The android mentioned them."

"Hopefully, you won't run into them any time soon."

"Who *is* this 'adversary' anyway?"

"You'll meet soon enough, but don't be fooled - the adversary is determined to thwart you at every turn."

He didn't like the sound of that. This 'adversary' sounded dangerous.

The android looked upwards toward the ceiling as if distracted by something, then cracked a sly smile. "By the way, the Major has just wiped out a world for you."

"What?!? 'Major disaster' has struck again!"

"Yes, just now as we were talking."

"It *figures*!" Then he added "We'll see about wiping-out worlds!" as he stormed out of the room, the doors having opened as if anticipating his egress.

"That's my boy!" Muttered Metatron to himself with a smile, just after Harvey was out of earshot. Then he followed the captain out the door.

Pymander's personality returned to him as he left the room. He looked around and noticed the 'missing time' as well as having just left the room.

"Darn it! It's happened again! I suppose you're not going to tell me what happened in there either!" He sounded both upset but almost amused.

"I just made a long distance phone call." said Harvey dryly.

The android sighed. "Jolly joker." he said as he shook his head. Harvey laughed, slapped him on the back said "I've got to run. See you later!" and went back to the bridge, leaving the android alone in the hallway.

"I hate it when they do that!" he griped as he began to trudge down the long corridor back to the bridge.

Harvey appeared at the bridge door, which got everyone's attention because they weren't quite used to the way the doors worked, and someone just appearing at the doorway was still a surprise. Besides, they thought that he would be angry over their pulsing[9] a star.

"Sorry sir, but we kinda outdid ourselves..." said the Lt., trying to break the news to him gently.

"That's okay, at least we know more about what the ship is capable of doing." he said as he looked over the Butator report of what had just happened. Somehow, deep down, the details seemed familiar - as if he had already known them.

"Damn straight!" said the Chief.

Everyone else was glad he wasn't furious over them destroying a star and consequently a world, possibly wiping-out an entire population... so nobody asked any questions. Two for two was the score, and they were beginning to not want to play with the controls anymore.

Seeing that he had everyone's attention, he asked: "How would you folks like to do your 'good deed for the day?'"

There was a general murmur of agreement. After all, who does not want to do a good deed? Especially after what they had just done.

"Good, because our first assignment is to stop a world war." he said as he walked toward the captain's chair and sat down. "One that has been raging for decades."

There was an overall cheer at this. Obviously the crew thought that this was a great idea!

"The planet is called 'Ambriel' by some and 'Giel' by others. Set a course helmsman, if you please."

---

[9] *Pulsing a star simply makes a smaller nova that re-coalesces back into a star. This process takes about two years to cycle.*

"Right away sir!" said the Lt. as he sat back and closed his eyes. The Butator interpreted the request and sent them on their way.

# XIX
# PEACEFUL GREENERY

Vegetarian: "Mr. Wizard, I reject my predatory ancestry and wish for
a vegetarian ancestry."
Wizard: "Are you certain that's what you want?"
Vegetarian: "Absolutely. My mind is made up."
Wizard: "As you wish."
Vegetarian: "Moo!"

As they approached a particular planet, surfing as they were, the helmsman noticed a dramatic drop in life-signs. He naturally slowed at discovering this.

"What's up?" asked Linda, noticing what he was doing.

"A planet is dying, and it *doesn't* look like 'natural causes'." he replied.

"How can you tell..."

"The ship can detect bio-photons[10]."

He pointed at the main screen where he had the readings displayed for her.

"Wow, that's probably worth checking out!" she said.

He used the slingshot maneuver around the star as he had before, to 'skid' into a stationary orbit, making his best attempt to do it smoothly and with style.

"Show off!" she said.

He grinned and gave her a curt salute as if to say; 'Guilty as charged!'.

"Captain to the bridge." she said on the ship-wide intercom.

"You know, you could call him directly no matter where he is."

"I know, but I've always wanted to make an announcement like that."

Harvey and Pymander arrived on the bridge, convinced that there was some sort of emergency.

---

[10] *'Live' photons given off by life, making life itself detectable.*

"What wrong?" asked Harvey.

"We found a dying world, and thought it was worth a look."

"Good enough."

He was not too concerned about delaying arrival at their first assignment, because the war had been raging for decades. Given that, a few more days or hours didn't seem to matter. Further, he didn't have a clue as to how he was going to stop it. So, any delay bought him time to think.

"What have you got?" he asked the helmsman.

"Looks like a sudden drop in life-signs. I scanned the cities and there does not seem to be anybody left in them, except for *one*."

"Pathogen?" he asked the Azbuga who was arrived on the bridge just after the captain.

"There's nothing unusual in the environment." came the reply as he looked at his sensor readouts. "I think we can rule-out biological warfare, it's just like all the animals and most of the humans have been, well... *killed*."

"Could this be the work of the adversary?" he asked the android.

"Most assuredly so."

"Who?" asked the Lt.

"The bad guys."

"Oh." he said then he asked "There's *bad guys?*" to no reply.

"Dare we take a closer look?" Harvey asked the android.

"Do whatever you like, you're the captain."

He looked at Linda. "Wanna look into this with me?"

"Well, it's not what I envisioned as our first date, but I'll go." she said playfully.

He blushed, and the Lt. looked away to hide the smirk on his face.

"I'll take Pymander, some S*I*P*Es for protection, medical crews to examine the biology, Linda, the Chief and a few technicians with me."

"Very good sir, but might I suggest standard equipment too?" said the android.

"Standard equipment?"

"Come with me." he said almost disappointedly.

The android led him to a lab that was just down the hallway from the bridge, only closer to the bridge than any door that they had found earlier. The room was full of neatly organized equipment. Most of it looked more like wardrobe than anything else. The android approached rows of sunglasses and hats. There were also rows of coats, backpacks and other various bits of clothing and equipment one might need on a camping trip.

Pymander picked out a hat that was Harvey's size and handed it to him.

"That's nice, but I don't usually wear a hat."

"Actually, it's not *just* a hat." said Pymander holding one out for the captain. "It's a *Kirtabus.*[11]"

"A what?"

"A type of translator."

"Oh, I see... and what do the sunglasses do?"

"They translate written language, and reveal hidden things."

He tried them on and looked into the mirror. He looked like a 'man in black'. A look that he loathed.

"Is there another way?" he asked hopefully with a slightly pained look on his face and a slight sigh.

"Well, if.you don't mind sleeping for a day or so, you could take some Penemue pills, specifically designed for this world."

"That sounds better. I don't like the way I look in this stuff." Then he thought about it, "But, do I *really* want to learn their language *permanently*?"

"The Penemue pills are a special *temporary* formulation in a case like this. In two weeks you'll have forgotten almost everything about how to read and speak their language and, I might add, the pills have the added benefit of infusing you with antibodies to any normal infections that may be present on that world that your immune system isn't already used to. So you won't have to go to the infirmary for shots."

---

[11]*Kirtabus: Intelligent translator.*

"Oh, hadn't thought about immunization. I wish I could say 'Let's do that instead' because I hate the way I look in a hat. But since time is probably of the essence here, I'll say: 'hats, sunglasses and flue shots all 'round.'" He thought for a moment, and added: "In case this takes a while, maybe we should take the pills too."

"Suit yourself." he said as he opened up a door that led to a long hallway lined with shelves upon shelves of bottles filled with Penemue pills. He looked up the planet Loam, and pulled a bottle from the shelf, handed it to Harvey and said: "Give one to each member of the landing party."

"Understood." He made a false start for the door because the age of the ship suddenly occurred to him. "Wait a minute, how old or out of date are these pills?" he said as he looked over the bottle for an expiration date. "Will their information be up to date?"

"When you were visiting with the Emperor, I knew it would take a while so I took the opportunity to re-supply the ship. Everything *is* up to date."

"Oh, that makes sense." he thought about it for a moment. "What about the owner's manual pills? Did you get any more of those?" he asked hopefully.

"The ship makes them since they are *specific* to the ship, and to order replacements for the general knowledge part would be to admit that we lost the old ones. I thought you'd want to 'save face' in that department. Besides, those particular knowledge pills aren't that critical anyway, they're just convenient."

"Oh."

He was somewhat disappointed and really didn't like having to ask so many questions. Those pills would have filled-in a lot of gaps!

"Don't worry, you'll pick things up as you go along. That's one of the reasons I'm here." he said with a smile. "Besides, you'll probably do better not knowing certain things until they are relevant."

He got the feeling that the android simply wanted to be needed more or depended on more, but the more he thought about it the less he thought it were true.

# THE HALO EFFECT

* * *

Those that were to remain behind could not believe the weird language that the landing party was jabbering in while wearing the hats. They made a game of it, placing the hat on the head and removing it mid-sentence. They thought it was a laugh-riot.

Linda and Harvey were watching them with some degree of disbelief. This was very juvenile behavior after all!

"Small things..." said Linda.

"You said it." replied Harvey.

"How are we going to understand any transmissions?" asked DeSoto who had opted to stay behind on the bridge.

"Two ways." said the android. "They still can speak your original language, and the communication devices can translate for you as well."

"Oh." and he shuffled off to his favorite console.

"It looks like they're ready, what's next?" said Harvey.

"Pick a craft."

"What do you mean by that?"

"This ship is equipped with many forms of shuttle craft; fighters, freighters and transport ships to name a few. In short, a complete compliment."

"Where?"

"In the main shuttle bay, around the ship's equator."

"I though that that was a cargo bay." said Harvey, remembering how the Lt. had brought aboard some equipment with some sort of 'tractor beam'.

"That's just one of the decks around the equator. You have a deck that is virtually full of ships."

"Really? Show me!"

The android brought the whole party down a not so long corridor to a hangar that appeared to be a recess in the outer hull of the ship and looked to go on forever. There was ship after ship, many varying in design and all were ready for flight.

"Is this, uh, 'hangar', *full*?" asked Harvey, not knowing what to make of it.

"Almost, there *is* room for additions to your collection if you like. Also, there are additional decks."

"This is so cool!" said Linda as she ran around the hangar. She stopped at a sleek looking shuttle craft that could obviously carry the whole landing party. "This one, take this one!" she said excitedly.

The Major Shrugged, and motioned for his S*I*P*Es to board.

They skimmed over the surface of the planet for what seemed like hours, not finding any life signs other than plants and insects. The plants were dying, and the oxygen level on the planet was higher than the android had ever seen on any world. As a result, some of the insects were growing to record size, which caused more than one of them to 'freak out'. There was also no sign of any pathogen of any kind in the atmosphere. They landed at a few recently deserted sites, but found no one, time after time.

"*Now* can we go see the only place where Human life signs show on the scanners?" asked the Lt. after the ninth deserted city.

"Okay, I've seen enough." said Harvey in a 'far off' tone.

He was appalled at the sight of so many empty cities. Something bad was happening here, and he wanted to put a stop to it. He only hoped that they *could*. Checking out abandoned cities was not a waste of time as he saw it, because he wanted the crew to see the scale of what was happening, to motivate them, and hopefully find some survivors other than the group they were now approaching, but there was no one and nothing. Time may have been a factor, but he believed that they needed to see this.

The Lt. made a 'beeline' as he called it, for the only place on the planet that they had detected Human life.

When they arrived they found a large, yet strangely thin crowd of people. They all seemed to be peacefully headed toward the focal point of what looked like a cross between a baseball diamond and the Hollywood Bowl. They filed in, but there seemed to be no outlet.

"Perhaps they're going into a shelter of some kind." suggested the Major hopefully, in a low voice.

Harvey gave him an appreciative nod since this seemed to be out of character for that man, and Linda cracked a small smile as she scanned for underground structures.

"They're a particularly united culture, perhaps they are..."

"My God!" exclaimed Linda, cutting the Chief off. "It's a disintegrator! Land! Land this thing *now*! Don't you get it? It's mass suicide!"

The Lt. looked at Harvey for approval but he shook his head.

"What?!?" said Linda almost horrified. "Aren't we doing to do something about this?"

"Look, I agree with you, but how do you propose we stop them?"

"Oh, I see, there's thousands of them, and if they are committing suicide..." she said as her faculties began overriding her adrenaline.

"They won't be afraid of weapons." concluded the Lt.

"We couldn't cut them all down anyway. Some are bound to take cover." said the Major dryly. "Does this ship even *have* weapons Lieutenant?"

"You can't *kill* them!" said Linda. "That would be pointless!"

"Relax, I wanted to merely *stun* the crowd, then we could disable the disintegrator at our leisure without, I might add, anyone getting hurt."

Linda beamed at the Major, impressed with his logic. Perhaps he wasn't such a total jerk after all.

"Yup, we've got stun!" announced the Lt. triumphantly.

The Major, the Lt. and Linda all looked at Harvey for approval.

"Do it." he said.

* * *

The crowd was going to sleep for at least twelve hours which was plenty of time for the crew to wade through the sleeping masses and disable the disintegrator.

"That's quite an achievement for their level of technology." said the Chief, looking around at the other signs of unusual technological development.

"What's to stop them from repairing it or making a new one when they wake up?" asked Linda.

"Nothing, all we're doing is delaying them." said the Chief over his shoulder as he examined what appeared to be an access terminal.

"Can we wake one of them for interrogation?" asked the Major.

"No problem." said the Azbuga.

"Well, let's pick one for starters." said the Major, looking around the rather widely disbursed unconscious bodies, "let me see now if I were the ring leader, I would be..." he spotted a finely dressed man collapsed on a small platform, near the back. "...YOU!"

The Azbuga went over to the man the Major had indicated and began to revive him.

The man woke slowly, and stayed lying on the ground, unable to get up. The Azbuga didn't want to wake him fully in case he were to become unmanageable in some way.

"What's happening? Is this *paradise*?" asked the man as he half-opened his eyes.

They were surprised and slightly unnerved to see that the man's lips did not match his words - an effect of using a Kirtabus.

"Don't worry, you're all right now." said the Azbuga.

He looked over the crew, in puzzlement. They were all wearing black hats and sunglasses just like government agents on most worlds. The exception was Linda. She was not only a woman but her hair was very long and with it flowing under the hat, she looked very strange and out of place in contrast to the others.

"Can you tell what is happening here?" asked the Major.

"The cleansing! Is it over?" he asked hopefully.

They all exchanged looks. This sounded too much like 'ethnic cleansing' to them.

"Do you mean this mass suicide?" asked the Major dryly.

The man tried to get up but was too weak. "No, you must not stop the cleansing! We need to save our planet!" He almost passed out again. Obviously he was still groggy from the stun weapon.

"Maybe we should wake another; this one sounds whacked." said the Chief.

"Agreed." said Harvey. "Pick a straggler, which might be an 'un-believer.'"

The Azbuga, went to work on one of the last in line, while the major continued to query the ringleader.

"Why must you all die to save your planet?"

"Carbon dioxide! We exhale it you fool! We are creating greenhouse gasses just by living!" The man was so stressed with this he passed out.

"Could they really be that...well... *stupid*?" asked Linda, quietly.

"Let's find out." said the Major as he approached the man that the Azbuga just revived.

"How are you?"

"Where am I?" asked the man.

"Don't worry, you're still on Loam."

"Oh, thank Apharoph! Who are you? What's going on?"

"We were passing by and saw that your world was dying, so we thought we'd try to help."

The man reached up and grabbed the Major's uniform. "Yes! Help us save our world!" The Major thought they had another fanatic until the man continued with his next labored breath: "Stop this suicide madness! Pleeeease!" then he collapsed.

The Major turned to the Azbuga. "I think you can wake this one up fully."

He nodded, and gave the man a shot which took a few moments to take effect. The man sat up, shook it off a bit, then got to his feet. The Major and the others gave him room to stand. He looked around at the crowd and then at the crew.

"Thank you."

"For waking you?" asked Linda.

"Well yes of course, but more for stunning everybody."

"You're glad we stunned everyone?" asked Linda.

"Yes indeed. Now we have a chance to stop this madness."

"So you're not onboard with all of this? uh?..." She didn't know what to call him.

"Sorry, my name is Iealo Astad, I'm a... a..." He looked back and forth over his shoulders then whispered; "*Scientist.*"

"Pleased to meet you, you can call me 'Major'". said the Major uncharacteristically warmly. "Can you tell us *exactly* what it is that is happening here?"

"'Loam in the lurch' is what's happening here."

"Come again?" asked Linda.

"That's a book on pseudo environmentalism."

They all looked puzzled.

"It is full of lies, flawed logic and propaganda. It's hardly scientific." he said.

"A *book* caused all of this?" asked Linda.

"You have to understand, it caused an environmentalist movement, based on false information."

"But... *mass suicide*?"

"Well not overnight! But it *is* a *very* convincing work."

"It would have to be!"

"It 'explains' that there is global warming and a hole in the ozone layer due to mankind's interfering with the environment."

"Sounds familiar." said the Chief. "They tried that on our world, but we scientists didn't buy it because we knew the truth."

"What happened on your world? How did it turn out?" asked Iealo

"We, the real scientists of my world, tried to tell the public the truth, but most didn't believe us. Our governments even passed laws based on the lies." Then he added "But it never came to anything like this!" answered the Chief.

"Well, here on Loam, it started with reducing industrial emissions of greenhouse gasses."

"That doesn't sound so bad." said the Major.

Linda backhanded the Major and gave him a glare. That was one of the most draconian laws they had passed back home.

"That's how it works! Little steps that sound reasonable at first, but each one is closer to the unacceptable. Once they get there, it's too late!"

"How did it come to this?"

"In order to get rid of all greenhouse gasses, they banned carbon-dioxide infused beverages, then malted beverages that gave off that gas then anything that gave it off, and eventually decided to kill all animal life because they exhale it! Now they decided that we all have to die for the good of the planet! Can you believe it?"

"Didn't you explain the truth to them?" asked Linda.

"I tried and so did other scientists, but to no avail. I showed how the oxygen levels were climbing but they took that as a sign that the atmosphere was 'normalizing', just as the book predicted. It's pure madness!"

"That explains why a lot of the plant life is dying out; not enough carbon dioxide for them - they're choking to death." said the Chief.

"We tried showing them that, but they still wouldn't listen. The book has answers for almost any argument in it. It's well worked-out madness, I'll give it that. It's like some twisted religion!"

"What about the ozone hole, didn't you explain that it had to do with natural sun cycles?" asked Linda.

"We tried, but the book told them it was caused by too much use of hydrocarbon fuels, so we switched to hydrogen and electricity. By the time that the ozone hole naturally closed, they cited it as proof that the book was correct. Things went down hill rather quickly after that."

"They tried that on our world too, only they blamed it on refrigerants." said the Chief reassuringly.

"In our ancient history, some could predict eclipses, and they pulled the same trickery, to force favor from the leaders. I thought that we were beyond that by now." said Iealo.

"It would seem that Human nature is the same everywhere." said Harvey, "What can we do about this?"

"Beats me, many of us have tried for years to stop it, and so have most my colleagues. After the ozone thing they killed every scientist who refused to give up technology, ordering that everyone abandon all forms of it. Well, except the weapons they used to subdue the non-believers that is."

"How did they get the disintegrator then?" asked the Chief, curious that they had discovered how to make one.

"Believe it or not, the last of the scientists, myself included, made it as a means of recycling refuse. We never dreamed it would be used to wipe out our race! It's a horrible nightmare!" Iealo said as he began to sob.

"There has to be *something* that will stop them." said Harvey to the rest of the landing party.

"Well, it's not like you're sent by emperor Qayin or anything." said Iealo, recovering somewhat from his anguish.

They all exchanged looks.

"What if we were?" asked Linda guardedly after a long silence.

"Well, if you could prove it, then you could just *order* us to stop." said Iealo, gaining even more composure, with a hint of hopefulness in his voice.

"Would that work?"

"It might not have until now, fanaticism can blind people you know. It's not like they fear for their lives, but if you truly are his representatives, you would have the power to destroy our precious planet, and that's the last thing they want."

They all exchanged looks again.

"Tell me you came here from NOD?" said Iealo hopefully.

Harvey cracked a sly smile. "Indeed, we *did!*"

* * *

"I think it was a good idea to call in one of the other ships to guide that world back to reality." said the Lt. "What was it called again?"

"Thanks. It's the Suriel. It's a good thing that they can restock the planet with animal life too. They tell me it stands a good chance to get

158

the atmosphere and environment back into balance within a year or two."

"So many died for an insane idea. It boggles the mind." said Linda.

"Remember our world wars?" said Harvey rhetorically, with a twinkle in his eye and she frowned at him for it. It seemed that Human nature *was* the same everywhere, but she wanted to believe that there was a better place, somewhere out there.

"It's amazing what some people will do for power, in any form." said Pymander. "Bending others to your will, is the root of all evil."

"I thought it was money." said Linda.

"Money is a simple and indirect form of that kind of power."

"Indeed." muttered Harvey. "Let's get going back on track." he said to the Lt. in an attempt to change the subject.

"Right away sir!"

"Lieutenant."

"Yes sir?"

"Good call. I'm glad you stopped."

"Thanks, me too. It's still depressing though, what they did I mean."

"That, is why we're out here."

"I thought it was about saving our world?"

"That's part of the deal: in salvaging theirs, we're a step closer to saving ours."

The Lt. smiled slightly, though a little puzzled about what Harvey had said, so he found himself instead wishing that all of this on Loam had never happened or that they could have arrived years earlier. But then again, had they arrived sooner, could they have done anything about it? He thought that he might never know, but the truth is that he would soon see the answer first hand.

# XX
# Pantherion Lost

"I thought YOU parked the car!"

The door to the Pantherion's sickbay slid open to reveal a stocky, distinguished looking man with salt-n-pepper hair.

"Let me guess, you couldn't sleep again?" asked the ship's doctor.

"I knew I kept you onboard for a reason." said Captain Nitibus Hofniel as he entered.

"Nightmares again?"

"Yes."

"Same ones?"

The captain just nodded with a pained look on his face.

"You can't go on like this sir, you're losing sleep over nothing."

"Am I? Did I imagine that spy we caught last week and that she confessed Captain Batna knows everything?"

"She probably said that to cause this very effect. Even you are not as effective when you're tired."

"You're probably right, but I just can't shake the feeling..." He was cut off by the ship being hit by a powerful blast, followed immediately by a red alert klaxon.

He gave the Doctor a look.

"Go." was all he said, and the captain was at once off to the bridge.

When he arrived he could see that they were under attack by Captain Batna's forces. This proved that the spy was not lying after all.

"Glad to see you sir!" said the first officer as the captain arrived.

"What's the situation Kal?"

"We didn't detect any ships at all, then suddenly we were surrounded. Before we could hail them, they fired on us."

"How many?"

"Over a thousand sir."

"Hmmmm....Let me see the tactical display."

# THE HALO EFFECT

It was punched up on the main viewer, and indeed, there was no avenue for escape. The Pantherion was at least three times as fast as any of the Kurzian ships, but there simply was nowhere to run. It was a tough warship, but it couldn't bear up to the combined firepower of over a thousand ships, and ramming enough ships to escape was out of the question. Their only hope was the new, untested weapons.

"They must have perfected their stealth technology sooner than expected." said the first officer.

"I think that this whole mission was a trap from the very beginning."

"Sir?"

"They leaked the information about their invisibility screens and the possibility that we could duplicate the technology. It's the only explanation that fits. The whole thing was a trap from day one. They even sprang it sooner than I anticipated. I think that they've had invisibility all along."

"Did you inform the admiralty?"

"Of course, but they didn't believe me. They actually said: 'We've never seen an invisible ship.' Can you imagine?"

"Now what do we do?"

"That's up to Captain Batna. Hail her for me would you?"

The main screen showed the image of a woman, with black hair and an attractive black uniform, standing on the bridge of the frighteningly designed battle cruiser directly in front of them.

"Well well well, if it isn't Nitibus Hofniel of the doomed Aban alliance and captain of the Pantherion, well at least for the next five minutes." she said with a very condescending tone.

"Hi Satrina, how've you been?"

"I've been plotting your death, how have you been?"

"Fine, just fine. You know, death is only an inconvenience for some of us."

His eyes fixed on the new weapons control panel. He was asking his weapons officer to arm the antimatter torpedoes. She complied, and had her finger ready to fire on his command.

"Really?" Her attention was distracted by one of her bridge officers, that showed her a readout that indicated Hofniel's intent. "Tisk tisk, you men just never learn do you?"

With that there was a large explosion on the aft of the Pantherion and it began to list out of control. A suicide squadron had slammed into her engines from behind - destroying them. Now, it was no longer the fastest ship in the spiral arm. Before Captain Hofniel and his bridge crew could regain their balance, there was a flash of light. Every one of Batna's ships fired at once, wiping out the Pantherion's rather extensive array of weaponry. It was dead in the plenum, and unable to strike back. The trap had worked.

"Prepare to be boarded." said Captain Batna. "Any resistance will be met with the destruction of your ship and the death of your entire crew. All we want is your captain. The rest of you may live." With that, the screen went blank.

"We're prepared to fight to the end sir." said the first officer. Indeed, the entire bridge crew was smiling at the captain, as if they believed he had an ace up his sleeve, as always.

He sighed, placed his hand on the first officer's shoulder, and said: "Not this time Kal." in a very defeatist tone.

There were a lot of blank looks. No one knew what to think of this.

The captain turned and addressed the entire bridge crew: "Let her have me and none of you will be harmed."

"What about self destruct?" asked the first officer hopefully.

"No old friend. I want all of you to survive, to carry on the fight another day."

"But sir!" protested the worried first officer.

"Just have faith. Things will work out for the best."

Kal's head bowed because he knew what that meant.

They all began to sulk. Their captain was about to be taken prisoner by the Kurzi Empire, and he wasn't going to fight this time. Seventy-nine successful missions and now, on their eightieth, he was beaten. The 'wizard of warfare' beaten? How could it be? But here they were, defeated, and about to be boarded by the Kurzian hoard.

# THE HALO EFFECT

Captain Batna's flagship, the Zebuleon, which looked much like a robotic scorpion, extended several of it's 'legs' to capture the Pantherion, steady it and dock with it. A boarding party was led by Batna herself. She arrived on the bridge momentarily. Her troops were armed with very powerful rifles but she just had a regular handgun.

"Nitibus!" she said, as she walked into the bridge. He turned toward her, smiling. To the shock of the bridge crew, she managed to shoot him twelve times before he fell to his knees, gasping for half-breaths.

"DIE ALREADY!" she screamed.

He looked up with such conviction that she looked up too to see what he was looking at.

"Pisqon, old friend. I hope you're right." That was all he said. By that time she had her sword out, and cut his head off for good measure. His lifeless carcass collapsed in a pool of blood.

"It doesn't hurt to be sure." she calmly explained to them with a shrug as she wiped off her blade on the only bloodless part of the dead captain's shirt.

The bridge crew, some horrified, some almost crying, were speechless. A great hero of the Aban alliance had just been senselessly killed. This was the kind of enemy they were up against; barbaric.

Captain Batna turned to the commander of the boarding party. "Put them on a slave barge and take them down to the planet. I'll let their people know where to find them."

"You are letting us live?" asked the Pantherion's first officer.

"Only to let you tell your leaders how futile it is to fight us." she said coldly. "Put his body in with them, I want no doubts in their minds that he's finally dead."

The boarding party commander saluted and motioned for two of his men to pick up Captain Hofniel's head and body.

When they had left her alone in the bridge, she rubbed her hands together, grinned evilly and said to the ship: "At last! You're *MINE!*"

# XXI
# EUGENOCIDE

"It is not enough that I succeed; everyone else must fail."

1:30 AM, Monday, December 24th, 2012 Anno Domini

The Ezrael went surfing down the star valley between two spiral arms, only to discover a battle between two vastly different ships.

The smaller, less powerful ship was obviously for a single occupant as it was barely larger than an escape pod. It was roughly heart-shaped, but angular and it glowed slightly. The attacking ship was larger than an aircraft carrier, looking somewhat reminiscent of a giant cat ready to pounce. It was firing some sort of energy weapon and barrages of missiles on the smaller ship that seemed to be shielding itself, and trying to escape. This had the look of a bully picking on someone smaller and weaker. So what else is new? The ships danced about the area erratically like two birds in flight. The important thing to note is that the smaller ship had no weapons of any kind - a fair argument for arming oneself in a hostile environment.

As the Ezrael approached, attracted by the flashes of light the 'battle' produced, the helmsman naturally slowed and observed.

"Hmm. What have we here?" asked Harvey.

"Looks like a fight." said the Lt. with a grin as he opened his eyes and looked at the captain.

Harvey gave him a look. The question was rhetorical, and the Lt. knew it.

"Looks more like a beating." said Harvey dryly as he indicated the display that showed the armament capability of both ships.

"Ouch!" said the Lt., who didn't approve of that sort of bullying either.

"See if you can contact both ships, would you?" he said to the communications officer who immediately busied himself with the task.

A moment later, the face of a beautiful woman appeared on the screen. She looked up and simply said "Help!" Seemingly very busy with the business of staying alive. Then the image of another woman, with black hair and an attractive, if not revealing black uniform, standing on a bridge, appeared on the other half of the main screen.

"Captain Batna of the Pantherion, who are you and what are you doing in *my* space?"

Harvey raised an eyebrow as the Butator displayed information about Captain Satrina T. Batna, 'her' ship, her fleet, and the Kurzi empire that she served. He thought that this was pretty cool, complete information at his fingertips and he didn't even have to lift a finger!

**Butator display:**

**The Kurzi Empire: A religious sect that fervently believes that the adversary is the just ruler of the universe, and that cruelty is for those that are weak.**

**The Kurzi Empire spans the outer edges of most of the spiral arms, and they have a plan to encroach until they can directly challenge Grand Emperor Qayin himself.**

**He is well aware of this but knows that you will begin showing them their place, very soon.**

**Detail on Captain Batna:**

**Captain Batna is a prominent member of the malevolent Kurzi empire, she is immortal, and the enemy of all mankind.**

**She has stolen the Pantherion a few weeks ago in an act of piracy, from another, benevolent fleet: the Aban Alliance of the Libra arm of the galaxy, and made it her flagship because it was so large and powerful. The ship was crippled in her attack, and their refit engines and weapons are inferior to the original designs. However, the ship's hull remains incredibly resilient.**

**Typically, once a world had reached a nuclear age, they manage to bomb themselves back to the stone age. If, by chance they managed to achieve world peace and then travel into space, they**

**usually get squashed by something like the Kurzi empire, which isn't too much more technologically advanced, because it doesn't have to be. Besides, Batna and her descendants, known as 'the sheeple', are not very creative and therefore have difficulty in advancing technology on their own.**

**The Pantherion's technology is roughly equivalent to what the end of the twenty-first century on your world might have developed. Weaponry included positron cutting beams and antimatter missiles. The hull is three feet thick and is composed of an extra-tough titanium alloy. Top speed is currently 0.997 C.**

**The original crew was placed on an unstable planet, and left there to be rescued by their fleet.**

Dwarfed by the Ezrael, the Pantherion could be docked inside without difficulty. This fact didn't seem to phase Captain Batna, who took a very arrogant stance. Harvey had authority due to the fact that he officially worked for the galactic empire, and this smaller, more malevolent empire agreed to obey common galactic laws and allow such interventions to avoid being wiped out altogether.

Linda was curious about this 'multiple empire' situation so she checked her Butator display:

**Butator display:**
**The galactic empire is broken into smaller empires, and they are allowed to expand by taking over or conquering worlds of other empires, thus making the whole alliance stay strong and relatively stable. Also, these little empires are like states and the Emperor they serve is like the federal government. Many like the Kurzi empire believe it is important to bomb civilizations into the stone age to "keep them down"... so convenient low-tech exists on most worlds as a result.**

"My name is Harvey, captain of the Ezrael." he said, indicating the ship. Obviously he was not used to this sort of thing.

166

"The *Ezrael?*" She recognized the name, and got visibly nervous, looked around the bridge to access the reaction of her crew and ordered the barrage to end with a hand signal. The pilot of the other ship looked frazzled, and groggy. Obviously she was very shaken and couldn't speak just yet.

'Why would Emperor Qayin send his *flagship*?' Satrina asked herself.

"What are you doing here, Captain Harvey." she asked, assuming it to be his surname.

"Well, we just noticed this little lop-sided fight of yours as we were passing by, and we thought we'd find out what was going on." he said innocently.

"Well, if you *must* know, we caught that *abomination* and were in the process of eliminating it when you showed up."

"Abomination?"

"Yes, she's impersonating an angel, so I am within my rights under *galactic law.*" She was smug about it, assuming that Harvey would be compelled by this statement to let her do as she wished.

He looked at the screen, and information he sought was already displayed.

**Butator display:**

**Amitiel says that the inhabitant of the smaller ship had never made that representation, she merely *looks* like an angel to the uneducated eye. Also, deliberately impersonating an angel *is* indeed a capital offence under galactic law.**

He wondered for a moment who 'Amitiel' was, and got this display.

**Butator display:**
**Amitiel is the one who knows and speaks the truth without fail.**

Harvey thought to himself: 'Good, a truth subsystem. Now nobody can lie to me. Wonderful!' His confidence swelled.

"What makes you think she was impersonating an angel?"

"She's been to half the worlds in the Kurzi empire, flying around on her wings and bedazzling the populations."

"Okay. What's your point. Surely flying is not an offence." He double checked the Butator display after he said that, worried that perhaps it was after all.

**Butator display:**

**Flying is not illegal.**
**NOTE: All angels have two or more pairs of wings and all flying humanoids have only one pair.**

He quietly sighed in relief.

"How many pairs of wings does she have?" he asked.

"PAIRS? *One*, of course!"

"Well there you have it then! Everybody *knows* that *all* angels have *more* than one pair of wings, *that's* how you tell them apart from flying humanoids. So how could she be mistaken for an angel?"

Captain Batna seemed perplexed. Obviously this little reminder embarrassed her. She thought about it for a moment and replied; "That does not matter, it's the *perception* that matters... the people must not believe in such things. Too many have seen her already. Besides, many others of her kind have made the claim." This verbal squirming had the air of 'My dog ate my homework!'

The Butator concurred:

**This individual is innocent of stated charges. 'Guilt by association' is not applicable. She was not a member of a group that was making such a claim collectively, and simply being of the same race as others that had made such claims is not an offense.**

After reading this he said: "I'm afraid I must *insist* that you *desist*." which made Captain Batna fume. By this time, the other woman was recovered enough composure to communicate.

"Captain Harvey? May I speak?"

Her voice was sweet and angelic, though it sounded weak. The Butator identified her as Gladrina Urim of the planet Thummim.

Captain Batna frowned, she had Gladrina on her screen too.

"By all means." he said sweetly.

This made Linda's ears perk up. She turned her narrowed eyes toward him, watching him closely.

"First of all, thank you for interceding. I might not have survived the next salvo."

"You are *very* welcome." He beamed, happy to have 'rescued' this beautiful creature.

Linda said: "Down boy!" out of the corner of her mouth.

With that, Satrina sent another salvo, but the Lt. caught it with the Ezrael's shields.

"Deactivate her weapons!" said Harvey in disgust.

The Major fiddled with a control, and Satrina fumed over being disarmed by remote control.

Harvey looked satisfied and turned back to Gladrina: "You were saying?"

"As for the charges; I would like to state for the record that I was only looking for others of my race."

Captain Batna put her hands on her hips, shook her head in disgust and scowled.

"What about the flying around and such?"

"I asked people if they knew of anyone like me and sometimes I had to demonstrate what my race looks and acts like, which includes flying."

"Did you ever represent yourself as an angel?" he asked, already knowing the truth of course, but half wanting to test what the Butator display had showed him.

"I never claimed to be anything but a Tummin. If they mistook me for anything else, I am unaware of it."

"So why are you looking for others of your kind?"

"To bring them home."

"For what purpose?"

By this time, he was getting curious. He also felt drawn to her. Not only was she beautiful but there was something pleasing in her voice that he did not want to end.

"Our government decided to recall all our people so that those guilty of those very crimes may be dealt with, *severely.*"

"So I take it that you are operating with the authority and approval of your planetary government?"

"That is correct."

"Thank you."

Harvey looked at the Butator display:

**Amitiel says she is telling the "truth, without omission or attempt to deceive."**

He thought about clarifying that statement and the display added:

**She is not being deceptive by omitting anything that would contradict her statement, or wording it in such a way as to be deceptive.**

It goes without saying that lawyers almost never pass that test.

"There, you see? A simple misunderstanding." he said to Captain Batna with a big smile. Then he looked at her firmly. "So you can go about your business and forget about her. She's not your problem anymore." He said that last part rather firmly, with a note of finality in his voice.

Captain Batna was furious. Obviously, there was more to the story. The screen showed that she had a personal grudge against the Tummin race, and was determined to wipe them all out, no matter the cost. Since the Ezrael had disarmed her ship and Harvey had the authority to intercede, there was little else she could do at that point in time. So she scowled, shut off the transmission without another word, and took the Pantherion rapidly out of the area.

"Are you all right?" Harvey asked Gladrina.

"I'm a bit weak, thank you... that attack took a lot out of me."

**Butator display:**

**She is weak because her ship is a Laghima type: powered by her own personal energy. Therefore, an attack on her ship was an attack on her person. Given time to rest, she will recover completely.**

By this time, Linda was taking notice of how all of the men, not just Harvey, were reacting to Gladrina. They seemed to be 'drooling' over her. This made Linda jealous. She may not be very beautiful in everyone's opinion, but she was *pretty*, and she was beginning to like the fact that most of the men on board looked at her with a little longing. Now this creature comes along and they all act like teenage boys in the presence of a super model. She didn't like that one bit.

"Perhaps our doctor should take a look at you. Would you like to come aboard?" he asked sweetly.

Linda gave Harvey a light, playful backhand to the stomach, folded her arms and said: "Down boy." under her breath again. He grinned. Jealousy was a good sign.

"I would be glad to, though I doubt that I need medical attention... just *rest*."

"I'll *bet* you do." muttered Linda.

A big grin ran away with Harvey's face. Linda really *was* jealous! Wonderful!

\* \* \*

When Gladrina disembarked, most of the bridge crew were there to greet her. She was beautiful indeed, and wearing such slight and sheer clothing as to leave very little, if anything, to the imagination.

The men upon noticing this being gentlemen after all, averted their eyes. The Lt. simply said: "Oh my...!" and looked at the ceiling, obviously torn between wanting to look at this practically nude, 'drop-dead gorgeous' woman, and knowing that Linda would be upset with him if he stared. After all, Gladrina must be an exhibitionist, or more likely her culture saw nothing wrong with revealing the human form. She sure looked human, except for the wings of course.

She smiled warmly at Harvey who maintained eye contact. That way, he thought that she would know he was not gawking.

"Have you no *shame*?" asked Linda just before Gladrina fainted.

Linda rolled her eyes, sighed and shook her head as all the men, doctors included, fell over each other to rush to Gladrina's aide.

Back on the bridge, when they were about to leave the area, they spotted the Pantherion, obviously going at full throttle intending to ram the Ezrael. The chisel-like nose had been designed to maximize the damage it could do.

"What to do, what to do..." muttered Harvey, hand on chin, finger tapping his jaw, as he scrutinized the 3-D tactical display showing the relative positions, speed and trajectory of both ships.

"The shields will protect us from the impact." offered the Lt.

"That's not it. I was wondering if we should catch them or let them kill themselves."

"Oh..." said the Lt., who thought about it then added: "Good idea!"

"Yes, I think we should open the docking ports and let them in, don't you?"

"Uh oh... Looks like the naughty Captain Batna has escaped in her yacht." said the Lt.

It was a bit awkward carrying on a conversation with a helmsman who had his eyes closed, but it was the way the ship worked. The captain used the main display and the helmsman was being careful to get more detail with the ship's sensors directly.

172

The main screen now clearly showed a smaller ship on escape vector, and a Butator-generated course back to the Pantherion. Harvey nodded approval at the Lt. who was now looking up at him as if asking if he should do something about it. When he got the approving nod, he smiled broadly and went to work.

"Not so fast little lady." said the Lt., as he engaged a gravity beam to stop her escaping craft.

"She's not going to be too happy about this." said the Lt.

"I'm not so happy that she's sacrificing her ship and crew, not to mention trying to kill all of US in the process."

"Looks like there's no one on board the Pantherion."

"Well, that's *something*, anyway." He thought about it for a moment. "I hope that they're all right."

The Lt. nodded in agreement. "mmm huh." he muttered as he closed his eyes and concentrated on the task at hand. The Ezrael matched the velocity of the Pantherion, and through delicate changes in velocity and direction, guided it precisely into a landing bay. This was some trick, but it went off without a hitch. The Lt. was becoming quite skilled at piloting the ship. Next, he finished pulling Captain Batna's yacht into another bay.

# XXII
# THE BRIG

*"There's a way out of every cage..."*

The furious Captain Batna was involuntarily removed from her yacht, but it was neither immediate nor easy.

The S*I*P*Es were very good at this, so the advantage was theirs. Or so they thought.

She was using a defense system that was built-into the yacht, and since this was the Pantherion's yacht and the fleet the Pantherion belonged to was benevolent, it didn't have a 'kill' setting. "I'll have to rectify that." she muttered to herself as she turned the controls up to 'full stun' - the worst that she could do.

There was a force field around the yacht that successfully repelled bullets and tear gas canisters. They found that they could get past it physically if they leaned up against it and pushed slowly. Two squads went in and got stunned into unconsciousness in the first few feet.

"We're not going to be able to flush her out until we can get past that thing." said the Major, in a defeatist tone. "We're up against technology that's ahead of ours."

"If only we knew more about the high-tech stuff on this crate. There's gotta be something that we can use."

The rest of the S*I*P*Es were scratching their heads as to what to do. No armor could protect them, and even the Azbuga was stumped. "That's a 'neuro field', they're highly effective, and I don't know of any way to counteract it." he said to the Major.

"How the hell am I supposed to get that woman out of there?" said the Major.

Mongo was watching all of this, thought about it for a few moments then volunteered. After all, nothing he ever knew could harm him so he had no fear, and he felt obligated to help his new friends.

"I will go and get the bad lady for you." he said as he trudged into the ship.

The Major looked surprised, and watched - as did all the others - in anticipation. There was the muffled sound of gunfire, followed by Captain Batna screaming: "CALL HIM OFF!" and then a muffled squawk, ending with silence.

Moments later, the triumphant Slurdrahk came strolling out the door, dragging the kicking and squirming Captain Batna by her feet.

"Here you go!" said Mongo as he handed one foot to Lt. Argent and the other to Cpl. Swanson. She squirmed as far away from Mongo as she could, obviously terrified of him. She could not believe that they had domesticated a Slurdrahk, but there it was, doing their bidding. *Impossible*, but true!

"Thanks big guy!" said the Lt. as he patted the nine-foot monstrosity on the arm. Mongo appreciated the gesture and smiled broadly at the Lt., his fangs gleaming. This terrified Captain Batna all the more.

"This one's a wildcat!" Corporal Swanson commented to the Lt. who nodded and grinned in agreement.

Lt. Argent looked down at her exposed ankle and saw it to be quite hairy. He lost his smile immediately. "Now I know why women back home shave their legs!" he joked.

Swanson looked down and pretended to have a queasy stomach, then they both chuckled.

They dragged her, literally kicking and screaming all the way into a doorway and were at once in the brig. She gave them no choice but to make a wide circle so that they could drop her and go right back out of the door, but not before she managed to bite Cpl. Swanson on the ankle. He merely jumped back, making the tear larger.

Her hair was mussed-up and she was seething with anger. As the two S*I*P*Es backed out of the door she lunged at them. Knowing what was going to happen to her, they grinned at each other as they disappeared into the doorway.

She had drawn blood and had a small amount of skin from Swanson's leg on her teeth. Having fallen flat on her face she grinned, got up and produced a small container and spat the skin and blood sample into it, sealed it and returned it. Then she wiped the remaining blood from her mouth, and chuckled softly.

Meanwhile Swanson went to the infirmary to have his leg looked at and to be checked for rabies.

"You never can tell!" he joked to Lt. Argent as he headed out, exaggerating his limp. He was always in good spirits, even when wounded.

Back in the brig, Satrina could not figure it out. She had landed on her face, on the floor of the brig. She looked around and was certain it was the *same room*. In her rage she had run out of the door several times only to wind up in the *same room* time after time. She tried ruffling the sheets on the bed, and they were ruffled in exactly the same way when she entered yet again. How could this be? She walked out of the door, and would up walking into the same door. At first she had thought them idiots to not have a door on her cell, which had to be only a few feet away from her yacht, but it seemed that there was no escape.

She went over it and over it in her mind, then she remembered that the men had *backed* out of the room. Could it be that easy? She tried it only to be all the more frustrated. She saw the room fade as she backed into the very room she had just left. Something weird was happening in that dark threshold in the doorway, and after nearly two hours of attempts, she finally gave up on that approach.

"There's a way out of every cage, and I shall find it." she sobbed to herself.

Looking around for another way out, she eventually managed to scratch the wall by using the chair, which gave her hope of escape, but her hope faded with the scratch. Defeated, and sobbing, worried that her luck had abandoned her after all this time, she dropped the chair, crawled into bed and went to sleep. She dreamt about behaving herself and working for the betterment of mankind rather than the domination and destruction of it. The ship was trying to get her to reform. She was in the brig after all! To her, this was not a dream but a nightmare!

Meanwhile on the bridge, Harvey was curious as to why Captain Batna was so terrified of the Slurdrahk, so he looked it up on the

Butator. He would have when he first met Mongo, but at the time he wasn't sure how.

Here is what he found:

**Slurdrahk: Silicon based generically engineered life form.**

**Planet: Cerv. Apparent immutability of the life forms indigenous to it. All are silicon based and there is no record of any of them actually being killed.**

**A Slurdrahk is the result of a forced kludge between a Slurkinoid (vampyric life form, looks like a teddy bear with long fangs. Short, expandable tummy, and insatiable thirst) and a Dirkenrahkster (Spinal cord-eating gorilla, looks like a gorilla with normal fangs. Tall, very muscular knife-like fingers- for tearing out spinal cords.)**

**Note: When the two are mixed 'the other way' they form a Rackhasa, instead of a Slurdrahk. Rackhasas tend to eat Humans rather than drink spinal fluid, which slows them down in the battlefield, so it was decided to make Slurdrahks instead.**

**This genetic offense was committed by the Kurzi empire, which uses Slurdrahks to invade, or more often destroy the populations of planets. A Slurdrahk does not seem to need to eat, but it enjoys the ingestion of human spinal fluid through its hollow fangs.**

**The Kurzi ship will typically drop Slurdrahks from orbit onto the target planet. The numbers used vary according to population but range from one hundred to one hundred thousand. The Slurdrahks then typically slaughter the population mercilessly until there are no Humans left.**

**It should be noted that truly immortal beings, although unable to die from a Slurdrahk attack, find it very uncomfortable to have their spinal fluid drained. It takes a while for them to recover, so they avoid Slurdrahks like the plague that they are.**

**Slurdrahk factory: As discovered by Captain Callicrates, of the Ezrael.**

Slurdrahks are 'manufactured' for want of another word, in a factory located on Cerv's largest moon of 'Ksoppgh'. Once a Slurdrahk is fully grown, it is assumed to be programmed to be a ruthless killer of all humanoid forms. Most attacks involve the destruction of the spine. They are uncontrollably unruly and for that reason are put into hibernation once said programming is completed. They are then shipped to a planet the Kurzi empire wishes to depopulate, and are dropped from orbit without a parachute. The heat from entry and resulting impact are sufficient to wake the slumbering Slurdrahk, which then begins it's unending rampage. A Slurdrahk is capable of killing as many as ten thousand in a day, as they do not tire nor do they need sleep, making them effective in destroying entire populations in short order.

Intelligence is just above animal level. They are thought to be incapable of independent thought, and mental development is retarded by the fact that they are a kludge of two dissimilar species. This may also be a result of not being able to sleep as such, since sleep is essential to learning. It is estimated that it learns at an imperceptible, but measurable rate.

Vulnerabilities:
None known to exist.

The only cases of someone escaping or defeating a Slurdrahk involve leaving the planet or trapping it in the planet's core. However, the Slurdrahk may eventually climb out of an active volcano. Using a tractor beam to drop one into a star seems the only way to get rid of it. Suspending it in mid air is effective until the anti-gravity field fails. No weapon short of nuclear explosion or disintegration seem to have any effect short of getting a Slurdrahk's attention, which is something to avoid at all costs.

Since Slurdrahks are silicon based life, their natural state is invisible, so with little effort they become very stealthy.

**Warning: Once a planet has been infected with Slurdrahks, it has almost never been reclaimed by carbon-based life. The only exceptions have been where there were generation-long programs of dispatching them one at a time.**

**This makes it one of the Kurzi empire's most powerful punitive weapons.**

Further curiosity about how they could possibly have one of these onboard that was friendly and intrepid, he searched for related information and found a log entry made by Callicrates:

**We finally found the source of the scourge known as Slurdrahks, the planet Cerv, in hopes of finding their natural enemy. When we arrived there we found no direct evidence of their existence, however related life forms abounded on and below the surface. Upon investigation, we discovered a manufacturing facility on Cerv's largest moon of Ksoppgh.**

**I had always known that Lilith was despicably evil, but never dreamed that she would design and build such a facility. We managed to extract a 'sample' in between the completion of the manufacturing process and what was labeled as the 'programming phase', in hopes of being able to control the beast to the point of being able to study him and discern a weakness. The creature was dubbed 'Mongo' by the crew, and I must admit the moniker suits him.**

**Unfortunately, the ship's Azbuga assures me that the Slurdrahk had to comply with examinations for anything significant to be learned. It proved entirely unruly and completely wild. After multiple attempts to get through to the creature, we finally gave up. The only thing the Azbuga learned was that a Slurdrahk has the capacity to learn, but it takes considerably more time to learn things than carbon-based life, as his thoughts and knowledge are literally set in stone. It does not seem to sleep, rendering temporary**

memory into permanent memory is next to impossible. The difference in learning speed is gauged in orders of magnitude. The technique the Kurzi empire uses to program these things eludes us.

However, due mostly to his unruly behavior, he was eventually transferred to a hibernation chamber with an educational program running continuously. I harbor little hope that Mongo will learn to 'play nice' in fewer than ten thousand years. That's a little too long to wait, so we will attempt to find another way to defeat this scourge.

In the meantime, the captive Slurdrahk will just have to stay in hibernation and learn at it's imperceptible rate. Perhaps the next captain of the ship will enjoy more success with Mongo than we have.

Addendum: We eventually managed to isolate the Slurdrahks on a planet and quantum teleport them all into the local star, where I am told they will never escape, but probably not expire. Even though they are rabid alien killing machines, I can't help feeling sympathy for them. A better way must be found to deal with the problem. Even a means of killing them would be kind in comparison to this hellish fate.

Harvey felt sorry for the Slurdrahks, and realized how lucky they were that the educational system and ten thousand years had done their job. It also meant that he had even more homework to do.

"So what are you going to do with our guest?" asked Linda, as she approached.

"I haven't decided what to do with Captain Batna just yet. But, I have an *idea*." he said, looking up from the screen. He was a little detracted by what he was reading, and was intrigued with the concept of a working quantum teleporter. He also wondered why they were not using that kind...

"Not HER, I mean 'Droxina', your 'whittle fwend!'" she said in her most taunting childish voice, cutting off his train of thought.

"Huh? Her name's *Gladrina*." finally regaining his composure.

"What*ever*!" Linda chided in her best 'valley girl' accent.

Sensing her jealousy at last, he said: "Let's go see how she's doing shall we?" with a twinkle in his eye. It was his turn to tease *her*.

"Okay *Romeo*, let's visit your little girlfriend." She was certain that he just wanted to see Gladrina's revealing outfit again.

* * *

"I had hoped that I could have spared you the ordeal of the rehabilitation protocol my dear." said a voice that woke Captain Batna from a deep sleep. She sat bolt upright. "Locating you took a little more time than I had anticipated."

"Who the *heaven* are you?" she demanded of the man that was standing over her.

"Allow me to introduce myself: Cornelius Morax PH.D., at your service." he said, bowing as if his name would be familiar to her. Actually it was but not the way one might think.

She shifted her weight to lie on her side half sitting up, then looked him up and down. She cracked a sly smile. "With a name like that, you must be one of mine." Perhaps her luck hadn't changed after all!

They proceeded to craft an alliance. She promised him immortality and power. He pledged his services. Totally evil men with psychic powers were in demand, and she demanded a lot. However, she was evil to no end and her promises came with a hidden price. Her thinking was that if he managed to overcome the trap she was sending him into, he would be worthy of her service, and in the meantime she got out of her current predicament. A win-win situation for her, so she told him about the true Ankh, and in return he would convince a sleeping captain to release her.

* * *

Harvey and Linda appeared at the doorway to the infirmary.

181

"Not you too?" asked the Azbuga, then he realized that Harvey was accompanied by Linda. "Oh. It's just that all of the men from time to time have tried to come in to get another look at her." he said.

"Indeed. How *is* the patient?" asked Harvey.

"Sleeping quietly."

"What have you found out?"

"Well, she's a genetic conundrum."

"Come again?"

"She has been modified genetically."

"*Really*?" sarcastically.

"Oh yes, and very extensively I might add. It looks as though she was originally Human, or what's more likely, her parents were at one point."

"Okay, this is from a scientific perspective mind you, but how does she have such an affect on the crew?"

Linda gave him a sly smile.

"Pheromones." the two medical men said in chorus.

"Ah *ha*!"

"What's worse, is that she produces a pheromone specific to the man closest to her, making her as irresistible as possible."

"Then why aren't you two affected anymore?" Linda asked.

"We've developed an antidote." said the Azbuga.

Actually it was entirely his work, but he wanted the Xenobiologist to share the credit.

"Maybe you should distribute it throughout the entire ship." muttered Linda, sarcastically.

"We've been making batches for that very purpose." said the Xenobiologist with a glint in his eye.

Harvey agreed. "Good. What else have you got?"

The Azbuga showed them over to a wall where there were several displays showing live readouts from medical scanners.

"Am I reading this correctly? Does she have TWO hearts?" asked Linda.

"Yes. She has two of almost every internal organ, as far as we can tell." said the Xenobiologist.

"How *old* is she?" asked Harvey, to a scowl from Linda. "What?" he said, shrugging at Linda. "If she has redundant organs, it stands to reason that she can live a long time."

"That's right, but as far as we can tell, by certain isotopes locked in her bones, not to mention the number of layers, she must be well over a thousand. So it's much more than we expected." said the Azbuga.

"Yikes! That's more than I thought possible!" he exclaimed as Linda chuckled softly, obviously amused at the man's reaction to the age difference.

"There's more."

The Xenobiologist indicated a microscopic enlargement of cells growing and dividing at an alarming rate.

"What are we looking at?" asked Linda as she closely scrutinized the display.

"Her cells, they grow and divide but the DNA strands don't have any telomeres."

"How is that possible?"

"You've got me, but it seems to work, effectively making her immortal."

"Immortal huh?" muttered Harvey. The idea actually made him feel excited in some way.

"Yes, it's a dream of mankind and now the secret is staring us right in the face, and frankly we're stumped."

"*Both* of you?" said Harvey, almost glaring at the Azbuga.

"Yes, both of us." said the Azbuga. "I know a few techniques of course, but this one is new to me. The pills haven't shown me everything just yet."

"Keep on it, I want you to figure out what you can about her before she wakes."

"Here you go." said a nurse as she handed him a small glass of light brown colored liquid.

"What's this?"

"Gladrina antidote." she said with a knowing wink and nod at Linda.

Harvey held it, gave Linda a mischievous look, wiggled his eyebrows and quaffed the 'antidote'.

"How long until it takes effect?" Linda asked the nurse.

"It works almost immediately." she said reassuringly.

"That's good enough for me. I've got some work to do." She nodded at Harvey and said: "Be *good*." in her best 'ET' impression, and left the room.

Harvey smiled out of the corner of his mouth. Then he noticed a large oblong tank in the corner. "What's that?" he asked.

"A tissue sample we took. What do you think that display is from?" said the Azbuga.

"Why such a big tank?"

"It appears to be growing into a full-sized copy of her, so we put it in a tank that was large enough."

"A clone?"

"Yes, but there's no sign of any wings on this one yet." said the Xenobiologist.

"That's probably because Gladrina's are grafted on or something." said the Azbuga.

"We shall *see*."

Harvey walked over to the tank, and could make out the outline of a human form in the opaque nutrient-rich slurry.

"How long?" he asked, his voice almost trailing off.

"We figure it will mature in another day or so."

The Xenobiologist was nodding in agreement.

"That fast?"

"Her cells are reproducing at an alarming rate, just like cancer does. As long as there is food, they will divide and grow like the dickens."

"Hmm."

"Call me when she wakes up."

They looked at each other, puzzled. "Which one?" they asked in chorus.

"Either." he said as he headed to the door. "Keep me informed, this is fascinating... and make sure the whole crew has a dose of that antidote. I don't want anymore of that nonsense she causes."

"Don't worry, we've almost got enough for that now."

# XXIII
# MEHUMAN

"Did you ever have the feeling that you wanted to go...
And still have the feeling that you wanted to stay?"

10:00 AM, Monday, December 24th, 2012 Anno Domini

After having a night of fitful sleep on it, Harvey appeared as a hologram in the brig.

"It's about time you showed-up." said Captain Batna calmly.

"I thought I'd let you get a good night's sleep first." said Harvey.

"What are you going to do with me?" she asked, almost sweetly.

"That depends on you."

A sly look came over her face, and she began to smile. She knew what was going to happen next.

Harvey marooned Captain Batna on the same planet that she had left her crew. He also confiscated the Pantherion as well as the yacht as a 'slap on the wrist' for being 'naughty' as he put it. He said that he planned on returning it to it's rightful owners. The truth was, he simply didn't want to 'keep her in irons'. What was he going to do with a prisoner? This seemed like the better option. After all, help was already on the way, and she could tell her fleet how futile an attack on the Ezrael can be.

He hoped that she would learn something from this. However, to change the habits of immortal beings that have already lived millions of years is an uphill battle, to say the least. For some reason, consulting the Butator, the android or Metatron didn't occur to him this time. Something was fogging his mind on this issue and he didn't much like it. In the end, he erringly chalked it up to the 'Gladrina antidote'.

He hadn't seen the last of Satrina Batna, and she told him so as he left her on the planet's surface. Somehow, he didn't mind so much. If the stolen Pantherion was the mightiest ship at their disposal, he had little to worry about from the Kurzi empire. What he didn't know is what they lacked in firepower and technology them made up for with sheer numbers. The Kurzi empire would deal with him as a swarm of bees deals with a bear. At least that was the plan she was formulating at the time.

That night, when both the doctors were asleep, an alarm went off waking them. It seemed that the clone was about to wake up. They paged the captain, who showed up immediately. He couldn't sleep, so he was, reading about galactic history on his personal Butator terminal when they had called him.

"What have you got?" he asked, expectantly.

"The clone is about to wake, ahead of schedule, and you said to call." said the Xenobiologist.

"Wow! That's fast! How's Gladrina doing?"

"She's still out. Apparently the battle almost drained her to death." said the extra sleepy Azbuga. Indeed, he was yawning and barely able to keep his eyes open. Perhaps those pills were coming back with a vengeance. True, they do tend to make one sleep a lot more than usual for an extended period of time as they release their information to one's brain.

"Well, let's take a look at this clone then."

"It should prove interesting to see what a fully-grown clone acts like." said the Xenobiologist. "I think that she'll have a genetic memory, so she'll be sentient right away, but 'Bug-face' here says she'll be dumb as a post."

The Azbuga yawned, covering his mouth with one hand and waving dismissively with the other. "You know, there are a lot of trees out there that would be offended by such a comment."

"What about the scanners? Can't they tell?" Asked Harvey.

"That's the problem; they show engrams appearing which makes *me* think a mind is forming, but he thinks it is just a minimal pattern to allow it to function at all." Said the Xenobiologist.

"Well, let's take a look." said Harvey as there was a slosh from the tank, and a wingless Gladrina clone sat up, and took her first breath.

187

They all exchanged glances, and Harvey approached her. She wiped the nutrient goo from her eye sockets, looked at him and smiled broadly.

"She recognizes him! I was right!" said the Xenobiologist.

"Wait for it!" said the Azbuga confidently.

"Graayyyk!" said the clone, and threw-up on the floor in front of the captain who reflexively jumped backwards.

The Azbuga looked at the Xenobiologist and raised an eyebrow as if to say 'See? I told you so!'

The nurse helped the unsteady clone out of the tank and into the nearby shower to wash off the nutrient goo that covered her, and a good thing too. It obscured just enough detail to keep the men honest.

After the clone was cleaned-up and clothed in an examination gown, she staggered into the main room of the infirmary, looked around and smiled when she saw Harvey. She made a sound not unlike a happy baby and waddled towards him with her arms outstretched.

"I was afraid of that." said the Azbuga.

"Afraid of what?" said Harvey.

"Since you were the first living being she saw, she has 'imprinted' on you. In short, she thinks you are her mother."

"Hummumph!" he said as he received a smothering hug.

The Azbuga turned to the Xenobiologist. "Now he'll never get away from her."

They both looked at Harvey and the clone, and shook their heads.

"I think it's a left-over function of the bird DNA used for making wings." said the Azbuga.

"You're *reaching*! I detected the reptilian DNA for wings, and there aren't any!"

"I beg to differ."

"Then where are they?"

"I am certain that they manifest at a further stage of development like antlers on elk. That's why I told you they wouldn't be on the clone."

0"You're guessing! Just guessing!"

"Never mind that, what am I going to do about this?" asked Harvey as soon as he was able to get some air. "I can't raise a hundred and twenty pound baby!"

"We'll take care of her. In the meantime, may I suggest you go back to your quarters, we'll do what we can for her." said the Xenobiologist as the nurse gently led the clone to a bed.

"Perhaps Gladrina here can tell us what to do with her clone when she wakes up. Given the nature of her cells, and how it happened, this sort of thing can't be all that unusual." said the Azbuga.

"You *wish*." said the Xenobiologist.

"*Will* she wake up?" asked Harvey.

"Oh yes, I can safely say it only going to be another few hours at the most." answered the Azbuga. "She should be awake by morning."

"Good, I'm going to get some sleep myself. Call me when she wakes up." he said pointing at Gladrina.

"Count on it."

He paused at the threshold of the doorway. "One heck of a birthday, isn't it?"

He looked confused for a moment, then checked the calendar on his watch. "Oh yeah! I suppose that it is!"

Satisfied with that, he went back to his quarters. He stopped worrying and was so tired that he could sleep though anything.

"Give the clone a sedative, and we'll deal with her in the morning." said the Xenobiologist to the nurse. Then they retired to their respective quarters for the remainder of the night.

A few hours later, the quietly sleeping clone awoke, due to her advanced ability to flush-out and neutralize foreign substances like sedatives and poisons. The Azbuga might have guessed this but he was too sleepy to have thought of it at the time.

She sat up, looked around and slid out of bed, effectively removing her hospital gown. She staggered around a bit making 'happy baby' sounds looking for Harvey. Then she spotted the doorway, and staggered into it.

Harvey was sleeping like a log, and didn't notice the nude woman crawl into bed with him, nor did he notice her snuggle-up to his back, and put her arms around him. So there they slept; one blissfully unaware and the other simply blissful.

Linda had awaken earlier than the others. She was not only a 'morning person' but had gone to sleep sooner than the rest. This business with Gladrina had the whole male population of the crew awake until the 'wee hours'... that is until they got the antidote. By that time it was later than usual. So, she had the ship pretty much to herself. She got up and ate breakfast, wandered around a few labs and the bridge, looked for Harvey in specific places rather than having the ship send her to him. She was feeling playful and enjoyed the 'hunt'. She wanted to apologize for being jealous of Gladrina. It wasn't as if they had proclaimed their feelings for each other, but she had decided she wanted to be with him, and was relatively sure he wanted to be with her as well.

Today, she was going to tell him how she felt. Perhaps it was the way Gladrina had looked at Harvey, or just the feeling of 'competition', but she just thought that it was high time to clear the air if nothing else. He was a good and decent man after all, and he made her feel safe and secure when he was around. From the moment she first saw him, she was delighted with him.

After a while she found she didn't want to search anymore, the butterflies in her stomach were getting to be a problem, so, hoping that she wouldn't catch him in the shower or doing something even more embarrassing, she took a deep breath and walked into a doorway, thinking about him.

Harvey was still asleep, and so was Gladrina's clone. Linda didn't wait for long to yell; "WHAT'S THIS!?!"

Harvey, who was about to wake anyway, jumped like he had just heard an explosion. In a way, he had. The clone rolled over and moaned, stretched out on the bed, opened her eyes a bit and smiled at Linda.

"I *trusted* you!"

Harvey was confused and now wide awake. "What?" Then he saw the clone in his bed and noticed the lack of wings.

Linda was so upset that she didn't notice was that he was fully clothed.

"But...but..." was all he could muster.

"Don't you 'but but' ME mister!" She was furious at being wrong about him. Even after he got the antidote, he was all about one thing! Typical MAN: His mind was in the gutter as often and as deeply as a woman's mind was in the refrigerator!

"It's not what it looks like!" he protested.

Linda was furious. She shouted: "Just... *GET LOST*!" Her trust shattered, she stormed out of the room, headed for her quarters.

The clone looked up at Harvey, stretched out her arms for a hug and burbled "BurrraaakkK!" at him, giggled and grinned coyly.

"Oh boy." was all he could say.

Just then, the intercom came on, it was the Azbuga. "Captain, Gladrina's clone is missing."

"Couldn't you have told me that *five minutes ago*?"

"What do you mean?"

"She apparently found her way into my room while I was sleeping, and Linda just walked-in, afterwards."

"Oh my." said the Azbuga as he held up the empty hospital gown that the clone had been wearing. "I can guess what she must be thinking!"

"I'll bring the clone by, but could you explain things to Linda for me?"

"I'd be glad to. But it might not help much."

"I'll take that chance."

* * *

"Why a sheet?" asked the Xenobiologist, as Harvey and the clone appeared in the infirmary.

"I didn't have anything for her to wear, and didn't want to bring her over in the buff."

191

"It's only though *one* doorway!"

Medical doctors are notorious for not being bashful about the human form. Go figure, so they wondered how a grown man like Harvey could have a problem with the clone in her birthday suit.

"Look, I don't want to see Gladrina OR her clone in the buff, I only want to see *Linda* that way!" he blurted quite oblivious to what it was that he had just revealed.

The Xenobiologist gave him a look. "It's high time you told *her* that."

"At this point, I don't think she'll listen to me." he said, blushing intensely.

"What are you going to do?" asked the Azbuga.

"I'm going to do what she demanded! I'm going to *get lost!*"

"I thought that was impossible in this ship." said the Xenobiologist.

"Well, I'm going to *try*, then I'm going to have a stiff drink!" Then he turned to the Azbuga and said in a milder tone: "You'll explain things to her?"

"Yes, but that alone won't patch things up."

"It never does, but it's a *start*... and make sure you *show* her the clone, I don't want her to think that it's a 'story'. She's a scientist. I'm betting her intellect will take over."

The Azbuga nodded, and Harvey stepped out the door. "Never underestimate the power of a woman." muttered the Azbuga.

# XXIV
## One little drink... from a certain fountain.

"I did not know how empty I was, until I was filled."

Harvey wondered aimlessly around the seemingly endless halls of the ship. The way he was walking, it was as though he had been going at a frantic pace until he was nearly exhausted. His head kept rolling back and he stumbled frequently although there was nothing to stumble over other than his own two feet. He was extremely sleepy as well as physically worn out.

Linda's words kept echoing through his head, "I trusted you!" and "Get lost!" Her disappointment echoing through his head again and again. He could kick himself for what had happened. What was worse, it was not what she thought it was, and he had no way of preventing it from happening. It was all a misunderstanding of circumstances beyond his control. He knew, that she would learn the truth eventually, but the damage was already done. She would never think of him in quite the same way again. He knew enough about women to know that much.

After what seemed like an eternity, he finally reached a doorway. The space beyond seemed as though it had been intended for large numbers of people. The room had double doors on it, not just a doorway like so many others in the ship. In short, they were saloon doors.

Harvey pushed in the middle and the doors opened wide. He slowly entered and noticed immediately that the only other person there was the bartender, who stood there minding his own business, polishing a glass in the classic bartender-with-nothing-else to do fashion. Although Harvey had never seen this man or this room before, he seemed unalarmed by this unusual turn of events as he walked up to the bar.

"Can I help you sir?" the bartender asked the approaching captain.

"Thirsty." was all he could blurt out as he slowly and stiffly sat on a barstool as if he were in pain.

"You look worn out. I've got just the thing..." The bartender began searching for the ingredients to the drink. "Whatcha been doing?" he asked as he worked.

"I've been trying to find my quarters. I think I'm lost."

"Funny, I though you couldn't get lost in this ship."

"I was told to 'get lost', and now somehow I've managed it."

The bartender just smiled as Harvey continued.

"I've been wandering the corridors for what seems like days. Now all I want is something to drink and a good night's sleep."

He collapsed into his arms for a moment, took a deep breath and looked up and around.

"Where the *hell* am I anyway?"

"'The Right Place.'" came the reply.

"No really, where am I?"

The bartender smiled. "You are in a *bar* sir, the name of which is 'The Right Place'." he said while pouring a drink behind the bar.

Harvey looked puzzled despite the clearness of this assertion.

"Also." The bartender continued' "You *are* in the right place for you to be in right now Captain." as he produced the glass and slid it across the bar.

"What's this?" asked Harvey as he looked at a glass that appeared to have a piece of sky in it. It was incredibly blue with a few fluffy white 'clouds' that appeared to be dissolving.

"It's called 'Eth[12]'" Leaning forward and lowering his voice as if to avoid being overheard though there was obviously no one else around: "It's a very special concoction, and I'm the only one who knows the recipe." He leaned back and in a loud clear voice said: "So drink up!"

"I saw you make it, there's only two ingredients. How secret can that be?"

"One has to know *what* the two ingredients are, and let me tell you; it's a big universe with *lots* of possibilities."

"I see, and you still seem to have me at a disadvantage."

---

[12] *Eth: Time.*

"Name's 'Mumiah Zethar', you can call me 'Zeth' for short. Everybody does."

Satisfied with this, he stared into the cobalt blue liquid as if he were a child on Christmas morning. It captured his imagination and seemed to be the most important thing in the whole world. He stared more and more deeply into the liquid and finally broke away and asked: "What do you mean by saying I'm in the right place for me to be in right now?"

"You're thirsty, and this is just the right thing to quench it." motioning to the drinking glass of delightfully blue fluid. It was so blue as to glow with blueness. A pure blue that seemed to put the sky back home to shame. "I might add, you're thirsty for more that just fluids. This is the drink you need, so go ahead. You're allowed." he said reassuringly, like a parent.

Harvey stared at the drink. He still had questions. Somehow on an instinctive level, he knew that this drink would change him, so he asked: "Is there any going back?"

The bartender smiled and said: "It wouldn't be worth it."

"What wouldn't?"

"Mortality."

He still just stared at the drink, wondering what the bartender meant. Was this really what an immortality potion looked like? And why was he being offered it? Was this really happening? He was so tired that it *seemed* like a dream. Indeed, the night before he had dreamed of immortality and flying, possibly because of Gladrina's arrival.

The bartender continued: "You don't *have* to drink it if you don't want to. As always, the choice is yours. BUT..." raising his index finger "...it's ill-advised to turn down this *particular* drink once it's been offered - because my dear captain, the offer may not be repeated."

Satisfied at this, he picked up the glass and took a small sip. He felt a flood of good, warm energy pass over him. A feeling of robustness, energy and heath that was more than he'd ever felt before. He felt more alive than when he was in college and had been in the best shape of his life, playing on the hockey team. He felt wonderful! Looking up, he found the bartender to be gone.

195

"Thanks! Zeth! This is great!" he said looking around.

He sat there and finished the drink and left the glass on the bar, tossing a gold coin onto the counter as he walked out of the room. Where he got the coin from didn't seem to matter to him. The next thing he knew, he woke up in his bed.

Had it all been only a dream? Whatever it was, he felt more rested and alive than he ever had before. His "blahs" were gone, and now he was raring to go! He felt what he'd been lacking so far. He felt... *ENTHUSIASM!*

# XXV
# MUPIEL

"Out of the mouths of babes..."

11:30 AM, Thursday, December 27th, 2012 Anno Domini

Fully recovered, Gladrina woke up while the Xenobiologist was listening to her left heart with a stethoscope. She opened her eyes, looked up and him and said "Doctor, I never knew you cared!" (If I have to explain this, you're out of luck!)

He very quickly removed the stethoscope almost embarrassed. For a doctor, that was difficult to do. She smiled warmly at him and was amused by his growing change in complexion.

"I guess I was more worn out that I thought." she said. "Three *days*, wow!"

"How did you know how long you were asleep?" asked the now puzzled doctor.

"I have a sense for the passage of time. A sort of internal clock, which is reasonably accurate."

"To say the least." he replied - almost astonished.

"Where is Captain Harvey?" she asked as she sat up. "I'd like to thank him for intervening when he did. One more salvo and I might have been *history!*"

"He's on the bridge but he'll be here soon. He wanted to talk to you as soon as you woke. Are you sure you're all right?"

"Yes, I'm fine now." Looking herself over, she noticed the hospital gown. "Are these the clothes you'd *prefer* me to wear?" She appeared to be totally unconcerned with how she had been changed into it. Truthfully it was a female nurse that changed her clothing, because the Doctors kept sighing as they looked at her, and the examination gown, being open at the back, worked well with the wings. She was looking over her shoulder, and playing with the opening as if attempting to remove it.

197

"Uh...you *might* want to just leave that on for the moment. In the meantime I'll see to it that appropriate attire is delivered to you."

"*Thank* you!" She beamed at the doctor, and placed her hand on his arm for a moment. He instinctively pulled away mostly because, it felt very good... He was a married man, though his wife was back on the home world and was probably gone. She had been seeking a divorce before the incident that launched the ship, even so he felt it was absolutely inappropriate to even think about getting involved with a patient. Her being so friendly, and 'touchy-feely' made it all the more difficult for him. The antidote could only do so much!

"Also, there's been a... *complication*."

"Complication?"

"Waaaaaaaaa!!!" echoed down the hall and into the room.

Gladrina slowly turned her head and gave the Xenobiologist a coy look as she cocked her head.

Linda had been designing new, less-revealing outfits for Gladrina for the past few days. "I never guessed how challenging it was to make clothes for someone with wings." she muttered to herself, as she finalized the details on her 3-D monitor. The ship's ability to quickly manufacture anything she could design was a constant delight for her. She had already made a number of smart new outfits as well as pieces of test equipment; a combination only a female scientist could appreciate. Now that she had had an explanation of the clone incident from the Azbuga, she felt like she should make amends. Besides, 'tis the season. If that took the form of offering Gladrina less revealing outfits, which would help stop some of the problems, so much the better.

When Linda arrived at the infirmary, Gladrina was sitting on a bed with her clone. They were face to face with their foreheads touching. Both had their eyes closed and their eyes were moving rapidly back and forth just like someone does when they are dreaming.

"What's she doing?" she asked the Azbuga.

"She's teaching Aniyel everything she knows, telepathically."

"Aniyel?"

"That's the name she chose, it's apparently their name for the goddess of love, like Venus in our culture."

"Oh... that's, uh... *interesting*. How long will this process take?"

"I don't know, but if their combined neurological activity increases one more time, I'm snapping them out of it."

"It's dangerous?"

"Right on the edge, even for them. Look." He indicated a monitor that showed the synchronized activity of both brains to be *beyond* what 100% *should* be. "I think she's giving her all her memories too. This clone may become a duplicate in *every* sense after all."

"Is that *normal*?" she asked, examining the readouts.

"She said that cloning is the only way they can reproduce after they reach a certain age. She, and most the females of her kind have run out of eggs. Now they do it this way and transfer knowledge to the clone, making it an adult right away."

"Well, that gets you three off the hook!"

"*Three?*"

"Both of you doctors *and* Harvey."

The Azbuga just smiled. At that point, Gladrina moved a bit, took a deep breath and gently let the clone lie down and sleep. Then she turned to Linda and the Azbuga, and took a deep breath.

"Oh, hello!" she said, noticing Linda for the first time she arrived. "She'll sleep for a while now."

"It worked?" asked the Azbuga.

"Certainly. When she wakes, she'll have my knowledge and memories, but she'll also have a slightly different personality."

"Why is that?"

"She's a clone, she knows it, and she thinks Harvey is her mother for starters. You want more?"

"That'll do."

Linda deftly held out a large bag resembling those from a fancy store. "Here, I made these outfits for you and your, uh... clone. It's a tradition where I come from to give gifts on a certain day of the year. Actually it was Aniyel's uh, birthday. You were asleep for it, but that couldn't be helped."

"Thank you!" she said as she got up quickly and looked inside the bag. The clothes were matching outfits but one version of each was obviously made with the wings in mind. She looked at Linda and beamed, then started removing her examination gown.

They both cleared their throats and turned away to give her some privacy.

"She's really not bashful." said the Azbuga out of the corner of his mouth rather matter-of-factly.

"Well, I hope the outfits help." she replied in kind.

"Done!" said Gladrina.

They turned around to see her gladly showing off a tastefully conservative outfit.

"I'm glad to see you're not jealous... this is simply the naughtiest thing I've ever worn! It should drive the men back home wild!" She began admiring the outfit in the mirror. "I'm sure that Ani will love hers too!"

The Azbuga slowly turned his head toward the somewhat stunned scientist with a twinkle in his eye. "You see, she told me that the reason she's not bashful is that in her culture the more you obscure the body, the more you leave to their over-active imaginations, making nudity 'boring' and this a 'racy' outfit."

"That explains a lot!"

"Look on the bright side; at least she's covered even though she thinks she's being an exhibitionist. I think you've achieved pretty good symmetry there."

"I can only hope." she muttered as she walked up to Gladrina and got her attention by appearing in the mirror behind her. This only got her face to light-up and she turned around and hugged Linda to thank her. Linda had a slight look of disgust on her face. This was not quite the reaction she was hoping for.

"This'll definitely drive them wild back home! Thank you!" Then she wrinkled her brow in consternation. "Is there anything I can do for you in return?"

"Well, you could come with me. The captain would like to have a little talk with you."

Gladrina smiled, nodded enthusiastically, and went with Linda, who turned to the Azbuga as she walked toward the door, blew some of her bangs up and shook her head in mock frustration. This made him chuckle quietly as they disappeared into the doorway.

In the conference room, Gladrina insisted on a private meeting with the Captain, then he could decide if he wanted to tell her story to the rest of the crew. Linda and the others begrudgingly agreed. Once the last of them had left, she looked at him, smiled meekly and told her tale.

There had been many health movements on her world, which eventually led to an eugenics program. A scientist by the name of 'Meher Parvargigar' engineered the changes. One by one, they conquered genetic 'problems' ranging from aging to cancer. There were many who thought it unnatural to take the treatments, which consisted mostly of gene therapy. It didn't end there. Her people had learned a lot about genetics, and started adding 'extras', such as telepathy and telekinesis to name a few. These 'extra features' enraged the normal folk all the more. They claimed that monkeying with nature was just plain wrong and they wanted nothing to do with it, and they insisted that the augmentations not be forced on the masses. They had however, eventually agreed to the augmentations being optional, but insisted that 'antidotes' be developed and stored for those that may eventually wish to 'go back'.

At first, the wishes of the normal people were honored, but eventually, not only did the augmentation viruses get out of the laboratory and into the general environment, deliberately or by accident - no one seemed to know; a war broke out; the 'normals' versus the 'augments'. The normals thought that the augments were committing crimes against nature, and the augments thought that they were achieving perfection.

She hung her head as she revealed the next part, not proud of what she was telling him, and visibly ashamed that it had happened at all. He noticed that her charisma level substantially dropped and the room seemed very quiet. She continued her tale as a tear ran down her cheek.

Under the guidance of a star empire run by 'superior beings', not only did the augments win the war, but they were able to enslave and eventually exterminate all of the normal people on her home world. They were now long gone.

The augments renamed their race and planet to reflect their arrogant views of perfection, and proceeded to create even more changes, eventually growing extra parts such as large bird wings, until they hardly resembled what they once were. Some left her world to become gods on other worlds, with the blessing of the then governing body.

Over time, they became isolationists, thinking all other races to be inferior to the point of being not worthy of their attention. Visitors to their world were ignored, if not simply killed as a pest or 'nuisance', much like one might swat a fly.

After a thousand years of this, they received a visitor that somehow managed to remind them of their crimes. Perhaps it was the time involved - allowing them to get used to their new minds- perhaps it took that long for the depth of their crimes to sink in or egos to deflate, but the reminder resulted in a world-wide attack of *conscience*.

After literally decades of grieving, they came up with a plan. They wanted to somehow return to their original form. Mortal, prone to illness, ugliness and all it entailed. She was one of many sent out into the galaxy to retrieve her kind. They wanted to return to normal together, *collectively* as a race, so they wouldn't undergo the change until they were all accounted for. She was on such a mission when Captain Batna had attacked her small ship.

She had been hanging her head for some time. When she was finished, she turned her teary-eyed face toward the stunned captain. "I'm a *good* person. I really *am*. I was born this way, so I wasn't a part of the holocaust. Most of us that were, eventually committed suicide. All that is left at home is the second generation, like me." She sobbed like a little girl. "Now you know why I didn't want the others to hear. I didn't want them to know about it... or see me like this. It's so depressing!"

"It's okay. Don't worry about it. Can you tell me who these 'superior beings' were that ran that empire you spoke of?"

"No, only the original generation knows that, and the only ones left are somewhere out here, in the galaxy. All we have right now is the name: Lilith Kali Izorpo, as their leader."

Two of them were names Harvey knew: Lilith and Kali. Neither had anything good associated with them. Still, he wanted to be sure before he suggested anything. He calmly looked-up the names.

Lilith was indeed one of the greatest agents of the adversary. In fact, all three names meant the same person. Talk about redundancy! Three times? Three? Not the number three again!

"I know that name. If what I've read about her is true, and I have no reason to doubt it, she probably *started* your eugenics movement."

There was a glimmer of hope in her tear-filled eyes. She didn't want to believe that her people were evil at heart, and if an outsider had caused all of this by manipulating her society, it would mean that there was indeed hope for her people after all, and that there was a horrible monster out there somewhere.

He showed the information to Gladrina, who changed her expression. The display also showed that Meher Parvargigar was a good name that was often falsely used by one of her operatives to dupe worlds into engaging in eugenics programs.

"You mean we're probably *victims* and not the perpetrators after all?" she said with the sound of hope in her voice.

"Well, I might not believe that they were entirely innocent but yes, it is probable that they were indeed mislead by the adversary. It smells of it to me."

She beamed at him. This was the best news he could have given her. The weight of guilt was leaving her, even though she was not involved directly, she still felt responsible, but now it was somehow... *better*.

She turned her attention to the screen, and looked shocked as she called the captain's attention to it. Under "Lilith: Aliases", amongst others read the names "Satrina" and "Batna".

Harvey turned white. Anticipating his next request, the Butator displayed the words:

**She is the Lilith in question, and she is no longer on the planet you left her on as she has been collected by her forces. You will meet her again.**

The last sentence made him feel better and worse at the same time. Harvey and Gladrina exchanged a worried look.

"Well, that explains why she wanted to kill you."

"Yes, I'm part of the ruination of her plans. But what is troubling you?"

"I don't know what made me let her go."

She took a deep breath. "With your permission, I can find out for you."

"How?"

"Well, I am telepathic, and if you like I can read the thoughts that elude you. Your subconscious mind if you will."

"Does it hurt?"

"No, but it's *very intimate*." she said with a sly smile.

He thought about it for a moment.

"What if you see something you don't like, or I have thoughts that upset you?"

"Don't worry, I'd respect your privacy, above all things."

"Okay, I'm willing to give it a try. How is it done?"

"Lean forward, touch your forehead to mine, and let me put my hands on your temples. I'll do the rest."

He complied, and she was very gentle with his mind. He felt her gratitude and love of all things living. She felt the deception that Dr. Morax had planted in his mind and then broke contact.

"It was Dr. Morax. He influenced you while you slept."

"The BASTARD!"

"Don't worry, I helped your subconscious put up barriers that will keep him - or anyone else for that matter - out from now on."

"Thank you!"

"Besides his influence, you didn't know that she was a monster at the time, so you probably would have let her go anyway. That's the only reason that it worked. He could only nudge you a little, since you have a good, solid mental foundation."

There was a long silence.

"I think you ought to stay on board until we resolve your problem and this little 'Morax' thing." suggested Harvey.

"Thank you. I'd like that."

"Besides, we might be able to track your people and round them up more easily than you can, and your help would be invaluable."

"I'd be glad to help, but what about your crew? How will they react to *my* problem?"

"All they need to know is that Lilith did horrible things to your world."

"Thank you again Captain."

"Now go and rest, your eyes are red and the others will know you were crying if they see you that way. Come to the bridge when you feel better."

"Thank you captain Harvey. You are a kind man." She rose and gave him a peck on the cheek, and a small hug.

Harvey put his hand on his cheek where she kissed him and smiled as she left.

She hesitated at the threshold and said. "You really should tell her how you feel. She feels the same way you know."

"Did you read her mind too?"

"I'm a woman silly! It's obvious to everyone on board how she feels about you, but I understand your reasons for hesitating."

"You saw a lot in there."

"Enough to know that I wish I were her. By the way, your form of immortality is better than mine sweetie." She winked and smiled at him

205

then disappeared into the doorway before he could ask her what she meant by that.

* * *

Dr. Morax had been trying for days to get into the armory. Finally, he managed.

He searched through the swords placed here and there. Some were in various stages of being forged. He was here for a particular sword, and he found it in a case.

"Ahhhh! Here you are. HERE YOU ARE! My friend, you and I have a destiny!" he said to the sword.

He held it point up and admired it for a moment. It was a beautiful piece of work, with gold and platinum, diamonds and sapphires. A weapon fit for a ruler, and that's what he intended to become. After all, that's what Lilith had promised.

He sheathed it, and carried it out of the room, chuckling softly. He even began to sing to himself. He was surprisingly good at carrying a tune.

# XXVI
# From Arael, with love.

"Anything you can do, I can do better!"

After all the worrying about his first three assignments, the problem on Loam, a run-in with Captain Batna and Linda's wrath over Gladrina's inadvertent clone, Harvey was feeling stressed-out. He knew he was headed for problems if he didn't find a way to relax soon. He had licked the enthusiasm problem, but stress was beginning to take it's toll, and things were only going to get worse.

He sought out Pymander and asked him: "What did captain Callicrates do when he was in need of a little rest and relaxation?"

"Sometimes, when then stress was rather bad, he liked to go flying sir."

"Flying?"

"Yes, he found it to be quite relaxing."

"Isn't that what we are doing now?"

"Yes, and no."

"Huh?"

"We are inside something that is flying, but Captain Callicrates used to actually fly."

Harvey looked perplexed. He made a wing like motion with his hands and Pymander nodded.

"You mean shut-off the gravity?"

"No."

"Jet pack?"

"No." Pymander rolled his eyes, sighed and said: "You'd best come with me sir and I'll *show* you."

Harvey followed Pymander as he had before, allowing the android to take him through the seemingly endless corridors of the ship. They arrived at a room that was behind a large ledge on a high cliff over a valley that was full of tall growing grasses.

"Wow! What a view! Great for hang-gliding, right?" said Harvey as he took a few quick steps to the edge. "This is good!" He turned back to look at Pymander and saw several pairs of what looked like large wings mounted on the cliff wall behind the android. As if an a daze, he walked up to a pair, and they startled him by fluttering a bit.

"They're alive!" he exclaimed as he jumped back. Then he thought about what Pymander had said earlier and the whole reason they were here.

"You've got to be kidding me!"

Pymander simply shook his head.

"Really?"

The android nodded.

"Just like Gladrina?"

The android nodded again, this time closing his eyes. "Very much like her." he replied half under his breath. "In fact, exactly like she does."

"How do you...?"

"Just put them on, much like a backpack."

"That's it?"

"Well, you have to gain control of them after they merge with your body."

"Ewwww, that sounds gross... and painful!"

"I've been told that it's rather like a big, warm hug."

Harvey grinned like a small child. He timidly reached toward a pair of wings. They fluttered again and he partially retracted his arm as if they would bite.

"Allow me." said Pymander, examining the labels above the pairs wings, settling on the very same pair that Harvey had approached. "These *match* your blood type, interesting you picked the right ones on your own. Good instincts on your part."

Harvey seemed pleased with himself, but somewhat anxious. Pymander lifted the wings off of their life-supporting wall mount. Apparently this was still part of the ship. How the ship bordered with or had a valley inside of it was something Harvey took in stride. The ship almost seemed like it were magic at times.

The wings spread out a little as if anticipating the flight to come. It was like the balancing reflexes of a large bird as it's perch is moved.

"Take off your shirt and turn around." instructed the android. The excited Human enthusiastically complied.

"Have you ever wondered why the shoulder blades are arranged as they are?" He asked as he fitted the wings on Harvey's back.

"Yes, as a matter of fact I have."

"That is so that you can wear wings like these."

"You mean that we are *designed* to have these?"

"It's more like what you might call a piece of 'optional equipment'."

He felt the 'warm hug' of the wings merging with his body. They attached to his skeletal system; Shoulders, down his spine, rib cage and even hips! Finally, they merged with his nervous system and he became aware of them like he was aware of his arms and legs. It was like he had had wings before and feeling was *returning* to them. He thought about that and wondered if this feeling wasn't just due to the fact that since he had never had limbs *added* to his torso before he simply had no reference for comparison. Funny how it seemed like he remembered them though. The whole process, although rather invasive, didn't hurt. It was a warm, comfortable feeling. When it felt like it had finished, he asked: "Now what?"

"Control them." came the reply.

"How do I do that?"

The wings began to flutter a bit more as he thought about them and then they opened slowly as if he were stretching his arms.

"It takes a moment, but your brain will remember."

'Remember?' he thought to himself: 'How did he know? Callicrates must have told the android about this part too.' Then he continued: "How can I remember something I've...never..." his voice trailing off as he *remembered!*

"Almost everyone knows instinctively how to fly." Pymander explained; "That's why mankind dreams of flight. For you, that dream is coming true right now."

"Indeed." said Harvey as he was testing his new wings. He looked over the right shoulder and flexed his right wing and then the left. Satisfied that they worked as he thought they should, he grinned like a very excited child. Dare I say; an *evil* grin?

* * *

The golden grain and other grasses shimmered in the sun and light winds as Harvey skimmed along the top of the vegetation. His right arm stretched out in front of him, as he had seen numerous comic book heroes do. He let out a "YAAAAAAAAAAHOOOOOOOOOOOO!" as he reached the maximum velocity and minimum altitude of his maiden flight. He laughed and giggled as he swooped to and fro, hovered, gained altitude, dived and bobbed. He was nearly exhausted as he landed lightly on the ledge to find Pymander patiently waiting.

"Was that fun?" Pymander asked rhetorically.

Harvey was out of breath but managed: "You bet your transistors it was!"

"I don't have any..."

"That's okay! You know what I mean!"

"Indeed."

"Exhausting though!" as he was puffing and sweating heavily with a very large grin. Then he continued: "The others have just *got* to try this!"

"Careful, there are only so many pairs."

"Oh Yeah, how do I get these off anyway?"

The android paused.

"You CAN take them off can't you?" Harvey asked almost panicked.

"Of course."

"Whew!"

"All you need is a scalpel."

"A what?!?"

"Merely an attempt at humor."

"You are going to have to work on that."

The android grinned sheepishly and said: "You didn't see the look on your face!"

Harvey glared at him.

Pymander just nodded and continued: "They come off as easily as they went on. However, if they are left on *too* long, they would become a permanent part of you."

"How permanent?"

"As permanent as your arms. Then it really will require a scalpel!"

"Ouch! How long does that take?"

"For them to become permanent?"

Harvey nodded slightly.

"Roughly two to three days, depending on how quickly you normally heal."

"Gotcha. Though they'd be a little difficult to explain at parties, it wouldn't be so bad, having wings that is." he muttered as he played with their range of motion. Discovering that they can compress: "Hey! They tuck behind the back rather nicely, don't they?" Harvey folded the wing closely to his back, the tips hiding behind his thighs, and they took-up surprisingly little space as they hugged his back. He turned his head over his shoulder in an attempt to look behind him. Pymander looked and nodded.

"Captain Callicrates used to hide his that way, but he couldn't keep it up forever and, I might add, it still looked like he had a bit of a hunchback, or at least a severe slouch. Chairs become a problem, you have to start sleeping on your stomach, and none of your shirts would fit anymore."

"Yes, I suppose you're right, it'd be just like it is for Gladrina. I'd hate to have to get a whole new wardrobe, and sit only on stools. Hey! are you saying Callicrates wound up with them permanently attached?"

"How do you think I found out it takes a scalpel to remove them?" said the android with a wink.

All Harvey could do to that was wince. He motioned with his hands to have the wings taken off.

They removed the wings, and it actually felt sort of *good*, Like a scab being prematurely pulled off an itchy wound. A curious feeling. As he was putting his shirt back on Harvey looked at his back, and noticed a few red marks on the skin.

"No bleeding?" he asked.

"The flesh is sealed, but there will be a little tenderness for a day or two - nothing to worry about, and I wouldn't do this again until it heals completely, as it might tend to cause rather permanent marks."

"Gotcha."

As they left the room, Harvey looked back at the wings as he left and grinned. He was going to come back here!

# XXVII
# SECOND SKIN

"Great minds think alike, and fools never differ."

Monday, December 31st, 2012 Anno Domini

They finally arrived at the planet of their first assignment, so Harvey couldn't delay anymore. He hoped that he would be able to solve this planet's problems and move on.

The planet was called "Ambriel" by "Sagras" - leader of the Northern Alliance[13], and it was called "Giel" by "Saraiel" the leader of the Southern Alliance. Because of this, Harvey referred to it as 'Dichotomy'.

Note: Sagras uses the symbol of a bull and Saraiel uses the symbol of a ram on their standards.

After arriving at Dichotomy, they scanned the planet. The population, environment and natural resources were all devastated. They were locked in a war of attrition - neither side giving quarter. It seemed that the people were as polarized as they could get.

"Well, Pymander, do you want go down there with me and talk to those folk?"

"Certainly, but since we are entering a combat zone, might I suggest some precautions first."

"What do you have in mind?"

"Personal protection, primarily."

"Mmm!" This intrigued the captain, and they left for the armory.

When they returned to the bridge about thirty minutes later, Harvey looked more confident than ever. He leaned forward to whisper something to the android, who then approached Linda.

---

[13] *Not to be confused with the radio show of the same name, Saturdays 11AM to 3 PM CST on WWTC AM 1280 "The patriot" Minneapolis/St. Paul, and simulcast on www.am1280thepatriot.com (plug plug, nudge nudge wink wink. Will that do Mitch? May I have my cat back now?)*

Linda had not yet resumed her habit of standing by Harvey's side after all that nonsense with Aniyel, and he felt more nervous than ever in her presence, even though the air had been cleared. So they maintained their distance for now, and made certain that they were never alone in the same room together. This is why they began using the android as a 'go between'. Childish I know, but people can get that way when they're in love.

While preparations were going on, she took the opportunity and met up with the approaching android.

"Uh, Pymander."

"Yes?"

"May I just *borrow* you for a moment."

"Of course."

She led him away from the bridge to a lab she was used to working, as if pulling him aside to avoid 'prying ears.' Then she gave him a strange look.

"What can I do for you?" asked the puzzled machine.

"Well..." she started, as if pondering a long story, or something she wished to avoid but had to face none the less. "I don't want to sound like a wimp or anything, but since we're headed toward a potentially dangerous situation, I was wondering if there was anything on the ship like, supertech *armor*?"

"Certainly, as a matter of fact, the Captain has his already and instructed me to offer some to you as well, which I was just about to do."

"*Oh Really*?" she asked rhetorically, then she muttered to herself: "It seems that 'great minds think alike.'"

"'And fools never differ.'" offered Pymander.

This got a mischievous twinkle out of Linda's eyes. "Let's go!" she said playfully, glad to experiment further with the ships technology.

When they arrived in the armory, a moment later, the android continued; "What the ship offers for armor is a form of 'skin' that protects without being noticed."

"Un, '*skin*'? Surely you mean some sort of 'outer covering?'"

"No, I do mean skin as in 'second skin'. It covers you completely, and I do mean utterly and completely."

"That sounds awfully cumbersome."

She was thinking of the armor of centuries past made of metal, that covered completely, and she was only looking for something like an updated version of a bullet-proof vest, or a personal force field or *something* like that.

"It is completely unnoticeable by anyone I assure you, in fact the captain is wearing his now."

"I didn't see...oh... you don't mean...?" she said as the concept formed in her mind.

"Yes I do. Here you go." he said holding a small coin like object in his extended hand "All you need to do to activate it is to place it over your third eye."

"My *third* eye?" Obviously the android was malfunctioning. Humans only have two eyes!

The android, noticing her puzzled look, rolled his eyes and said: "Place it on your forehead to start the reaction."

"Why didn't you say so in the first place?"

"You are able to see the captain's badge of authority with your third eye, so I was assuming you were aware of it, just like he is."

She gave him an odd look, took the object and looked at it, turning it over and over in her hand. It was simply a small coin-like disk that was completely black with no markings of any kind. She puzzled over it for a moment or more before she asked, "How does it work and what does it do? I want you to tell me everything about it. I'm not doing this until I know what I'm getting myself into and whether I can get out of it."

There was a glint in the android's eye, which made her worry a little more, as he continued.

"Firstly, it is a single molecule, engineered to be partly living and intelligent - much like everything else on the ship, so it knows how to do it's job." She nodded in understanding. "Once you place it on your...forehead, it unfolds and covers you entirely inside and out..."

She cut him off: "What do you mean *inside*?"

215

"It can protect you from poisons that way."

"Ingested *and* inhaled?"

"Yes, it is an intelligent membrane and a virtually impenetrable molecular layer at the same time."

"'*Virtually* impenetrable'. You mean it *can* be breached?" Linda was used to ship's technology seeming to be infallible.

"A high-powered crossbow bolt, armor piercing bullet, guillotine or other such thing such as a large battle ax can pierce the armor. However, it will repair your injury and itself over time and try to keep you in one piece if it is breached."

"It can repair my *injuries*?" asked Linda as she held it up between two fingers as if a different angle would give her more insight as to it's construction.

"Somewhat. It can hold cuts together until they heal properly, but in the case of life-threatening internal injuries where it has to hold in large quantities of blood and major organs, but its efforts may only be a temporary measure."

He placed his hand on her shoulder reassuringly, "Don't worry, it takes quite a lot of kinetic energy to breach."

This seemed to reassure her somewhat.

He went on: "It protects from heat and cold as well and biological agents. Anything harmful to the body, including UV light, poison gasses and even binary poisons, are filtered out entirely."

"*Binary* poisons too?"

"Yes, as I said it is intelligent and knows it's job well."

"Huh." she said as she looked it over once again before flipping it like a coin and catching it with her other hand.

"So what *else* does it do?" she asked with a smirk on her face, knowing full well that the ship's equipment is multi functional.

"It also has the added benefit of allowing you to see telescopically, in other spectrums and hear in a wider range and see a virtual 'heads-up' Butator display of important information. To mention a few."

"Sounds like it needs a rather large manual."

"It comes with a built-in manual that works like the Penemue pills. Basically it works the way you expect it to, within reason meaning that it cannot ignore the laws of physics."

"Uh, now I remember my other concern... *can* it be *removed*?" she asked, worried that there was 'no going back', like with a tattoo.

"It can only be removed by you, but all of this is in the manual."

"What about the 'heads-up' display you mentioned, how does that work?"

"It sends an image into your visual cortex, much like the helmsman's chair does, and occasionally, to get your attention, it might display information directly into your eye."

"Why would it do need to get my attention?"

"It has automatic sensors, so it can alert you to the approach of dangers and will do what it has to get your attention if you ignore it."

"Like everything else on this ship. it sounds like a technological *miracle*! You know, as a scientist, I feel completely superfluous at times on this ship... but that doesn't matter." she said as she put her arm around him for a moment. Then she thought better of it, remembering the jokes the S*I*P*Es made about a high-tech vibrator. "So there is no surprising drawback to this thing?"

"The only thing worth worrying about is avoiding panic when it is unfolding on your skin."

"Why? Does it *hurt*?" she asked, suddenly concerned.

"No. But I might add that some have reported it as feeling a little snug at first, but that is purely psychosomatic as the armor adjusts itself to fit the subject perfectly."

"How many of these do you have?"

"Plenty of them, but only a few select people can wear this kind of device as it takes a 'quiet mind' to operate."

"Oh, like you mentioned earlier to Lt. Argent. So do all of the fun toys require such mental discipline to use?"

"Only the ones that read your surface thoughts. I might add that there is also 'less sophisticated' or more conventional armor for the others to use. I've already informed the Lt. and the rest of the S*I*P*Es."

"Understood." said Linda as she pondered 'taking the plunge'.

She knew she would need such a thing, and had never had any reason to doubt the ship's technology or the android. This whole thing seemed weird, but she couldn't shake the feeling that the android might be holding something back. The final logic was that Harvey has done it and the need was there, so she decided to try it out. After all, the android said that she could remove it. She glanced at her microscope on the table, but thought better of it. She didn't want to see the structure that was soon to be hugging her skin, as it might 'gross her out' and change her mind.

"So I just put it on my forehead?" she asked.

"Yes, then it holds itself there and automatically unfolds."

"Okay." she said with a little nervous apprehension. "Like this?."

She placed the disk on her forehead. It stayed there as she hesitantly let go of it. A moment later it appeared to spread. It looked like a black spot that grew. She grinned as it worked because the tomboy in her liked to play with all the fun toys as much as the boys did.

The dark patch grew and grew, it covered her face and her scalp and each individual hair. It covered the inside of her pores, and she almost panicked as it began to cover her eyes. It went clear there, and only there, to allow her to see. It continued to spread. She looked like a shiny black statue with almost glowing white eyes. It went into her lungs and coated them, it went into her mouth and coated her insides, and tickled where it came out to meet the other, shall we say 'side'. In short, it went *everywhere*. It looked and felt like a rubber fetishist's wildest dream. The moment it finished covering her, it appeared to vanish. She looked at her arms as it did this, and was amazed. Tempted to ask where it had vanished to she instead exclaimed: "You didn't tell me it felt like this!" She had never felt so healthy or 'stimulated' in her life! She danced around in circles, grasped the android's hands for a moment, said "Thank you!" and practically floated out the door.

The android shrugged, and said: "I hate it when they leave me on the far side of the ship." to himself as he headed for the door. Then the lack of something caught his eye. "Oh NO!" he exclaimed. There was a very

218

important sword missing, so rather than burden the captain with it now, he thought he had better tell him about it after the current situation was dealt with.

* * *

Just to be on the safe side, Harvey and Pymander took the first trip to the surface, leaving everyone else behind.

They managed to contact General Sagras by radio who invited them to the surface, and gave a location to land, which was toward the north side of the DMZ. Better known as 'no man's land'

They set down in a small wadi near the location they were given. This was to afford protection for the shuttle when it was on the ground and allow them to walk the short distance to the rendezvous point.

There was nobody waiting for them. It was a desolate rock-strewn open area with some 'high ground' nearby.

"I don't like this." said Pymander nervously.

"I agree, it seems like a great place for an ambush."

They looked around a bit more, contemplating leaving the scene to regroup aboard ship.

They were being observed through telescopic sights.

"Well?" demanded General Sagras.

"Only two of them sir."

"Good. They should be far enough from their craft to drop them both before they can get away. Carry-on."

The general waited with his arms folded.

The sniper focused in on Harvey, and hesitated.

"What's the matter soldier? Take your shot!"

"I thought I saw..."

"What?"

"Nothing sir. It must have been an optical illusion."

Then he took his shot.

"OW!" exclaimed Harvey as his head jerked to the side as if it had be smacked with a hammer.

219

"Are you okay sir?"

"What the hell was that?" he asked as he put his hand on his temple, where he had felt the blow.

Harvey had been shown specifications by his body armor but didn't recognize a pneumatically propelled projectile with a triangular cross-section.

"That was a *bullet* sir. Your body armor saved you from injury, but some blunt trauma remained, in order to let you know you've been attacked."

"That felt like a baseball bat! Do you think the armor could be adjusted to be a little more *gentle* about it?"

"Your reaction needs to be accurate, and keep in mind that the armor cannot ignore physics, besides this is not the time or place to discuss such things. Someone is trying to kill us." he replied as a bullet ripped past his head. "They seem to be going for head shots. I suggest that we *skidattle*."

The android sounded worried and began to crouch nervously. Afraid or not, he positioned himself between the shooter and the captain, but seemed torn between shielding the man and ducking for cover. This puzzled Harvey, as he thought that neither of them were in any real danger.

"You seem *afraid*." he said as yet another bullet whizzed past their heads.

"I am, a *little* actually." he replied nervously.

"But I thought you couldn't be 'killed'." he said, indicating quotation marks with his fingers as he said 'killed'.

"Well, not as *such*, because I'm not alive in the same was as you are sir, but I do dread head wounds..." His voice trailed off as a bullet hit him squarely in the temple, leaving a neat triangular hole accompanied by a muffled sound of shattering glass. His head twitched slightly with the impact, a single drop of red liquid rolled out of the hole and a blank expression came over his face. Harvey watched with some degree of horror as he thought he saw the 'life force' fade from the android's eyes as he dropped to his knees and then fell over, a small quantity of red liquid continued to leak from the wound. This was of course his coolant, but it seemed eerily like blood. Harvey took the hint and feigned a collapse.

"They're both down." said the sniper coolly, after he watch the android fall and Harvey duck down. He felt badly about it somehow.

"Excellent! Now we can retrieve their craft and glean all that high-technology from it." said the general. He was certain that Harvey's shuttle would yield the technological advantage he needed to turn the tide of the war.

# XXVIII
# MOT

"If Meshabber comes for electric sheep, does Azrael come for electric Bo-Peep?"

Harvey was stunned. It was like watching an old friend die. He fell to his knees, and looked over the android's 'lifeless' body, which then began to shudder. He thought to himself: 'Death quivers?' the shuddering began to accelerate so he stepped back as the android began to implode. Then he remembered that the android had an teleporter inside, and it could not transport the android 'in one piece'. He supposed that with the complete systems failure, the teleporter took over and transported the whole mess back to the ship.

He was partially correct. The system was set up to do this, as power failure alone could cause this effect, but it was to effect repairs on board ship and keep the technology out of the hands of possibly 'unfriendly forces'. After all, the android had just been totally disabled, and that usually meant a deliberate act with malicious intent. It was better to be safe than sorry.

In moments the entire android had disappeared into itself, as if it were folded or being sucked into a black hole. The teleporter folded into this effect as well, destroying itself in the process. This too was a technology they didn't want to fall into hostile hands. He thought at this point that he had best take the android's advice and 'skedaddle' back to the ship.

He didn't want to let those that were firing at him to know that he had survived, so he mostly crawled back to the shuttle even though the shooting had stopped as soon as he had ducked out of view of the highest peak when the android fell.

He had a score to settle over this one. "Some 'no-brainer!'" he muttered to himself as he climbed into the shuttle. "I hope I don't get any bruises from this." He had been hit several times and each felt like a pretty heavy blow. Despite this, he was more worried about whether or not his technological friend was as beyond repair as it seemed.

He went into the shuttle and engaged the invisibility cloak, to avoid being shot at by anti-aircraft guns, and then hurried back to the Ezrael.

Back on the ship, he learned that the bridge crew had been watching, and that the android had indeed been teleported to the robotics lab. The engineers were working on repairs. Most of the crew seemed to be upset at the developments. He didn't know if it was due to the android being damaged, him being shot or the lack of progress toward ending the war. In any event, his dander was up, so he decided to take more direct action.

"Linda?"

"Yes."

"Is there some way we can use the ship's power to stop the fighting?"

"As I understand it, the rule of thumb is; if you can think of it, the ship can do it."

"Good, I want you to be ready to erect a force field along the entire DMZ, on my signal."

"All of it? All around the whole planet?"

"Is there a problem with that?"

"No problem." she said with a smile, and returned to her console. She knew just what he was thinking.

Seconds later she said "Ready when you are."

He raised an eyebrow. "Communications, get me that jerk I talked to earlier!"

A few moments later, after the communications officer talked for a moment on his console, a voice came over the main speaker.

"This is General Sagras."

"General, this is Harvey Johnson again."

"How did you get away? My snipers assured me that they had dropped you."

"That was my assistant."

"Oh, I see."

"Why the deception?"

223

"Did you really expect me to believe that you are who you said you are?"

He looked to Linda and said "Now." She activated the control.

Just as Linda was about to activate the control, there was a nice-looking man with long 'salt and pepper' hair standing in the very place where the war initially broke out decades earlier. He chuckled softly as he bent over and pulled a rusty old iron knife out of the ground. It appeared to have been pushed in under the heel of a boot. In fact, *his* boot. He looked it over, flipped it and caught it. Then he smiled broadly and looked up at the Ezrael in orbit. "Go get 'em tiger!" he said to himself, and walked towards his shuttle, just as a force field of great intensity formed like a fence on the planet's equatorial region; the DMZ.

"I think you'll find the proof in your DMZ right now General." said Harvey.

There was a lengthy delay, as if the General was checking things out.

"My God! There's some sort of invisible barrier around the *whole* planet! *Now* I believe you! Please accept my sincerest apologies."

"Perhaps later. Right now, I am not going to let either of you fight, until you are ready to talk."

"Anything you want, you obviously have us outclassed." he said with a hint of fear in his voice.

"Can you help me reach General Saraiel too?"

"He can be reached on this frequency and is probably listening in right now."

"I am indeed Sagras, old friend." came a slightly sarcastic voice over the speaker. Apparently he was trying to sound as if he were not as rattled as his opposite number.

"Good, now that I have the attention of both of you, I want each of you in turn to talk to my people, no tricks, or I'll end this war for you in a way that you won't much like; understood Sagras?"

"Understood."

"And what about you, Saraiel?"

"I will comply."

"Good, now I will turn you over to a negotiator who will work out the details. I want you to meet my people in a day, to give you time to cool off and adjust to the idea that I won't tolerate battles breaking out while we're negotiating." His voice sounding harsh and impatient.

Many of the crew darted glances at him out of the corner of their eyes. They were made nervous by this because he sounded very angry, and they knew all too well what the ship's capabilities were.

He nodded to the Major, who was glad to speak to military men of another world. He then arranged for each to be visited by a delegation consisting of only two each, at the capitals of each faction. Now all Harvey had to do was to get four volunteers for a dangerous mission. He found he was not short of any. Linda and a S*I*P*E would visit the south, the Lt. and another S*I*P*E would visit the north.

The two generals wanted the emissaries to arrive unarmed, but Harvey would not have it. He didn't want his people to be vulnerable, so the S*I*P*Es were armed in full battle gear, hopefully it would impress the generals. After all, his home world was more advanced than this one, to be sure and the S*I*P*Es were the latest and greatest troops. They should be impressed.

Harvey looked around the bridge that was humming with activity. Everyone was working to make this happen. He thought to himself that it was funny how harmonious a group of people with a common goal can be. He cracked a smile. This made him feel better, and he calmed down.

Linda, having noticed that he was in a better mood now, thought she might take advantage of the opportunity. "Harvey..."

"Yes? What is it."

He didn't seem particularly miffed.

"What about tonight?"

He thought that she was referring to a date or something - which was something he would have remembered!

"What do you mean?" he finally asked.

"It's New Year's Eve!"

"You want a *party* at a time like this? Besides, I think it would be appropriate to start using the galactic calendar now."

She felt the pit of her stomach sink. There went her plans of kissing him at midnight! She was just going to have to try something else, that's all.

He noticed her looking at him with 'puppy-dog eyes', and it puzzled him.

"If you must, have the party. I've got more important things to do."

His voice almost cracked. He had always dreaded New Year's Eve. That midnight kiss was on his mind too, but in a different way - he thought that there was no one to share that moment with him. Sure, he secretly wished it could be Linda, but he didn't dare admit it, especially to himself.

"No, you're right. We shouldn't enjoy ourselves when we're in the middle of a world war."

She almost seemed angry with him, but he couldn't figure out why. He gave her a longing look, imagining for a moment what it might have been like to have an excuse to plant one on her. Then he headed off to the robotics lab, hoping for good news.

There wasn't any.

"What do you mean there's no way to fix him?"

"We don't even know how he was manufactured. You must understand, this technology is quite a bit ahead of ours."

"Well, keep *trying*." he muttered in frustration as he stormed out of the lab, frustrated again. He simply had to find a scientist that was 'up' on this kind of technology!

* * *

The Lt. was the first to return to the bridge. He informed Harvey that the Northern alliance was Socialist.

"Well," he said slowly, "It looks like we'll be supporting..."

"Don't you DARE support those Southern Communists!" snapped Linda who had just arrived at the door.

"...a completely different solution." He recovered with a sly grin and a twinkle in his eye.

"Those two systems are almost identical! How could they be fighting over *that*?" asked DeSoto.

"Remember our country's own civil war? They fought tooth and nail over fewer differences." said Harvey.

"You've got a point." he muttered, somewhat disappointedly.

"Both of you, conference room, now." said Harvey to Linda and the Lt.

They looked at each other, shrugged and followed Harvey into the conference room.

"So as I understand it," said the captain. "The North is Socialist and the south is Communist and neither will accept the other's system, even on pain of death. Is that about it?"

"That's right sir, that's what started the war." said the Lt. Linda nodded in agreement with the synopsis.

"Now, I have a question for you two to put to the respective leaders, and depending on the answers we get, I might just have a solution for them."

The two looked at each other again in puzzlement.

* * *

After checking with their contacts, Linda reported to Harvey: "The South answers 'yes.'"

"Good!"

The Lt. added: "The North also says 'yes'."

"Fantastic!" He thought for a moment. "You DID make it clear to them that this was not an order, just a question as to whether they were open to the possibility, right?"

"Right!" they said in chorus.

"They're as sick of the war as the other side, so they are willing to explore *any* solution short of compromising what they've been fighting for all this time." explained Linda.

The Lt. nodded in agreement. Apparently both sides felt the same way for the same reasons. Good. Common ground!

He turned to the Major. "Do you have all the books I requested?"

"Right here." he said as he patted a book bag that he had slung over his shoulder. "All translated and ready to go." He could scarcely hold back a chuckle. He really liked this solution.

"Great!" He turned to Linda and Argent.

"Well, have them come aboard, I think it's about time I gave them my 'sales pitch.'"

They looked at each other, still puzzled, they shrugged and headed for the bridge to communicate with the respective contacts once again.

* * *

The Communist and Socialist generals, their respective staff officers and other support personnel sat at opposite sides of the large negotiating table, glaring at each other until Harvey walked into the room. As soon as he appeared at the door, this juvenile behavior stopped and everyone stood at attention. What they didn't know was that he had been observing them on the monitors before he had entered the room, so they weren't fooling anyone.

"As you were." said Harvey dryly and they all sat down nervously.

He worried that their compliance was mainly due the fact that they recognized his power and authority to destroy their world. What he really wanted above all was *honesty*, and the long-term fate of their world depended on it. If they managed to fool him, they might return to the war after he left the system. That he would not forgive. So he planned on leaving a spy satellite behind to keep an eye on them, just in case. He was determined not to fail on his first official assignment.

"I assume we all know each other."

There was a general murmur of agreement.

"All right, let's get down to business then. Shall we?"

Harvey dug into the book bag he had brought into the room with him. He handed two identical sets of books to Linda and the Lt., who handed each set in turn to the respective leaders of the two factions. They looked them over and looked up to Harvey in puzzlement.

"They're two new systems that go hand-in-hand, called: 'capitalism and democracy'." he informed the puzzled generals. "I think you will find it can do wonders for you *and* your people. Oh, and I recommend a 'democratic republic' as the best form of government."

There was a collective "Oh!" followed by murmurs as they began to study the volumes.

\* \* \*

As the meeting was adjourned, Harvey cautioned them one more time "Now I want it to be perfectly clear; don't ever return to your old habits or I'll be back... and I won't be as *forgiving* as I was this time."

There was a murmur of happy agreement. After hearing his lecture on how these new systems worked, they were all for it.

"That was brilliant!" said Linda after the last had left for the shuttle bay.

He looked at her approving eyes and said: "You really think so?"

"You bet!"

"Well, let's hope that it works out for them. I'd hate to return to teach them a lesson about war and peace."

"Hmm" muttered the Lt. "I must admit, you stopped the war cold in it's tracks, and set them on a course they should rebuild their world. Well done sir!"

"What puzzles me is why neither of *us* thought of it." said Linda. "You'd think it was obvious."

"Well, I think you were a little too close to the problem, having met with the leaders and listened to how they see it as a choice between two systems. A third option didn't enter into it, so it didn't occur to you."

They both nodded in thoughtful agreement.

"So how did you see another option then?" asked Lt. Argent.

"Well, part of it was that I was able to stay a little detached. Besides, I've always believed that if there seems to be only two alternatives and neither is acceptable, then one should look for a third."

"I see. Now I'm only curious mind you, but in your view, is the glass half full or half empty?" asked Linda, thinking that she had cornered him with a question that had only two possible answers, as had been done with DeSoto earlier.

"The way I look at it..." he said as if pondering for a moment "...is that the *glass* is too *large*."

"Oooooh!" they exclaimed in chorus.

"Now let's see about getting that android fixed!"

Linda and the Lt. exchanged a look as Harvey headed for the door. It seemed to them that he was taking to this job like a fish to water.

# XXIX
## Flight of the Mizgitari

"I thought that they were angels,
but to my surprise,
we climbed aboard their star ship
and headed for the sky!"

As Harvey slept, he had nightmares about rescuing someone against insurmountable odds. In most of the dreams, he, or others, got 'killed' over and over. Each time though, he would awaken, realize it was just a dream, then fall back asleep. At one point he finally succeeded, then decided that enough was enough and headed for the bridge.

"How is everything?" asked Harvey as he entered the bridge.

The bridge was manned at 'night' by the few S*I*P*Es and as luck would have it, the Lt. was feeling a little unable to sleep that night too, so he was manning the helm.

"Nothing out of the ordinary sir."

Just then, as if to contradict him, an emergency signal was received and popped-up in the main 3D screen - an unusual event to be sure!

There appeared the bust of a young man with platinum blonde hair, and fair complexion, almost like that of an albino. He reacted as if pleasantly surprised, as the ship translated. The man had a slight, almost British accent. "Thank Apharoph! An Hyperachii ship! Boy! Am I glad to see you folks! I am desperately in need of rescue!"

The captain's Butator display informed him that he had asked the ship to locate a scientist that could not only repair the android, but would be willing to join the crew. Apparently this fellow matched those criteria.

Harvey nodded at the image and stepped forward to talk to the man; "Actually, this is the *flagship* - The Ezrael."

The young man let out a low whistle and exclaimed: "The ship of the sixth power? Even better!"

"Who are you?" asked Harvey.

The man bowed his head almost as if in shame.

"Forgive me Simkiel! I have arrogantly grown accustomed to my reputation proceeding me! My name is Raphael, the leading scientist of the planet Alberion. I am currently trapped in my research laboratory."

Harvey glanced at his Butator display again and the ship understood his request and displayed:

**'Simkiel' is a title some worlds hold for someone in your position. It means he knows you to be judge, jury and executioner of worlds. He seems to be fixated on the 'punishment' aspect of your position, hence the apprehension and show of respect. It's yet another manifestation of the 'Halo effect', which you can expect wherever you go.**

Harvey turned his attention back to the image before him and the ship turned the sound back on.

"You say you are *trapped*?"

"Yes, the masses have 'gone back to nature', and they've become militant about it! They have been systematically destroying all technology and *killing* all of the scientists. I'm the only one left on the planet that hasn't joined them, escaped or been killed - YET!" There was more than a sense of urgency in his voice.

"I see. What caused them to do this?"

"A book, entitled 'Loam in the lurch', written by a pseudo environmentalist."

It was *THAT* book again!

"Yes, we've dealt with the aftermath of that particular book before." He and the Lt. looked at each other and shrugged. It was indeed a small galaxy.

"They have me cornered, and the only thing keeping them at bay is a force field, but sooner or later they WILL breech it - and then of course, I'm *done for!*"

Harvey looked at the records officer, who reported "Thirty-seven planets in the galaxy that go by that name sir, seven with that language and only one with a famous scientist named Raphael."

"Well done, punch it up."

Another three-dimensional image emerged below the first. It was a representation of the entire galaxy, showing a route to his world, which seemed to be about as far away as it could be and still be in the same galaxy.

After studying it for a moment, and giving a nod to the helmsman Harvey said: "How long can you hold out?"

"My best guess is no more than a few days."

"No problem. We'll contact you again from orbit."

Raphael sighed with relief. "Thank you!"

His image vanished, and the image of the map stayed up. Harvey looked at the helmsman and said "Don't spare the horses. I'll be in my quarters going over the entries in the Grigorian[14] database, I want to know as much about this man as I can before we arrive." The Lt. nodded and began to work.

Harvey left the bridge to go over the information privately in his quarters before they arrived.

He read everything he could about this Raphael person. It seemed that this scientist was from a world where science was revered. He was the leading researcher and was widely respected throughout all of the worlds involved in traded with them. Alberion was a widely respected world in it's own right, and was considered the source of all of the best and latest technology and enlightenment. Indeed the people of that world were generally regarded as friendly, outgoing, open-minded and intelligent. Raphael was prominently mentioned.

However, recently there had begun a militant environmentalist movement based on that accursed book: 'Loam in the lurch.' This world was in the earlier stages, that of extinguishing most if not all science

---

[14] *Part of the Butator system that he had discovered had detailed knowledge about everyone. It contained details beyond even "big brother's" wildest dreams!*

and technology. Never mind that all forms of which on Alberion were 'environmentally friendly'. The wayward people of Alberion were not using much for technology with the exception of weapons: particularly a ground to air missile that could literally shoot down any atmospheric craft. A fact that disturbingly echoed his many demises in his recent nightmares. It seems that too much so-called 'open mindedness' can lead to problems. Indeed, anything taken to an extreme was not a good thing.

Although he did not approve of censorship, Harvey was now convinced that he would have to order the Mutuol Publishing company to have this book banned and recalled. It was causing far too much trouble and sorrow, since it had already destroyed at least two worlds!

Raphael was just what they needed to repair the android not to mention join the crew, and it seemed on the surface like a simple rescue. 'Caution' was going to be the operative word in this case because this paralleled his nightmares from a few hours earlier and he didn't like the look of it. Not one bit.

When they arrived, the communications device lit up again with the image of Raphael.

"Wow! That was FAST!"

"We aim to please." replied Harvey with a smile.

They had indeed 'spared no horses' in getting there, in order to impress Raphael, and it had worked. After all, it's not every ship in the galaxy that can cover 97,522 light years in forty-five minutes flat - without I might add, leaving 'second gear' though this was no Nash Rambler.

Navigating at such speed was beyond tricky, is was downright foolhardy. If it weren't for the self-preservation instinct of the ship itself, they might have crashed into something. As stated earlier, such speeds were usually reserved for the massive void between galaxies and superclusters. Luckily, the Lt. realized it was better to leave the plane of the galaxy, 'kick it down' as he would say, and get back into the galaxy once they were close to the destination.

"Now that we're here, we can get on with the business of rescuing you."

"Well, unless you have an invisible shuttle, I think we're stuck."

"Can you construct a teleportation portal?"

"No, I don't have the materials handy for anything like that, not even a quantum type."

"We can try sending down a shuttle under remote control with a portal inside - so you can bring up your belongings."

"You can TRY, but I assure you they WILL shoot at it. They feel that they answer to a higher authority now, the majority of them might not listen to you even if they recognize you for who and what you are."

"Sit tight. We'll get back to you when we think of something."

Harvey thought about it for a moment, it was just like on Loam itself. These people were the fanatics!

"Uh, 'teleportation portal?'" asked the Chief with his eyebrows raised.

"Yeah, they're pretty cool. I'll show you how they work."

"Thanks. But how did you..."

"The android showed me before he..."

"Enough said."

In the ship's science lab, Harvey, Linda and the Chief engineer were looking -over something that resembled a large globe, complete with moveable metal rings around the outer surface.

"So this is a *teleporter* is it?" asked the Chief as he looked at the sphere.

"How does it work?" asked Linda.

"With that one, you move the two rings to indicate a destination on the planet."

"So there is no mechanism on the other end?" asked the Chief.

"If there isn't one, you don't go there, otherwise, we could send a teleporter to Raphael."

"Why is it spherical?" asked Linda. "It's starting to look like a theme."

"I know what you mean. Well, it has to do with the event horizon."

"That's IT!" exclaimed the wide-eyed Chief engineer.

"Huh?" asked Linda.

"Don't you get it! That's what's been wrong with *our* research on this sort of thing!"

"Wouldn't a three-dimensional event horizon take even more energy?" she asked.

"Not necessarily. Look at it this way, how much energy would it take to squeeze you through a one-dimensional door?"

"Ewww! That wouldn't be too healthy for me either."

"Exactly, which explains the mess we get when we send someone through one of ours It would take a ton of energy, just like the calculations show, but if you encompass every dimension of the interfacing plane, then all you have to do is rotate it into the next higher dimension, and presto! A door. I don't know why it didn't occur to me earlier!"

"Ahhh! Skipping dimensions takes a lot more energy!" she exclaimed, as the light bulb went on in her mind too.

"I thought that everyone knew that a two dimensional surface like a wall, takes a two-dimensional door rotated into the third to breach it, and to get through three-dimensional space, you need a three-dimensional door to rotate into the forth to breach that." stated Harvey like it was old news to him.

They both stared at him.

"How long have you known *that*?" insisted the Chief.

"For decades."

"For...Decades or for a duration of FOUR decades?"

"I have known for about thirty years to be precise." Then he thought about it for a moment. "How *old* do I look to you?"

"How did *you* figure it out?" asked the Chief, shrugging-off the age question.

"My first clue was the power requirements, I took it that nature was saying that there was a better way."

"Where were you when we were doing research on this?"

"Someplace else evidently. You mean to tell me you were trying it with a two-dimensional event horizon... like in the book?"

"Yeah. We were."

"It's no wonder you failed."

"As far as I know, the research was ongoing, but I left the project because we were getting nowhere fast, and they began monkeying around with the power curves and negative matter. Dangerous stuff." He had a far-off look in his eyes, the he asked: "So, show me how this works?"

"It's pretty simple, you adjust the rings here to indicate a destination on the globe, and the nearest teleporter's location lights up. To activate you press the foot pedal here." He was pointing at a depression on the floor stand. The Chief looked at it.

"You mean to tell me that even with all this hyper-tech around here there has to be a mechanism at *each* end?"

"Ever been through a tunnel with only *one* opening?"

"Yeah, it's called a cave. I understand, but isn't that defeating the purpose if you have to already have a mechanism at the other end? I mean you've already found a way to get there?"

"What about the quantum method?" interjected Linda. "All you have to do is trade space with another location."

Both the Chief and Linda stared at Harvey.

"Well, the way the android explained it to me is that it is frowned upon."

"How so?" she asked.

"What I was told is that from a standpoint we cannot observe, it mess up the fabric of the universe, like turning a DaVinci into a Picasso."

"Are you saying the fabric of the universe is a work of art?"

"That's what I am told. Besides, there is a full time crew called 'Adoil' out there that fixes those 'glitches'. Think of it as environmental damage to the fabric of the universe itself, and I'd prefer not to add to their workload. Besides, do that too much and the universe itself could lose some cohesion and tear."

"That sounds staggeringly dangerous!" said the Chief.

"So are we *forbidden* to use it?" said Linda.

"No, but it isn't going to win us any twinky points with the boss if we do. But, if we let the subject step out of the area they appear in and quickly re-trade spaces, then it should repair the fabric."

"Okay. So that's why we don't send Raphael a regular teleporter that way." said the Chief.

"Right. It would be too heavy for him to move out of the way. Besides, I don't know how to do it even if I wanted to. It's one of those pieces of equipment that you need to know how to operate to get it to work. Probably because they don't want you doing it much. But, in an emergency, I am told it may be used."

After fiddling with the control rings the Chief noticed something. "This thing looks like it only works on the same planet."

"There are interstellar models. They refer to specific teleporters, not locations."

"What do those look like."

"Like this one over here." Harvey showed them to a larger sphere that resembled a massive ping-pong ball. "After he was damaged, the android folded into himself through the smaller teleporter he had inside his chest, and appeared through this one."

They stood there and looked up at it. You could ride an elephant through that thing." said the Chief.

"In fact, I am told that people have done that - on occasion."

"So how did he teleport himself through a smaller one and not leave it behind?" asked Linda.

"The Butator tells me that it is like folding a tunnel in on itself, it closes like a sock or cave, then collapses to the destination, destroying the sending unit."

"Why not leave the sending unit where it was?"

"To keep it out of the hands of the enemy. Even though it is smaller in size, they could still use it to send us their weapon of choice; an antimatter bomb."

"Oh."

"So how do these interstellar models work?"

"The Butator establishes a connection, and the wormhole is opened. You might recognize the event horizon, it's in almost every doorway in the ship."

"Hold the phone! If the doors work like that, and they have a two-dimensional event horizon..." exclaimed Linda.

"If you examine them closely, you'll see that they are actually curve, ever so slightly. Apparently the doorways are all side by side on the inside edge of a massive teleporter the size of the ship, and the fabric of the ship is a wonder of inter-dimensional engineering. That's why it's bigger inside than outside."

"What about the long corridors?"

"Straight lines across the inside of the sphere to a door on the other side."

"But, isn't inside beyond the event horizon?"

"Crossing the event horizon is what sends you, inside the sphere is usable space."

"My head is starting to spin."

"You think that's bad! He told me that the ship has no exact location."

"Ouch!"

"Parts of it are scattered all over the universe."

"Okay, I have a migraine."

"Well, anyway, these are the basic units; planetary and interstellar. In keeping with that, some of the doors on the ship actually send you to different worlds. Apparently you can teleport to many places the ship has been in the past, as long as it left one of these babies behind."

"Really? Like were?"

"A number of safe worlds that Callicrates visited. Apparently, he allowed the ship to inter-dimensionally interface with some of them. Walking through a doorway gets you to another doorway that is on that world. That's probably where the DMZ that the S*I*P*Es ran into came from. Also he left interstellar spheres all over the galaxy in his search for Earth."

"Darn, I was wondering if you would find the one to our Earth. No such luck huh?" said Linda

"Sorry. There was one in Nineveh Iraq, but it does not seem to be working right now. in fact, that particular one seems to have been non-functional for several millennia."

"Iraq?"

"Of all places."

They thought about it for a while.

"We can gather resources from any of those worlds, and we can all vacation on different worlds at once if we like."

"Why would he want to leave some of those doors behind on some worlds?"

"I don't know, like one is a world of mostly sunny beaches with no UV, and it never gets too hot or cold... you know, perfect. I don't know who would want to visit that place on their off time without the bother of taking the ship there." he said sarcastically.

"Okay, I get it."

The Chief approached Harvey, crossed his arms and turned his head away from Linda and spoke softly so as to not let her hear: "How do I get there?"

"The usual way." Harvey whispered back.

Linda smirked. She had very good hearing.

"What other toys do you have here?" asked Linda as she looked around the warehouse-sized room full of scientific equipment of every possible description.

"Lots, apparently. Look at all this stuff! The android was our only way left of understanding the gadgetry we have here, but this Raphael character should be able to explain a lot of it too. Besides, he just might be able to repair Pymander."

"You think?" asked the Chief.

"It couldn't hurt to give him a shot at it."

"Suits me!" said the Chief, "Lets get rescuing!" He couldn't wait to play with all that equipment and gadgetry.

They returned to the bridge to see what they could do about the situation.

"What have you tried so far Lt.?" asked the Captain.

"Well, we sent a remote shuttle."

"And...?"

"They shot it down."

"Did you try one with an armored hull?"

"It was! Our toughest one too! They used some short of shoulder-launch missile that apparently penetrates *anything*."

"What about turning it invisible?"

"They must have some sort of scanner, so they spotted it. Trust me, we took all *possible* precautions."

"What about stunning the crowd like we did on Loam?"

"Thought of that first thing, and the Butator insisted that the crowd is so thick this time that there'd be a 30% casualty rate with them falling on each other, and I though that was unacceptable."

"You're right. We don't want to kill any of them." said Harvey, deep in thought over just how to rescue Raphael. He looked up at the image of Raphael on the main screen.

"Do you think you can hold on for a couple of hours? I have an idea."

Raphael nodded and ended his transmission. He seemed remarkably mature for his years.

"Linda, Lt. Argent, Chief! I want to show you something else the android showed me."

They exchanged puzzled glances and left the bridge with him.

Harvey went with his gut feeling that the nightmares he had about this situation were a guide of some kind. Maybe his subconscious was working about a way to do this, or maybe the ship was talking to him in his sleep, helping him. Either way, his plan was based on the successful rescue in his dream and he thought it was worth a try.

\* \* \*

Inside a shuttle on their way to the surface, the Lt. said: "This isn't going to work!"

"It's a little too late for *that*, isn't it soldier?" asked Linda.

He shrugged, then muttered: "Craziest damn thing I was ever asked to do."

She had had the same thought, but at the same time knew that they actually did stand a good chance. She looked over at Harvey who was standing within earshot, grinning at her. She smiled knowingly back at him. She loved the idea, it *would* work, she was sure of it!

The crowd was trying yet another battering ram to break down a door that had been fused into the force field by Raphael. He was no dummy. This was a great tactic to let the masses think that the door was simply very well secured, and since it was made from materials widely known to be very tough, they did not learn too quickly that they were dealing with a force field and not just a strong door. Cooler heads might have suggested that they break-down the less-sturdy brick walls, but thankfully there were none there to be had. Funny how mobs are not that smart, but that's probably a good thing.

They were shouting and cheering as the door was bashed again and again with the ram, and even though they were not getting anywhere, they seemed happy with the attempt in and of itself. At least it kept them occupied for the time being.

The shouting and cheering went on and on and until a sky scout spotted something in the distance through his binoculars: "Look!" was all he could say as he pointed at the specks in the sky. The mob looked and gasped in unison and then fell to silence. High above, but not so high as to not be seen, there was a small flock of what appeared to be large birds flying overhead.

Gladrina appeared as if out of nowhere and "buzzed" the crowd. She hovered above them, glowed and streaked off into the sky in the direction of the others that were approaching on the wing. This had exactly the desired effect.

Harvey had noticed something in the information from the Penemue pills, that the others had ignored, which was that this culture was particularly fixated on angels. Hence the plan.

The crowd stopped battering the door and looked on in awe and the angelic figures. They didn't notice that one was carrying a small but usable teleportation orb.

"They seem to be buying it!" exclaimed Linda.

"I knew this would work!" shouted the Lt. with a wide grin and a wink.

"Remember, we're not impersonating angels, we're just going flying and letting them interpret this any way they want." Harvey had said.

"Nice touch sending Gladrina to buzz the crowd." said the Lt.

"You just think she's HOT!" exclaimed Linda. "Any excuse to see her... form!"

"You got that right little lady!" said the Lt. with a big grin.

"Gerrrr..."

They flew right over to the tower and were not bothered at all. The crowd believed that they were avenging angels that were going to give Raphael his comeuppance - *exactly* according to plan.

"Brilliant!" exclaimed Raphael as they arrived. "Just brilliant!"

"The eagle has landed!" exclaimed the Lt. as he landed gingerly on the balcony. Everyone but Gladrina and Raphael glared at him for that.

"What?" said the Lt., shrugging his shoulders as he noticed the icy stares. "Nobody got a sense of humor? Sheesh!"

Harvey approached Raphael; "We'd best get you and your equipment out of here." he said as he motioned for the Lt. to put the teleporter down and activate it, which immediately turned from a opaque white to a dark black and seemed to lose its surface to the blackness of it.

"It's the smallest one we had." said the Lt. shrugging. "I couldn't carry a bigger one anyway."

"It's still too big for me to move, and I don't know if everything will fit through it."

Under Raphael's direction, they began dropping his equipment into the sphere. The items seemed to fall into an endless chasm, getting smaller and smaller as they 'fell'. The Lt. was puzzled by this and even tried looking under the sphere. All he got was the same view, no matter what angle he looked at the sphere.

"Hey, that's pretty neat!" he said to Raphael who was watching him.

"That's the way they work." he said dryly not knowing what to think since it seemed like it was the first time the Lt. had ever seen one in action, which it was.

"Now all I have to do is program the tower to self-destruct." said Raphael, "There still is some unremovable equipment I don't want them getting."

"You're not planning on anyone getting *hurt*, are you?" asked Harvey sternly.

"Oh no no no! Despite the fact that they want to kill me, they're still my people. I'm setting the disintegrator. The tower will just peacefully dissolve into the atoms, and drift off into oblivion. It won't harm a soul. I promise."

"How does that work?" asked the Lt. who had images of a really cool gun.

"It, uh, takes the spin off the electrons, turning them into harmless beta particles leaving the atoms behind with no immediate way of binding into chemicals... as everyone *knows*." This man must have been recently rescued from a primitive world, he thought. It's no wonder they glared at him over the eagle reference.

"Oh, I've seen one of those!" he said remembering Loam. Talk about 'parallel development'!

"Okay then!" said Harvey, sensing Raphael's puzzlement. "Gladrina."

She was the only one strong enough to carry Raphael, so she got the duty.

He looked at her and was immediately captivated. No surprise there.

"Okay, I'm going to carry you away, because that's what the crowd expects. We don't want them shooting at us if we leave without you now, do we?" she said to him.

"Anything you say!" he said with a sigh.

"I thought you took the antidote we told you how to make!" said Linda.

"I did." he replied without looking at Linda.

"I'd hate to see what he would be like *without* it!" she muttered to himself.

"Now dear, I'm afraid that when we fly out of here, you need to kick and scream as if you were terrified. Can you do that for me?" she asked sweetly.

"Even though I live and work in a tower, I'm actually terrified of heights... so there won't be much acting involved."

"Don't worry then, I won't let you fall."

"Okay. I trust you." he said slowly as she put her arms around his waist from behind and launched off the balcony into the air. The others followed.

The crowd below was treated to a show. Their sworn enemy, the last and most vile of all scientists, was being carried off by avenging angels. They flew over the mountains into the nearby valley where their shuttle had waiting. Once it was clear that he was gone the mob began to disburse, and then the tower dissolved, harming none - as promised. This pleased Harvey, as it told him that Raphael could be trusted. It also pleased the crowd, re-enforcing their new found beliefs, perhaps causing more damage in the long run.

# XXX
# BACKUP

"Button? Button? Who's got the button?"

**Johnson's Journal;**

The latest addition to the crew is named: Raphael Elroy Mergatroid. He's a famous scientist, so he should prove to be an outstanding asset. He elected to take a permanent language pill to learn English which was more practical than asking the rest of the crew to permanently learn his language.

I recruited him to repair and maintain the android, to be his physician of sorts, and to explain to the crew how to use the rest of this wonderful technology we find ourselves surrounded by.

Since he is rather well known, and I wish to keep as low a profile as I can when evaluating various places, I asked him if I can call him by his middle name. He agreed for the same reasons. What can I say? He *looks* like an 'Elroy'.

Once we were back on board the ship, I asked him how he wanted me to deal with the militant environmentalists below. This was of course a test.

He replied that we might leave them alone to choose their own fate; which probably meant mass suicide, but I allowed it... for now. If they follow the 'Loam pattern' it will be a year or so before they realize that they emit 'greenhouse gasses' just by breathing, and then decide to commit mass suicide to 'save their planet'.

There is time to save this world from such horrors. Besides, it is my hope that they will come to their senses on their own.

Well, One can hope.

[Ship, remind me when it is time to save Alberion.]

Harvey was having fun with the ship's ability to write down what he said, as well as to understand his verbal and mental commands. Keeping a journal seemed to be the thing to do. After all, he had read some of the entries made by Callicrates, and found them helpful. Although they were readily available, he wasn't ready to experience life *as* Callicrates from the thought records he left behind. Perhaps some day he might give it a try, but not today. Instead, it was time to see what progress was being made if any, in repairing the android.

Elroy looked over the jumbled mess, and shook his head. "There just isn't *anything* I can *do* with this." he said to the expectant captain.

"Why not?" asked Harvey, almost indignantly.

"There simply isn't any way to repair this." indicating the pile of shattered crystals, a lot of which seemed to be sand or fine dust. "Even if they could be fitted back together, they could not function again, as it is obviously optical and wavelengths of light are very short. The precision necessary to repair it is simply *not* possible, even with an army of nanobots. I mean, they wouldn't know how to fit each piece together. Besides, even if it *were* possible, it would take decades to accomplish. Although we were rather advanced on my world, we just never managed to develop anything like this, let alone any *true* androids."

"But I thought you already *had* androids on your world."

"Those were simply robots, with *very* sophisticated programming I might add, but they were still merely simulations of human beings. Androids are much more sophisticated. You might as well compare an ox cart to this ship."

"But don't you have enough parts to construct a new one?", indicating the plethora of spare parts occupying the room. It almost looked like a mannequin warehouse. There were indeed enough parts to build a veritable army of androids.

"It's not simply a matter of body parts, his *brain* has been destroyed. Even if it could be replaced, his mind and memories would still be gone. That's the one piece of technology that has escaped all who have ever attempted it."

Harvey still looked puzzled, recalling the earlier conversations the engineers had had with the android about this very subject, so Elroy continued with the explanation.

"The sheer computing power needed to duplicate a human brain well, *boggles the mind*. You could cover a planet with quantum computers and still not get there. I don't know of any way it could be done, let alone in a manageable size like a brain. Frankly, I don't know how this jumble of crystals even functioned in the first place. So even if I *could* obtain a replacement, *and* it worked, his mind would still be missing. It would have to start from scratch, just like a baby or a clone." Elroy had a distant look on his face, obviously he had pondered these very problems before, and to no avail.

"What do you mean, 'even if it could be replaced?' Isn't the *spare* any good?"

Elroy looked excited and startled at the same time.

"*Whu..What* spare?" he said in surprise, with a glimmer of hope in his eyes.

Harvey indicated the cabinet android had stored it in, when they first met. "It's in there. He referred to it as his 'spare brain'."

Elroy practically leaped to the cabinet and opened it enthusiastically.

"Steady, it's a little fragile." cautioned Harvey.

"You don't have to tell *me* that." he muttered with a grin as he gently removed it from it's stand in the cabinet and began to look it over.

"This is magnificent!"

"Will it *do*?" asked Harvey, almost facetiously.

"Perrrrrfectly." answered Elroy almost as if in a trance. Then he snapped out of it, because he had noticed something. "Funny, it seems to already be *functioning*."

"Well, yes, I had noticed those 'spaghetti-web' patterns of light before." Elroy got a glint in his eyes over this. Obviously the android was retrievable after all. Harvey continued: "He had intended to make his regular backup when we first met, right here actually. I was standing right there as you are, looking with wonder at those patterns. When I inquired about them, he rather quaintly called them 'dreams'." Harvey smiled broadly, appreciating what Elroy was going through.

Elroy carefully placed the spare brain on a stand on the workbench. "Do you know how often he backed up his mind?"

"I have no idea."

"That may be too bad."

"What do you mean?"

"Well... I'd say he can be brought back with this obviously, but I'm afraid he won't have any memory or knowledge that postdates the last backup. In fact, he may not even know you at all."

Harvey looked a little disappointed over this. "Do what you can." he said and left the room. After this exchange, he knew how the android must have felt when they had similar question and answer sessions. Actually, this explained a lot.

Elroy mulled over the spare brain, using various instruments to scan it. He looked very content as he worked. This ship was going to teach him a lot.

# XXXI
# ZACHRIEL

"Pardon me, but your hand is in my chest."

Elroy sent for Harvey, who dropped everything immediately. He wanted to be there for the new android's activation.

"Well, everything is in place, and all I have to do now is activate the power relay." said Elroy. Then he looked at Harvey rather sternly. "Remember, he won't remember *anything* after his last backup. Whenever that was. In fact, it may be possible that he does not even know you at all. So be prepared."

Harvey nodded. With that, Elroy reached into the android's chest cavity, and connected the power relay. There was a full body twitch, and the android's eyes opened, looked down at the arm, buried in his chest and then into Elroy's eyes.

"Uh oh!" exclaimed the android. "I got *killed*, didn't I?"

"How could you possibly know *THAT*?" The scientist demanded indignantly.

"Three things tipped me off." he replied. "First, I know this is my spare brain, which would only be used in such a case. Second, my last memory is making a backup[15] copy of my mind in case just such a thing would happen down on Dichotomy and third, your hand in my chest next to my main power relay as if you just connected it."

"Oh." said Elroy as he realized that his arm was still in the android's chest, and slowly pulled it out. "Sorry." he muttered with his head down.

"He's back!" said Harvey. "Pymander, this is Raphael Elroy Mergatroid, your new physician."

---

[15] *Since he made this backup just before going to the armory with Harvey, he was unable to remember that he had discovered that Morax had taken a particular sword. A fact he intended to inform the captain of later, but now he had no memory of that important discovery.*

"Pleased to meet you Raphael." said the android to Elroy, as he extended his hand for a handshake.

"Call me Elroy." he said as he shook the machine's hand.

"Pymander." he replied. "First things first. Given the situation, I'd best make another backup!"

"I'd like to observe that process if you don't mind."

"Not at all, in fact I'll explain everything to you, after all, if you're going to be my physician, you'll have to know everything about how I'm put together." Elroy beamed at this. Not only was this android his dream machine, but it was perfectly willing to explain it's workings to him. Oh joy! Oh Bliss!

"It's good to have you back." said the relieved captain as he slapped the android on the back.

"It's good to *be* back sir. Were you successful?"

"Yes indeed."

"Wonderful!"

Then he handed the machine a small, short piece of lead with a triangular profile and a blunted point at one end. "A little souvenir for you."

"It that what killed me?" asked the machine.

"Indeed."

The android nodded solemnly as he turned the slightly deformed bullet over and over in his hands.

"Well, I'll leave you two to it!" said Harvey almost joyfully, and he headed for the bridge to research their next mission.

# XXXII
# Meeting of the minds

"I've lost my mind!"

"Think. Where did you have it last?"

"Okay, so the ship made a new backup brain in a matter of hours, grown from a single crystal the size of a grain of sand. That's hard enough to believe, but a backup taking only a millisecond? That's just too much! How much data in how long?"

"It's a *parallel* process." said the android.

"I don't care how massively parallel it is! It should still take a while."

"It's not massively parallel, it's *totally* parallel; like a photograph."

"The backup right, not the brain?"

"Yes. The brain is a collections of neurons, just like yours. So it's incredibly parallel."

"I looked at the design and so far, it looks like there are not enough neurons - by several orders of magnitude I might add - to do the job. How do you explain that?"

"As you know, optics are able to operate at different wavelengths of light simultaneously without interfacing with each other, thus sharing circuitry and in effect multiplying the number of circuits, in this case neurons, by the number of distinct wavelengths used."

"Wow! That's brilliant! How many wavelengths do you use?"

"All of them, from the bottom of IR to the upper end of UV. Literally millions."

"THAT would do it! So your engrams are made up of doped pathways between neurons?"

"Exactly."

"But, light is faster than ions, so how do you avoid schizophrenia?"

"There are photochemical regulators at each synaptic gap. Just as water slows light, the interface slows it much more, making me think at a normal human rate."

"Wow! But how does it know what connections to make and what ones not to? It's always been a mystery: how a natural brain knows where to connect and where not to."

"A normal brain starts with a cloud of neurons and the patterns of engrams form the mind. The unused connections atrophy and all but disappear."

"Yes, we know that, our science indicates that the neurons somehow *know* how to form a mind."

"You're looking at the question too closely."

Elroy gave him a blank look.

"*sigh* Have you ever looked closely at a painting?"

"Yes, of course I have." he said, not understanding where the android was going with this.

"What do you look at? The patterns of paint or the fibers in the canvas?"

"The paint of course. It's *on* the canvas."

"Just as the mind is *on* the neurons, in the form of engrams instead of paint."

"So... it doesn't matter what canvas it is on, or how it aligns with the fibers of the canvas, but rather how the pigments relate to *each other*, it's still the same picture!"

"Exactly."

"I get it! For the first time in my life I get it! And it's so simple when we thought it was so complicated!"

"Humans often do that to themselves."

"You mean make things out to be more complicated than they really are?"

"Indeed, however here is where I think you encountered difficulty; In my *particular* case, the mind and brain *are* one and the same. There are no unnecessary or dangerous neuro-pathways available."

"A *hardwired* mind?"

"Exactly. But not all available neuro pathways are used at once, allowing for change."

"What about the backups then?"

"Memories, and new engrams. That's all."

"Hmm, let me get this straight; we've always believed that human brains work the way yours actually does, and human brains are actually very flexible in construction and are mostly independent of the distribution of the neurons. Is that about right?"

"That's about the size of it."

"So... since you claim that you are incapable of going insane or deliberately harming a Human, the only way that could be achieved is if the neuro-pathways required for such behavior don't physically exist..." His voice trailed off as if here were in deep thought. "...so you mind *had* to be hardwired for that to be possible."

"That's exactly right."

"But the intellect required to do that would be..."

"Awesome?"

"Yes!"

"It's really not that difficult - it's like in the brain of a dog. He knows to behave like a dog instead of a fish, and in the same way a fish knows how to be a fish. They are all hardwired within certain parameters. Mine is just hardwired *almost all* the way. Humans by the way are hardly hardwired at all. That helps you have free will."

"So if the enemy got hold of you and duplicated your brain..."

"They'd just get a duplicate of me - which would be useless to them."

"So what about all the security measures?"

"Just to fake them out. Besides, it might be dangerous for them to know of the concept of how my brain works in the first place."

"Brilliant!"

"And the 'blank' brains?" asked Elroy as he indicated a secret cache of 'less-sophisticated', blank brains for a different class of android.

"Those are *somewhat* dangerous because they are truly blank, and can be 'brought-up' under any value system, or worse yet, have the engramatic patterns of a living being transferred to them, thus effecting a form of immortality."

"I know a few Extropians that would go nuts over an android like that."

"Indeed, some have."

This made Elroy raise an eyebrow.

"So if the adversary's forces got hold of these android brains, they could manufacture an entire army... of killer androids!"

"Yes, but they'd be the same as a living army, but slower, with less endurance and less strength. They'd be much better off sticking with normal life forms."

"Hmmmmm."

"That's all very well and good, but I still have a problem." said Elroy.

"Which is?"

"At the center of each neuron of a Human brain is what appears to be a very powerful quantum computer."

"Go on."

"They seem to contain a form of pure energy, and when someone is past the 'point of no return', the energy dissipates."

"Do you know what a soul is?"

Guardedly, he answered. "Well, our science has measured it as form of energy that upon death, leaves the body and it comes to three quarters of an ounce." He thought for a moment "You don't mean...?"

"Almost." Elroy breathed a sigh of relief. "You see, there are various parts of a soul, and one part is responsible for intellect, creativity, humor and intuition. Those sort of things."

"Okay."

"Well, that part that is responsible for those things, resides inside the center of those tiny quantum computers as you call them, and that is where true intelligence comes from. It is the true center of intelligence, and the brain is an interface to the physical world."

"Hang on! You're telling me *you* have a soul? Just like I do?"

"I can't get anything past you, can I?"

"But.... but..."

"I'm merely a *machine*?"

"No offense, but how can that be?"

"You forget who designed me. Besides, humans are *organic* machines."

"Then doesn't that make you alive?"

"Yes, in a manner of speaking."

"You've been alive and in this form for tens of thousands of years though."

"Millions actually, but who's counting, and your problem with that is?"

"How do you avoid going *nuts*?" The android raised an eyebrow, which got Elroy thinking about it for a moment..."Oh yeah! Yet another reason for the design."

The android patted Elroy's shoulder reassuringly.

"So what manner of being *are* you?"

"I am one of the first ones. A prototype if you will, of all beings. We are called 'Favashi'."

"Ohhhh, I've heard of you! In legends..." He pondered it for a moment, then added: "I also heard that the Favashi were all female."

"Most of us are, and I am one of the few males."

"That could be a lot of fun, you know what I mean?" he said nudging the android with his elbow.

"After the first thousand years or so, *that* loses it's allure."

"Sorry to hear that."

"Not for me, for the females."

"Now I'm doubly sorry."

"I *told* you, we are *prototypes*!"

They both had a good laugh at that, but the android wound up with a worried look on his face. It had been a long time since he had been reminded of his little predicament.

"So, what is your first name?"

He signed and said "Zagzagel." in a defeatist tone.

"Giusendteight. Now I know why you go by 'Pymander'. "But, what was the *first* name you ever had?"

"I have been called that since my initial creation billions of years ago."

"Is this is the first time you ever 'died'?"

"As a machine, yes."

"You've had *other* forms?"

"Initially, and at my core I am still an energy-based life form, and as such not subject to death as you understand it."

Elroy looked at the android in wonder.

"Then I was given a physical body, but it wore out, and I grew a new one, over and over, sometimes taking an abandoned one - to live out its natural life and make a positive difference in that world. After a few billion years of this, the creator had a new purpose for me, so this machine form was designed to hold my intellect, where I have remained ever since. Had you not repaired me, I might have eventually grown a new, organic body."

Elroy stared in wonder. This machine was one of the oldest, and possibly *wisest* beings in the universe, and they were having a conversation. After a long silence, he got back to asking about how the machine's body worked.

"Tell me, how is the brain grown from a single grain of sand?"

"Put just the right 'spin' on something and a lot can be accomplished with a little. It is the nature of that particular crystal to grow into a brain."

"But the intellect required..."

"Are we going down that road again? He gets his jollies from the maximum returns from the minimum effort."

"Some have argued that his side is less powerful because of his frugal use of power."

"Ever play darts?"

"Yes."

"Ever walk up to the board and put a dart in the double bull's-eye?"

"Well, yes I have actually."

"Wasn't as good, was it?"

"You mean?"

"Exactly."

He didn't want to contemplate all of what meant so he got back on track.

"So, what are these muscle fibers made of? I haven't scanned them yet."

"Roughly half titanium, half nickel and a few trace elements."

"OH! We've made them before, they contract well, but couldn't get them to release quickly enough to be used for muscles. So how do you get them to work properly?"

"Instead of strands, they're tubes and I run coolant through them to let them relax."

"And the resulting heat?"

"Is dissipated through the skin and breathing, just like yours is."

"Oh, so that takes care of body heat, something we needed to create after using our polymers for muscles."

"Yes, the others over there work that way, since the electro-polymers last longer, are stronger but don't generate heat, they have to generate body heat if they wish to fool people into thinking that they're alive."

"Also, the coolant is a red liquid that thickens and hardens when exposed to air, simulating blood rather well."

"So you're an interlaced design; mimicking humans in many ways?"

"Actually, Humans are the ones that are patterned after my kind, they're just the improved, self-repairing organic model, with the added benefit of *free will* I might add."

"Woa! Now I know what you meant about 'prototype'! Did he switch to organics because the titanium/nickel muscles don't last long."

"No, it's another safeguard, by using them I am slower, weaker and have much less endurance than a Human, and I wear out frequently. It makes them feel safer if I am inferior. Humans were a forethought - even though I was built first. Besides, why do you think we have all of those spare parts for me? To create an army of owner's manuals?"

"Okay that's a lot to swallow, in fact all of this is, but I'm still curious about your power supply."

"I use simple, electricity."

"Do you mean... *batteries*?"

"Rechargeables!" he replied almost indignantly.

"You know, you're weird, but I like that about you."

"Thanks!"

They both had a good chuckle.

"If that's all for now, I'd like to get back on duty. The captain probably needs me."

"Yes, that is enough for now. My head is swimming as it is."

Indeed, he had received more straight answers in the last few hours than he had in a long time. This was going to take some getting used to!

"Thanks." said Pymander, as he headed toward the door. "Do you mind programming the door for the bridge, I hate the long walk down the hall, since I wear out so quickly."

Elroy smiled, got up, said: "Not at all." and held his hand on a panel next to the door and thought about the bridge. The event horizon changed slightly but enough to be discernible.

This was a seldom used feature, not available on every door, that didn't work if they both went through the door. It allowed anything to be sent anywhere with alacrity if need be. It also wouldn't work under duress. In fact, in such a case, the door would teleport the Human and only the Human even if they didn't cross the threshold. A good security measure indeed - handy in the case of a Gynoid attack.

"Thanks again." said the android as he disappeared into the doorway.

"No, thank you." he said under his breath after Pymander was gone.

* * *

"Well, how do you feel?" asked Metatron.

"I feel a sense of accomplishment."

"Not pride?"

"No, not at all actually. Just accomplishment. I feel happy *for* them."

"GOOD!." Glad that Harvey hadn't gone down the wrong path. Then he added; "It feels good and satisfying. Doesn't it?"

"Yes, quite fulfilling but..." His voice trailed off.

"So what's troubling you? You arrived at the right solution, saving their world from war and providing lasting peace and prosperity. They will do very well now, thanks to you."

"I just don't get it. How could their best minds have never come up with the same thing with all that time to think about it?"

"They were so polarized in their conflict that they never saw the possibility of another solution, so their best minds worked on weapons and tactics instead. You said so yourself."

"Which demonstrates the value of arbitration."

"That too, but you have the natural ability to see other options where most do not. Like the 'glass too large' thing - very impressive!"

"I keep forgetting... you know everything I do."

"Don't worry, those insights are some of the reasons you were chosen for this job."

"But... it all seemed too easy. Can it really be that simple?"

"Capitalism and democracy are *alien* concepts to them. You are from a world where those systems have worked and their systems had failed, so it was easy for you to see what needed to be done and how to bring it about. Besides, I told you that this one was a 'no-brainer', remember?"

"Oh yes, you *did* say that."

"In any case, that was a job well done. Don't worry, future assignments will be more difficult - but nothing you can't handle."

"That's both good and bad news."

"Now remember, you have two more worlds to visit. School's not out just yet."

"As I recall, with this next one I need to 'go it alone'."

"That is your safest bet."

"Couldn't I bring you, uh, the android with me." hoping that the answer would be different this time.

"In this particular case, I would say that it's not a good idea."

He looked puzzled. the android was supposed to be his 'right-hand man'.

"You'll understand once you've been down there for a while."

Harvey sighed, worried about the learning curve.

"The next planet to visit was renamed 'Asbeel' by the inhabitants, but it's original name was 'Orphieus'[16]." said Metatron.

Harvey though that name sounded familiar somehow.

"You are directed to visit three cities, Zahun, Rahab and the capital city of Moloch and meet with Jeqon Gaap, the ruler of the planet, who is expecting you. After you have seen the way things are there, you are to return to the ship and carry out your decision to destroy the planet."

"What makes you so sure that I'll destroy it?"

"Trust me, that world has gone so irretrievably wrong that virtually no man would allow it to continue to exist. It's one of the adversary's greatest triumphs. Remember, this is to serve as a lesson to show you just how bad things can get if you don't help those worlds that need it. That's the only reason I've spared it up to this point."

Harvey thought that he was going to have to meet this adversary one of these days, but when he was ready.

"Will I be *safe* there?"

"Your armor will protect you, but I suggest you bring weapons, just the same."

"Such as?"

"Well, there's a pretty nice sword in the armory."

"A *sword*? You've got to be kidding!" His memory flashed back to the guards on space station NOD.

"No really, they are popular because they don't require ammunition, and since the inhabitants have forgotten how to manufacture complex machines, there isn't much to be had. Frankly, you'll definitely run into situations where you'll have to use it... and don't hesitate to either."

"Okay, tell me about this sword."

"It's the sword of Katzfiel, which can emit lightning as a special attack. In addition, it is virtually indestructible, so it's pretty useful."

---

[16]*Orphieus destroyed neighboring planet Tiamott in a war, but not after committing unspeakable acts of cruelty to the population. The destruction of Tiamott created an asteroid belt, which they avoided except for the purposes of target practice. At least as long as they managed to keep space travel technology. The Orphieuns hated the Tiamottens so much that many of them died of aneurysms just thinking about it. (Think about it, or rather DON'T!)*

"But swordplay..."

"Takes years to master?"

"Yes."

"Here."

Metatron handed Harvey two pills that looked like the knowledge pills from the ship, only one was red and the other brown.

"Penemue pills?"

Metatron nodded.

"But why is this one red?

"The red ones are permanent. The brown one is for temporary knowledge, typically for culture and language, as well as antibodies."

"I never noticed before. So I take it that I'm going to keep using a sword."

"For a long time I trust."

Harvey narrowed his eyes, and looked at Metatron before heading for his quarters to take the pills before bed.

* * *

When he awoke the next day, Harvey took Pymander to the armory, and asked the android to find the sword.

"I don't know how you knew to ask for this particular sword, but for personal defense, it's a dandy!" he said as he dug through the bins of swords, looking for that particular one. There was one particularly beautiful one he ran across in the forge, that is; stuck in an anvil and he muttered to himself: "Never again!" He continued on to find the sword he is looking for instead.

"Ah! Here it is, Katzfiel's own lightning sword." Holding it up for Harvey to see. "Isn't it a *dandy*?"

The sword looked like a nicely made hand-and-a-half with a mirror-polished blade. In short, it looked rather ordinary, which was somewhat anticlimactic. Sensing that Harvey felt this way, the android offered; "If it were fancy and expensive looking, people might try to steal it from you."

Harvey nodded, still looking a little disappointed. Perhaps he needed a demonstration.

"Here." said the android handing the blade to his captain, "Try a swipe at the anvil over there... just let the blade drop on it."

The captain shrugged and complied. The sword had a nice balance to it, and the blade glowed ever so slightly blue, with the occasional crackle to it as if it were highly charged with static electricity. This made him more than a little bit nervous. Still, he stepped up to the anvil and let the blade drop, just as the android had suggested, full well expecting it to bounce off. Instead, the anvil was cleanly and easily cleaved in half. His face lit up. "I like this sword!"

"I thought you might. Now let's see about getting you some skill with it then." he said as he looked over a drawer full of red Penemue pills.

Harvey stood there with a smirk on his face, but Pymander had his back to him.

"You have to be careful about motor-skill pills because they have to be specific to your body; size and musculature. That's why there are so many in this big drawer - all the permutations."

He turned around to see if Harvey was listening and saw him swing the sword around in a flurry. "Nice balance." he commented. Satisfied, he sheathed it, and held it with both hands.

Pymander sighed, and rolled his eyes. "You could have told me."

"It was more fun to see the look on your face!"

"I can understand that. Well, it shows that you're catching on nicely."

"So, what else do I need?"

"Let's see, as a backup you might want a hand weapon." said the android as he approached a set of small drawers that resembled the card catalogue at a library. He searched a bit and started looking through a particular drawer, and pulled out a small and extremely thin disk.

"Unless you already have one of those too." he added almost sarcastically. Obviously, he didn't much care for not being informed about what Harvey had been up to in his absence.

"Ooh, what's that?"

"This, is as good as it gets." said Pymander almost gleefully as he handed Harvey the disk.

"That's like the body armor disk, only thinner."

"Actually it works *with* it, but it is a weapon, I assure you."

"How does it.... What do I..."

"Place it on your palm, and in a moment, it will seem to disappear." He did and *it* did.

"Now what?"

"Try facing that silhouette target on the frame over there, and extend your hand as if fending off an attack."

"Like this?" asked Harvey as he extended his palm outward with his fingers spread out.

As if to answer him, a pulse of kinetic energy emitted from his hand and the silhouette was pushed across the room and into the wall with some degree of speed and malice. Almost as if it were being swatted like a fly, with the speed of a bullet.

"Wow!" exclaimed Harvey. "What else does it do?"

"Isn't that *enough?*" asked the android.

"C'mon! *Give!*" He coaxed, knowing full well that most if not all of the ship's technology was multi functional.

"Well, with practice and mental effort, you can get it to throw heat, cold and actually lightning."

"Lightning!"

"The sword can do the same, and with considerably less effort I might add. With practice, the palm disk can be controlled to the point of being able to manipulate objects at a distance; moving them about and even retrieving them."

Harvey looked at his palm in wonder. Although he couldn't see it, he knew it was there... his mind could *feel* it.

"However, that takes a lot of practice and mental discipline to gain the necessary control." Then he said with a twinkle in his eye: "It's not something you can learn from a pill either!...AAAAK!"

Pymander was levitated into the air and floated there for a moment before he said anything. His arms folded, he was not very happy.

"You're a natural." he said dryly.

"Thanks!" said Harvey as he let the android down gently. "Well then, do I need anything else for this trip."

Pymander counted on his fingers as if redressing a mental list: "Let me see now; weapons, lots of gold, armor and communications... Nope! you're good to go!"

"Great. When do we get there?"

"We've been orbiting for the last half hour."

"Great." He thought about the preparations, the fact that he was going it alone and that he was destined to destroy this world, and wondered. "Am I going to be *okay* down there?"

"Don't worry sir, your armor will protect you, and the weapons are just to assure you freedom of action. If you get into a pickle, just call the ship with your armor's communications capability and we will rescue you."

Satisfied, he headed for the docking bay, leaving the android alone in the armory.

That's when he noticed the empty case on the wall labeled 'Mastema'. "Oh no...!"

# XXXIII
# BELIAR

Quadis: "Life is temporary..."

Irin: "...and death is forever."

In the docking bay, much of the crew had arrived to see him off. Harvey boarded a shuttle craft that looked innocuous enough to be mistaken for a domestic one, not wanting to draw too much attention. He was wearing appropriate attire, which included a cape. He climbed on board, gave a longing look to Linda and closed the door. He was worried about what he might find down there. The last they heard from him was his reminder: "Don't scan the planet. I don't want you to see how bad it is down there!"

Once three days had passed, the crew was starting to talk about a rescue mission when then they finally got a signal from Harvey. He sounded more mature, more serious somehow.

"I'm all right." he said.

"We though you might have run into foul play." said the Lt.

"Actually I did within five minutes after I landed, but it's all sorted out now."

"Gave you a run for your money did they?" asked the Lt.

"You could say that. I'll be docking in a few minutes, and I'll see you on the bridge."

Harvey walked onto the bridge his cape tattered and dirty with a few holes and scorch marks. With purpose and a certain force of personality he headed straight for the weapons panel.

"Just tell me what button to push to reduce the entire thing to rubble." he said firmly after a few small arguments with the Major. He was not in the mood to squabble, and apparently he wanted to destroy the world himself. The Major just flipped a switch labeled 'Rogziel', indicated a button labeled 'Mashit' and threw up his hands in exasperation. Apparently the Major wanted to do it. After all, he was a military man, this was his duty station and well, these guns were really BIG! Besides, he could handle it psychologically, and wasn't so sure that Harvey could.

"Don't worry Major, I'll let you do the 'dirty work' next time - it's just that this time it's *personal.*"

"What *happened* down there?" asked Linda, with a worried look.

"If I told you, you wouldn't believe me... not in a million years."

"Try us." said the Lt.

"Not this time. The android was right, that place is absolutely irretrievable." he said as he pressed the fire button with deliberate purpose. "Good riddance." he said under his breath. Only the Major heard that, a fact he would relate to the others later.

The planet was hit with an uproar of quakes that soon added its mass to a nearby asteroid belt. Not only had he disrupted the planet into rubble, but he turned off the gravity so the rubble could dissipate into a cloud that could be guided. The second shot pulsed the star. He wanted no life to remain. Since there were three more planets in this system that could later harbor Human life, he left the star short of total destruction. He hoped that good people could be 'seeded' on these worlds some day - which might make up for what had happened here.

"Isn't that a little *harsh*?" asked Linda, half appalled not knowing what to think.

"Actually it's poetic justice. I haven't slept, so I'm going to get some shut-eye, but first I'm going to take a three hour bath. Just visiting that world makes you feel scummy. I'll see you later." he said dryly, and shuffled off to his quarters.

The crew exchanged puzzled looks, but they weren't going to complain. Not just yet.

# XXXIV
# EATER OF SOULS

"Beware the eater of souls, for it will be the true death of you."

**Johnson's Journal:**

**I felt like I could sleep for a week, but it turned out it was only 14 hours. Pymander is at this moment giving the bridge crew a history lesson on Asbeel, it's destruction of Tiamott and the atrocities they committed, presumably to let them know why I chose to destroy it the way that I did. Somehow I doubt that it will be enough, even with all the atrocities the people - and I use the term loosely - of Asbeel committed. All I can do at this point is hope that Metatron knew what he was talking about.**

**I will record the details on my visit to Asbeel in the 'Captain's eyes only' file later, when my stomach settles...**

\* \* \*

Having noticed their wrinkled brows as they looked disapprovingly at him, Harvey decided it was prudent to take Metatron's suggestion after all.

"Set course for the Cygnus Loop supernova, and watch the main screen as we approach." said the Captain. "I think all of you will find this interesting."

As before, they were able to shift the light into the visible range and see the last few centuries of imagery fly by as if they were only a few minutes.

They watched in some degree of wonder as the star burst into a massive cloud of dust. It continued to expand and then an amazingly unexpected thing happened. A cloud of what looked like fireflies darted about the nebula, but seemed confined to the limits of the expanding cloud.

"Ooh! What are they?" asked Linda. "They're beautiful!"

"Souls. The ship allows us to see them." said the android.

"*Human* souls?"

"Of course. There isn't any other kind. They were released from the star when it was destroyed."

"You mean to tell me that Human souls go into the local star?" She could not believe what she was asking.

"Some do."

"Which ones?"

"Mostly the lost ones, like those from Asbeel."

"Now I get it, you're showing us what happens to the Asbeelians next." she said, eyeing Harvey suspiciously.

The truth is that he was just as surprised by this as she was, but he managed to hide it rather well.

"I suppose that's the 'go into the light' thing." she postulated.

"Sort of. Actually 'the light' as you call it, is trap set by Ophiomorphus; the 'eater of souls'. You're better off going the other way." said the android.

"*Eater* of..." She swallowed hard. "...souls?"

"Yes indeed! If you see him, go away from 'the light'!"

"And do what?" asked Harvey.

"Do you really want me to give away one of the secrets of the universe?"

"Yes, actually." he muttered.

The android just smiled and shook his head.

"I always heard that you were supposed to go into the light." said the Chief, sounding puzzled. "Please don't tell me that it's one of those 'backward planet' things." he added.

"Well, some people who say that just don't know any better, some others are trying to create their own belief structure but the worst of the bunch are the ones that know the truth and not only wish to destroy your culture from within, but also condemn you to oblivion after you die."

"But what do you call it when someone sees their loved ones in the light?" asked the Lt.

"Bait." said Pymander bluntly.

"*Eater* of...souls?" muttered Linda, still trying to wrap her mind around the idea.

"Look! *There* he is." said Pymander pointing at the screen. "*Literally* the stuff of nightmares!"

They all looked at the screen and saw a gargantuan snake with a head the looked reminiscent of a human skull, slithering around the nebula gobbling-up the small lights as it went. The snake appeared to be made of the same material as the nebula, perhaps as a form of camouflage.

"That's horrible!" exclaimed Linda, almost in tears. "Why are you showing us this?"

"To let you know what happens to people from worlds like Asbeel."

"To what end?"

"To motivate you to help other worlds avoid this fate." he said solemnly.

She looked into the thinning cloud of lights that seemed to desperately trying to avoid the snake without much success. It was gorging itself. She wanted to look away, but was somehow morbidly fascinated. Deep down, she felt that those lights somehow might deserve this, but was repulsed by the very existence of the beast. She turned to Harvey, her eyes tearing up.

"Was it *that* bad on Asbeel?" she asked, her voice cracking as she held back the tears as best she could. "Tell me it was *that* bad! I *need* to know!"

"Much, much *worse*, I'm afraid. I'd rather not talk about it, if you don't mind." he said dryly.

She noticed that the boyish innocence in his voice was missing, and hoped that it was temporary because it was one of the things she liked best about him. Truthfully it was the scene in front of them that was making him sound that way. Despite what had happened on Asbeel, this still seemed harsh.

"We've seen enough. Now let's get out of here." He turned to the Lt. who was awestruck. "Take us to Mehabiah, perhaps the contrast of the people living there called 'the Keel', will make us feel better." he said hopefully.

There was silence on the bridge as the Lt. set a course. No one wanted to talk about it, but they would all come to terms with it; in their own time and in their own way.

# XXXV
# HARVEST

**Johnson's journal:**

**We've been in orbit around Mehabiah for what seems like days. It has become somewhat difficult to keep track of time, since there is no real night and day aboard ship. In fact, the higher oxygen content and the slightly lower gravity combined with lord-knows-what, makes one able to stay awake for as much as 40 hours at a time with no ill effects. It took a while, but it seems that one rejuvenates quite a bit, when one sleeps onboard, in a way I can't quite put my finger on just yet. However, I digress.**

**I've been flipping a coin so to speak, trying to decide if there should be a landing party or not. If this place proves to be anything like Asbeel, then I don't want to know. On the other hand, if it turns out to be the opposite, as I have been told, then I am not exactly keen on carrying out the assignment. In other words, it will be very difficult to destroy a world that is teeming with civilized people. How can such destruction be a reward?**

**One other curious point: when I mentioned shore leave to Gladrina and Aniyel, they both seemed terrified, and were very unwilling to go, let alone talk about it. That worries me, and I can only hope that one day one of them will tell me what their reactions were all about. Meanwhile, they have disappeared into the bowels of the ship yet again. Presumably to avoid The Keel and Mehabiah.**

The final verdict was to go there and find out. Curiosity had won out, and not only for him.

This time though, they didn't need to use Penemue pills or even match the mode of dress that this world was accustomed to.

"You mean that we really don't need to at least learn the language?" Harvey asked the android.

272

"That's right."

"How are they going to understand us and how are we going to understand them then?"

"Apparently, their mental skills are so sharp, they will be able to learn your language in moments, using their telepathy. I am told that it's quite amazing."

"So they are *that advanced* then?"

"They've learned to use almost the total capacity of their brains, and as a result have achieved true civilization."

"Well, aren't *we* civilized?"

"Not really sir. For starters, *true* civilizations don't need *laws*. The law is for the lawless, you see."

"So, you are saying that 'true civilization' is anarchy... that *works*?"

"When the entire populace behaves themselves because it is their true nature to do so, it can be claimed that civilization has been achieved. Consequently, laws are not needed. So, the short answer is 'yes'."

"Wow! So this ought to be the complete opposite of Asbeel!"

Linda and the Lt. exchange a look, only beginning to imagine what it must have been like there, but their estimates were still falling short.

They approached on a rather plain looking shuttle craft. There was no challenge from the surface. In fact, no attempt at communication was made whatsoever. The truth of the matter was that they really didn't mind the intrusion at all.

When they landed in the middle of a park, they were greeted by a man that had been feeding the swans in a stream.

He approached them as they disembarked, and said: "Welcome, I am Daniel! I trust you had a pleasant trip?"

Linda gave him a puzzled look, as she was worried about telepathy and the stray thoughts she never dared vocalize. "Did you read our minds?"

"Not at all, it's considered the height of rudeness to do that, and rightly so. Someone's thoughts are theirs and theirs alone. I just noticed that you looked a little lost and thought I could help."

"Thank you, but how are you understanding me, and how am I understanding you for that matter?"

"Projected thoughts are another matter. You send out the thought you wish to communicate as you speak. I do the same, and our minds process the thoughts and correlate the vocalizations we make."

They noticed that his mouth didn't match what they 'heard' him saying.

"So it *is* telepathy then?"

"Of sorts, but I assure you, only your broadcast thoughts will be read. In no time, we will have learned each other's languages."

Harvey had a strong thought that he didn't vocalize.

Daniel turned to Harvey. "Just because we have the ability to do something does not mean we will. Not to worry!"

Linda had a strong thought too that she didn't vocalize either.

"He did what you just did. If you think it out loud *at* us, we can't help but hear it, so no, I was not reading anything more than broadcast thoughts, and no I'm not offended, it is I who should apologize to *you*." Then he turned to the Lt. "He's the noisy one." Then to the Lt. he said. "You talk a lot more than the others."

"No I don't!" objected the Lt.

"With a little mental discipline, we ought to do all right here." offered Harvey.

They all gave each other slightly worried looks. Such mental discipline might be difficult to sustain and if the natives discovered why they were here they might not like the idea.

"So, Daniel, tell us about your world." said Harvey.

"I'd be glad to give you the 'grand tour'." said Daniel. They agreed, "Of course you can find out anything you want from anyone you like, but I think it would be nice to take you to the capitol city, Tahariel."

"You mean we missed it?"

"Not by much."

"Lead on." said Harvey

Daniel spread his arms wide, and their surroundings seemed to change from a park to a town square in front of a very beautiful building. The motto: "Law is for the lawless." was inscribed above the main doors. Harvey and Linda were able to understand it due to the armor's ability to translate. Harvey however, recognized the expression, though it had sounded familiar when Pymander had said it earlier. If he could just remember where he had hard it before...

"Hey! That's some trick!" exclaimed the Lt. as he looked around in intense interest.

Harvey leaned over to him and muttered, "I don't think it was a trick per sé. I think he just teleported us somewhere."

"Oh." said the Lt.

"Is there a problem?" asked their new friend.

"No, not at all." answered Harvey. Then he asked "Didn't you hear what I said to the Lt.?"

"I heard it, but since it wasn't meant for me, I was unable to understand."

"You mean to tell me that I could say something to him in a loud clear voice and if I didn't intend you to know what I was saying, you wouldn't?"

"That's how the reading of surface thoughts works. In time, if I learn enough of your language, it won't work that way anymore, as I'll understand your vocalizations."

"Oh, I see." said Harvey.

"So how did you get us here?" asked Linda.

"Oh that, it's just a little trick we use to get around longer distances. It has something to do with folding space."

"Don't you understand it?" she asked.

"Not entirely, I've never been that curious about it."

"Then how do you *do* it then?" asked the Lt.

"Well, everyone on this world is in touch telepathically. It takes a larger mind than mine to teleport like that, so I borrow an infinitesimal bit of energy from everyone to do it, and allow the collective sub-conscious to guide it to the result I ask for."

"You mean collective *un*-conscious, don't you?" said the Lt. a little proud of himself for knowing something about metaphysics. He thought it might impress those 'brain boxes' he was with.

Daniel leaned toward him as if to speak to him alone, but the others could hear anyway; "Remind me not to visit your world when it wakes-up!" Then he playfully but gently elbowed the Lt. in the ribs.

"It's just that we have heard of the same thing on our world. It used to be called the collective sub-conscious but it got changed for some reason." offered Linda, to The Lt.'s defense. "Now that you mention it, one means that it is asleep, and the other means that it is incapable of being awake. Hmm....That's a big difference!"

"In any event, it is the collective mind made by the inherent telepathic link between all the sub-conscious minds of all people on a planet. Most worlds are in touch with it on some level or another." offered Daniel.

"That's pretty cool." said the Lt.

"What else can you do with that link?" asked Linda.

"Well, we use the collective sub-conscious for most things that we can't do on our own."

"I see, so is that how you do the things that other worlds do with technology?"

"Precisely."

"What about information?"

"Well, all the knowledge of our race is stored in complete detail and is available to all."

"Like a library of the mind?" asked the Lt.

"Something like that."

"Sounds dangerous to me. What if someone ran amok?"

"Firstly, the collective sub-conscious needs to agree to what you are asking, and secondly, the kind of malevolent mind that you are referring to would be denied access in the first place."

"You mean to tell me that you all have god-like powers and you can only use them for good?"

276

"Well, I wouldn't go so far as calling them that, and no one here wants to harm anyone else in any way. There simply is no need, so there is no desire, and, I might add that it would seem as though we were hurting ourselves if we were to hurt others."

"I see, and a mind that extensive would be more able to tell what was harmful and what wasn't, even in the long term." said Linda.

"I'm happy to report that as a result, we've all been living in peace and harmony for some time now, and we're all just tickled about it!"

"That must have taken some time to achieve."

"Well it did actually. Many factions arose over time, and some thought that their way was the best one and tried everything ranging from propaganda to war in order to force everyone to comply with their idiotic ideals."

"Can you give me an example?"

"Certainly. Some thought it was better to change certain words because of the stigma attached with them. By using kinder, gentler sounding words instead. They thought that it would make people *think* differently."

"Did it?"

"No, we learned that one must get rid of the *stigma*, not the word. No matter how you label something, it remains what it is."

"You mean: 'A rose by any other name would smell as sweet.'"

"That's very clever!"

"We had a movement on our world just like that." interjected the Lt. "It was called 'Political Correctness'."

"How did that end?"

"It eventually led to a war, actually." said Linda

"I'm very sorry to hear that."

"Thank you."

"How did you achieve this contact with the collective subconscious?" asked Harvey, in an attempt to change the subject from the race war, which was what he was thinking at Daniel.

"It came upon us slowly, over time. First a few individuals then groups. Eventually everyone was in touch with it." said Daniel.

"So it just happened spontaneously?"

"Funny, it did actually. Once we learned to cherish life and abolish all war, we discovered that people with the insight to make a better life for everyone, were not only naturally connected in that way, but they were amongst the ones that were historically getting killed in the wars. So it would seem that all a world has to do is achieve peace and the rest will follow."

"Wow." they said in chorus.

"Evil begets evil, good begets good."

"We have a similar expression; 'you reap what you sow'." offered the Lt.

"That's very clever too. You must have many wise people on your world." said Daniel.

They all stood there for a moment pondering. Then Harvey broke the silence.

"So, you were going to show us your capital?"

"Yes, this building you see here was the center of our government, but now it's only used for light administrative duties, such as dealing with aliens like yourselves."

"Oh, I'm sorry, are we supposed to check in with somebody?"

"Not at all! If you were supposed to, we would have contacted you on the way down from your ship."

"How did you... never mind, I get it." said the Lt.

"Those offices are used for diplomatic relations with other worlds and interstellar commerce, you know, the boring stuff that other worlds find so important."

"What if someone tries to invade?" asked the Lt. as they walked into the lobby. "What sort of planetary defenses do you have?"

The Lt. asked this knowing full well that one simply cannot become pacifist without some sort of protection. After all, this may be a peaceful world, but it's still a harsh universe out there. Something that was missing from the philosophy of the pseudo-pacifists back home that almost destroyed his country. After all, the Chinese monks that learned

Kung-Fu did so that they could practice their religion in peace, and fear no one.

"Usually, we use the power of illusion to make our world seem invisible to them, and if that isn't enough, we teleport them back to their home world over and over until they get the hint."

The Lt. chuckled. He *liked* that! "That's fantastic! Nobody gets hurt and your world is completely safe! I love it!" Like most soldiers he was opposed to war, not because he wasn't willing to fight or afraid of death, but because he didn't want to *kill*... unless it was absolutely necessary. Unlike the trigger happy psychopaths some people believe them to be.

"Has anyone tried to invade recently?" asked Harvey.

"Well, there was the empire of Barbiel[17] that sent us an iron asteroid recently."

"What did you do?"

"We made it into 37 trillion paper clips and sent them to their home world, with our compliments."

"37 *trillion* paper clips? Whatever for?" barely able to contain his urge to laugh.

The Lt. wasn't able to withhold his amusement, so he snickered.

"We figured that with an empire as large as theirs, they must have a great deal of paperwork, so we thought we'd help them out with a week's supply of paper clips. Besides, paper clips don't make for very good weapons."

"You people have a good sense of humor."

"Thank you!"

"So, if everyone in your world has all this power and information at your fingertips, what do you people *do* all day?"

"We *live* our lives, and improve our minds. We have everything we need. Besides, there's always something interesting going on, such as your arrival."

"So are all visitors treated this well?" asked Harvey.

---

[17] *From the Libra arm of the galaxy. "The Barbielians!" ;) - aligned with the Kurzi empire.*

"Don't worry, all are treated appropriately."

"So, basically, you are beyond any petty concerns."

"Well, that's our hope anyway."

"So there's no one you can't defend against?"

"None that we know of."

"Keuwl!" said the Lt. He wanted to retire there. Then he remembered the reason for their visit, and stopped grinning. He hoped that their host didn't catch his 'stray thought'.

Daniel just gave him a quick glance with a knowing twinkle in his eye.

At their requests, before they left, Daniel showed them works of art that were so beautiful that they made them weep with joy. He brought them to concert halls where they heard music that they could never describe, because it uplifted them and made them feel like they were in love.

The Keel had conquered all disease, crime and social problems, the last being the 'monsters from the id' as Daniel had put it. He also showed them that the wild beasts of their world were tame. In short they had solved all the problems of their world and had been living in a state of near bliss for some time. It was difficult for them to return to the ship, especially due to the nature of their mission. But in the end, return they did.

Back on the bridge, they were all enjoying some sort of 'high' from what they had witnessed down on the planet. Reluctantly, they followed instructions and set-up the weapons system to totally disintegrate the planet. Just before the Major fired, the sensors showed that every last person on the planet had simply disappeared!

"Is that their power of illusion at work?" asked Lt. Argent.

"No." said the android. "You can't fool the ship's sensors."

"So they're actually *gone*?"

"Yes, they are."

"Where?"

"Where do you *think*?" he said with a twinkle in his eyes.

# THE HALO EFFECT

This made them smile, and the Major felt better about hitting the button. Then he did not mind so much pulsing the star past the reconstitution point. There were no more habitable worlds in this system, and the surviving planets would become rogues that drifted between the stars.

The planet was made to disintegrate completely in order to prevent revisionists[18] from changing the past, and the star was destroyed as a signal that this world has reached it's conclusion. It became a beautiful nebula.

As they watched the spectacle unfold, they were all awestruck. Linda was once again by Harvey's side, and quietly without looking, moved her hand over to his. He quietly held it without looking either, and they stood there watching the scene unfold. Somehow the death of a star could be very beautiful.

"Uh, I hate to break it to you, but there's a little problem you need to be informed of." interjected the android.

Harvey's eyes narrowed. "Come with me." he said as they headed toward the phone booth and discussed the missing sword on the way.

\* \* \*

"Wonderful! Didn't I tell you that you could do it?" said Metatron.

"You did at that. You know, I feel a sense of accomplishment when I finish an assignment. Will it always be like that?"

"Only when what you did will work out for the long term."

"I suppose that's a way to tell if I did the right thing."

"Yes, it is indeed. Or when you are finished with it."

"One thing is giving me a little difficulty."

"Yes?"

---

[18]*Revisionists are a group of pseudo-scientists that gained control of a time machine, and went back and forth over time "correcting" the universe into a Politically Correct state. They are thwarted by destroying the good places to the point where they have nothing to get hold of to reverse time on it, since that is how it worked.*

"Where did The Keel go?"

"You know."

"I need to hear you say it." said Harvey solemnly.

"Okay... 'they're with *me* now'."

"That's just what had I hoped."

"I know."

"Okay, now that I get it, what do I do next?" asked Harvey after a long silence.

"Whatever you *want*." replied Metatron to a worried looking captain.

* * *

In a remote part of the ship, Dr. Cornelius Morax PH.D. finally uncovered the item he so desperately sought. He held up the Ankh, twirling it between his fingers, examining it closely. When he was satisfied it was the real one, he cracked a sly smile. His maniacal laugher echoed throughout the large chamber.

===========================================================

Harvey Johnson will return in: "Phul, of Surprises"

# THE HALO EFFECT

## An excerpt from the next book: "Phul, of Suprises"

"Sir! I agree. He's bluffing!" said Uvall's first officer.

"These guys *never* bluff!" he snapped.

"Why not?"

"Because they don't *have* to!" he spat. Being outclassed, was never a fun thing. Although he had a vast numerical superiority, he still had nagging doubts, if not due to the identity of Harvie's employer, not to mention the history of clashes with the Hyperachii fleet.

"The power emissions off that ship are several orders of magnitude *lower* than ever recorded. It's surprising that they can even maintain life support."

The General looked at the readout, and what he saw filled him with the confidence he needed. A sly smile crept across his face as he chuckled softly. He wasn't about to be bluffed by anyone. He assumed that Harvie was betting on the reputation of the Ezrael to bail him out of this. Of course! The energy needed to move an asteroid at that velocity over that distance would drain any *fleet* let alone a single ship! It had to be a bluff! He had to have caught them before they could refuel. Wonderful! His luck had not deserted him after all!

By this time, Harvey had his arms folded and his head cocked slightly. "If you are *foolish* enough to fire on this vessel, I promise you a quick and decisive battle."

"Oh...on that point at least, we agree." said Uvall coldly. Confidant that he was to be victorious and convinced that Harvie was ready to die a warrior's death. "See you in hell." He said as he terminated communication.

"Not today." muttered Harvey under his breath.

The bridges of the Ezrael and the Kunospaston both sprang to life.

"Great! He bought it! He he!" said Harvey gleefully, rubbing his hands together, almost jumping up and down.

"How can you be glad when we're running on fumes and they're about to fire on us?" asked the Major rhetorically.

Harvey just looked at him and raised an eyebrow, as if to remind him of a previous "Major" incident.

The Major's eyes went wide and he raised his index finger and shook it at the captain; "Oh *yeah!*" he said with a sly, gleeful look on his face. "You *sly* DOG!"

Meanwhile on the bridge of the Kunospaston "Signal all ships to fire on my command!" barked the General.  He waited a moment then spat "Goodbye and good riddance; *SIMKIEL!*... FIRE!"

The combined firepower of over a quarter million heavy attack vessels converged on the spherical ship.  It looked small in comparison to the attacking fleet.  At first the shields appeared to stop the assault, but Uvall ordered them to maintain fire.  After a few moments, it appeared that the Ezrael was shrinking, apparently being destroyed under the barrage.

"It's *working!*" exclaimed the helmsman.

Now beginning to laugh maniacally, he said "Of course it is!

www.ingramcontent.com/pod-product-compliance
Lightning Source LLC
Chambersburg PA
CBHW071300170626
46809CB00001B/290